Ordinary Angels

Mark Sippings

For those of us who got through it ...
And for those who didn't.

And for Millie Buttons, my own perfect fairy – I miss you x
Sometimes it's hard to find any magic at all ...

CHAPTER 1

Thomas Blueberry scrolled through his new phone. Its camera at least had proved a welcome revelation given the past couple of years.

Which, let's face it, had been awful.

He'd split up with his girlfriend and spent most of his redundancy money on a company that had promised to turn his novel into a bestseller. Instead, he had ten boxes of books.

These he shifted from the floor to the bed depending on what he was using. Even that manoeuvre was becoming difficult with the increasing mess. He should tidy up, but what was the point?

The programme on Netflix looked promising, however – swearing, violence, scenes that some viewers may find upsetting and scenes of a sexual nature. Bingo, the full works.

He clicked the remote …

And yelped.

A small sparrow-like thing fluttered at the end of the bed and Thomas pulled his knees up to his chest. He'd once read that birds were related to dinosaurs, which surely meant his fear was rational. A bit anyway.

'God, shoo … shoo … get away.' He scrambled under the quilt, shivering but feeling hot and a little faint at the same time. 'Mum,' he shouted. 'Mum.'

As he peered over the top of the duvet, it occurred to him that sparrows didn't hover. Nor did their wings buzz as if electricity were passing through them. And the bright colouring was all wrong too. A humming bird? No, not here.

He moved a little closer. The buzzing intensified and—

Not a sparrow. Definitely not a sparrow. Instead legs … a dress … arms, a face, hair. *What the—*

'What's wrong?' his mum called from the bottom of the stairs.

'It's okay. I've sorted it. The curtains fell down.'

'Burtons? They shut ages ago.'

'No … Don't worry, I've sorted it.'

'Do you want a cuppa?' his mum asked.

'No, I'm alright, thanks.'

The buzz subsided a little.

Thomas looked at the creature. It was tiny. Two shiny silver shoes and a shimmering green dress glinted in the light as she moved. At least he assumed it was a she. Her head darted from side to side, eyes wide, as if in a state of panic, then she bolted straight up into the lampshade. There was a fizz. The bulb flickered and a shower of golden sparks rained onto the bed. Wisps of white smoke rose from the smouldering fabric.

Thomas leapt forward and beat the cover with a book.

'Thomas? What on earth's going on?' called his mother.

'Just a spider,' he said. His mum was afraid of spiders – that would keep her downstairs.

The closing bars of *Coronation Street* floated up and the announcer proclaimed Jacobs Manchester as the king of the game shows.

'The wishes programme's on,' his mum said. 'You coming down?'

'I'll sort this out first,' he said.

The lounge door banged shut. A spider-proof barrier.

Thomas returned his attention to the bed. The tiny being was curled into a tight ball near the edge, wings beating so fast they were almost invisible. Thomas inched closer, holding his breath until he was less than a foot away.

It was a girl – he was sure. Just impossibly small.

And with wings.

He'd watched *Peter Pan* when he was younger. This creature looked very much like …

Thomas shook his head. Was this real?

Was there a fairy in his bedroom?

He picked up a pencil from his table and bent lower.

Shoulder-length blonde hair partly obscured her eyes, which were shut tight. He pointed the pink eraser end towards her, intending to give her a prod.

Her lids flashed open and she launched herself up and zipped into a gap between the ceiling and the wardrobe on the far wall, leaving a trail of sparks in her wake.

Thomas crashed to the floor, scrambled up and grabbed the office chair by his desk. He wheeled it in front of the wardrobe, and climbed onto the seat. It swivelled every time he moved, and he tried to steady himself with one hand on the chair-back and the other on the door.

Just as he leant towards the gap and grasped the top of the wardrobe, the castors elected to go in the opposite direction. The chair spun away from him, and his knees banged into the wooden doors.

Like a mountaineer on a cliff edge, he hung on, trying to glimpse the glow just visible at the back of the gap, but he couldn't bear his own weight. As he slid to the floor the buzzing stopped.

Thomas needed a Plan B.

CHAPTER 2

Iris Blueberry, now in her early seventies, was a Londoner born and bred, something she'd proudly tell people at every opportunity. She'd always been confident, could talk to anyone, make them feel like their story was the most interesting one in the room. Her vibrancy and happiness were infectious, and drew people to her.

Even as a child, Iris had been the leader. Despite being the youngest, her elders hung onto her every word as she made up games or led them through the narrow streets to the park.

Eric, her husband, had been the love of her life.

They'd met at a dance in the East End and she'd known he was the one the moment she set eyes on him. Dark haired, straight-backed and barrel chested, he'd danced with every girl except her that night. Iris had kept to the shadows and watched and wondered. And then, when the evening was over, and the last waltz had played, he'd come to her and invited her to dance.

Years later she'd asked him why he'd left it until the end. He smiled and gazed at her with such love, incredulous that such a question was necessary.

'You know I always save the best till last,' he'd said, and held her hand so tightly, as though he was squeezing every ounce of love from her.

And it had been true, whether it was a crispy roast potato, a favourite tipple, the sports pages or her. *The best till last.*

She'd loved him.

It was as simple as that.

Did she look back on their life together with rose-coloured spectacles? Undoubtedly.

It had been a struggle at first – living with her parents, hiding from the milkman on payday, wearing second-hand clothes. Eric had taken every hour of overtime he could get his hands on, often getting up at six in the morning. There'd been no central heating in those days, and many a time she'd felt a cold draught as the blankets lifted and he slid out of their bed, his breath misty, then watched him in the gloom as he removed his pyjamas and teetered into his Y fronts. She'd close her eyes and wish with all her heart that he could be back in the bed, warm and cosy and close.

She'd worked hard too – cleaning, cooking, apple-picking, shop work, and even a night club which Eric hadn't liked, saying it was run by the Mafia.

Gradually things had got better.

They'd bought a small semi in a cul-de-sac bursting with young families, each setting sail on their new lives. Once again, she'd shone, organising parties and BBQs, festivals and fireworks. Eric had been by her side, encouraging and complimenting. She'd grown accustomed to his praise but never taken it for granted.

'Are you trying for children?' the neighbours had asked, Iris thought it a strange question. Trying was something you did in relation to riding a bike, learning French, playing tennis (which she was), losing weight (that too). But trying for children?

She'd bat their enquiries away with a wave of her hand and a 'We'll see'.

They *had* been trying – but nothing had happened. And then, five years later, just when they'd thought they should visit the doctor, Thomas arrived.

They'd *tried* for more children but Thomas was their miracle. When the lottery started, they'd not bought a ticket. Eric had said no prize could ever be as good as the one they'd been blessed with.

It had been so difficult not to spoil him, though they'd always brought him up to be polite and kind. Perhaps to his detriment. Iris often wondered if this helped in the real world. Maybe it was better to be rude and take what you wanted.

Her favourite hour had been Thomas's bedtime. Eric had loved stories and she'd sit outside Thomas's room, the golden glow of the night-light dreaming through the half-open door, and listen as her husband told his tales. The giggles floating from the room warmed her and filled her with love.

Memories. Iris liked to remember, and spent more and more time thinking about those years. She often recalled the fine details of precious moments as she drifted off on the settee or in bed. And it was easier than talking about Eric. Ever since he'd died, she and Thomas had both been tiptoeing around each other, neither wishing to mention the past because it was beautiful, and remembering its beauty hurt.

With Eric's passing, her confidence had floundered and the spark she'd once been able to fill a room with had dimmed. When Thomas had said he wanted to write a book, Iris knew it was to be close to his dad, to make him proud and build on those magical bedtime memories. She couldn't think of a time when Thomas had shown such commitment.

He had pursued his dream relentlessly, working every day on his computer. But the dream had disappeared as quickly as his publisher's promises, and Iris had watched helplessly as Thomas had withdrawn from the world as much as she had, surrounded by a mountain of books that should have been flying off the shelves but instead lay piled on his bedroom floor.

A bang from upstairs snapped her out of the daydream and she leapt up, trying to make sense of the droning and all the voices. Momentarily, she was lost. There was something she needed to remember. Who was upstairs?

'Mum ... Mum,' came a voice.

Mum? Iris scanned the room, bewildered.

She couldn't remember his name, but the voice was familiar. He wanted to know about the men's clothes shop, and Iris didn't understand why so she said the first thing that came into her head: 'Do you want a cuppa?'

He didn't so she returned to the lounge, shut the door and pulled a bundle of white cards out from behind one of the cushions on the settee and read them.

Your name is Iris.

You have a son called Thomas.

Your husband died – his name was Eric.

You live at 35 Rosebery Avenue.

Your sister is Betty. She is married to Harry.

There was another bang from the bedroom. She looked through the cards again and took a gamble.

'Thomas? What on earth's going on?'

The voice didn't question the name, just mentioned something about a spider. Iris hated spiders.

But not the cards. And they'd worked again.

She'd got the idea a few months ago when it had become harder and harder to remember even the simplest of things. They had been a success but now she was finding it difficult to remember that she even had cards, let alone where she'd hidden them.

She flicked through some more.

The bus home is number 65. Try to count eleven stops.

Thomas's birthday is 8th June.

Your birthday is 9th October.

You have sold the house to Mr Lipscombe. Talk to Thomas.

Mr Lipscombe? She could vaguely remember a suited man coming to the house. He'd told her that to ensure her home went to Thomas, and that he avoided paying inheritance tax, it was a simple matter of signing a few forms; his firm would take care of the rest for a flat fee of £1,000 rather than forty per cent of her home's value. Forty per cent? She'd had no idea inheritance tax was so much. It didn't seem right, but she'd read about big companies paying no tax and pop stars investing abroad, so why shouldn't she? She and Eric had saved so hard for the house; it was their legacy, their gift to Thomas.

She hadn't told Thomas; there'd been no need. But now she'd received a business-like letter saying that everything was progressing well and Mr Lipscombe would visit during the week so she could sign the house over to Lipscombe Property Associates. That didn't sound right either. She must remember to talk to Thomas.

There was another crash from upstairs and she rifled through the cards again.

CHAPTER 3

The chair Thomas had found in the spare bedroom proved a far more stable solution. He tucked it up against the wardrobe and climbed on. The seat creaked as he craned his neck and peered into a space so black it could have hidden the brightest star. Thomas pulled out his phone and swiped on the torch. A tangle of cobwebs expanded and shrunk as the light touched them.

And there she was, huddled against the wall.

He gave the fairy a tiny poke with the rubber end of the pencil.

Nothing.

Was she dead?

'Come on,' he whispered. 'Wake up. I won't hurt you.'

He poked again.

Still nothing.

The idea of asking his mum for help lingered for a moment, then fluttered away.

Still, what should he do? He'd never been good with animals, and there was no knowing what this creature might do. She was small, yes, but so were birds and their beaks could peck your eyes out. And piranhas – they were tiny and look what they did.

Of course. Gloves.

He jumped down, pulled on the black thermals and resumed his position.

Fearing another flash of sparks, he turned his head away and used the tips of his fingers to feel the way. They found a soft lump, and he teased the delicate mass into his palm and pulled out his hand.

Thomas opened one eye.

He had her.

Her eyes were closed, but there was a faint buzz as her wings fluttered like eyelids in sleep. He laid her on the bed and tucked a freshly ironed handkerchief around her.

For twenty minutes, he watched. But for the shallow breathing and dreamlike twitches, she didn't stir.

Again, he wondered what to do. A doctor didn't seem appropriate. Maybe all she needed was time; they said it was a healer. So he checked her once more, then put on his earphones and plonked himself in front of the telly.

Try as he might, he just couldn't concentrate. Which was fair enough, he reasoned, given that a fairy was asleep in his room. He gave it another couple of minutes, then switched off the TV and checked the bed.

She'd gone.

He yanked the covers off his bed, toppling a pile of books. Nothing. He dropped to his knees and peered into the gloom beneath the bedstead. Still nothing.

'Damn it.'

Thomas stood perfectly still and listened. A faint buzz was coming from the corner where he kept his shoes. He tiptoed forward and lifted his Doc Martens.

And there she was, trembling, her tiny hands covering her eyes.

'Shh,' Thomas said. 'I won't hurt you.'

'You shouldn't have saw me. You shouldn't. Trouble it is. Trouble, trouble, trouble. It is, it is.'

She spoke quickly, enunciating each word perfectly. The tiny voice was high yet not squeaky.

'I won't tell anyone,' Thomas said.

'Someone finds out. They always do, they do. If we talk to people, we get banished.'

'Well, maybe this time they won't.'

'They will.'

She crossed her arms and slumped to the floor, looking so dejected that Thomas couldn't help but feel sorry for her.

'How did I get here? One flash and I'm with Baby Blueberry.'

Thomas shook his head. 'I don't understand. Baby Blueberry?'

'You. You're Baby Blueberry, you are.'

'Me?' Thomas pointed to himself.

'Yes, of course. I'm not your fairy, I'm not.'

'I see,' Thomas said, even though he didn't. He took a deep breath. 'So whose fairy are you?'

He thought she rolled her eyes. She most definitely sighed, as if it were the most ridiculous inquiry ever.

'Blueberry's,' she said.

'Hang on, I'm Baby Blueberry so my mother is—'

The fairy nodded.

'Okay, so my mum's Blueberry. Does she know? Why aren't you with her?'

'No one knows. Secret are fairies, but—'

'How did you get here?' Thomas said.

'In a flash and I'm with you. So frightened.'

'But—'

'I needs to be back with Blueberry. She's gone soon,' the fairy said.

A cold shiver wormed its way down Thomas's spine. 'What do you mean gone soon?'

The fairy waved her hands into the air. 'She's soon flying.'

'What does that mean?' Thomas said, though he had a pretty good idea. 'Does she have to fly?'

The fairy smiled and tilted her head. 'Everyone flies someday.'

CHAPTER 4

Thomas woke, and allowed himself to revel for just a few moments in the relief that always came after one of his dreams. They were frequent and vivid … he'd overpaid someone at work or been accused of something he hadn't done. The dawning realisation that it was nothing more than a nightmare was always so delicious that it made the trauma of the dream worth it. Well, almost.

And this one about a fairy of all things.

Then the buzzing began.

Thomas sat up, his heart thumping so hard it made him dizzy. At the end of his bed sat the winged wonder, matter-of-factly preening her wings.

'Mornings,' she chirped.

'Oh God, you're real.'

'Real? Of course.' She laughed and a golden shower of what looked like blossom fell onto his bed and disappeared. 'No one sees us, but we're real, we are.'

'Jesus ... I thought you were a dream. What ... what do I do? How will you live? What do you eat? You can't stay on my bed, can you? What about my mum? Is she okay?' Thomas spoke so fast that he ran out of breath and had to take in a large gulp of air. 'And what do I call you?'

'My name is Isabelle Millie Fluff but you can call me Isabelle, you can. I don't need looking after, I don't,' she said. 'We do the looking after.'

'Like you look after my mum?'

'Yes, my person, she is.' Isabelle stood and shivered her wings. More golden blossom fell onto the bed.

'Why are you here, with me, I mean?' Thomas said.

She looked away. 'I don't know. A flash and here I am.'

'And you can get your own food and stuff?' Thomas asked.

The fairy laughed again and fluttered up towards him. 'Yes, yes. I've been with Blueberry all her years, I have. Maybe I'm with you now.'

Thomas was keen on nature programmes and this little creature reminded him of humming birds gathering nectar, their bodies perfectly still while their wings beat so quickly they were invisible.

'But you shouldn't have seen me. Now I'm in big trouble, I am. I'll be sent away if they find out.'

Thomas extended his hand, intending to comfort her, but the fairy hovered higher out of his reach.

'Sorry. I was just—'

'You can't touch. You got dirty hands, you have.'

'I do not,' Thomas said, though he glanced at his hands before putting them behind his back.

'All people are dirty, they are,' she said with such conviction that Thomas didn't think it worth arguing.

'What does Baby Blueberry do?' Isabelle said, and flew back towards his face.

'What do you mean?'

'The purpose of Blueberry is making happy people. Smiles and warm hugs. I helps her, I do.' Isabelle pirouetted towards the ceiling, showering Thomas with gold. 'She doesn't know,' she added with a hint of pride.

Thomas beamed. It was true. He'd seen his mother work her magic, turning a quiet room into a party or making a sombre stranger smile.

'So what do you do?' she asked again.

Thomas racked his brains. He'd always tried to be nice to people. His father had told him tales of knights and princesses, dragons, kings and queens. There'd always been honour in the stories, doing the right thing, protecting the weak, finding true love.

Real life had turned out to be somewhat different.

He'd started out bursting with enthusiasm, so full of possibilities, so ready to make his mark, but his efforts had been rewarded with nothing but the mundane.

When had he last laughed?

When had he last cared?

His mum, starving children, abandoned kittens, life itself – he was apathetic to it all.

What was wrong with him? He did nothing, didn't believe in anything. What an embarrassment.

And yet ... and yet ...

He was talking to a fairy.

* * *

Thomas poured muesli into his bowl, then added cornflakes. It was 9 a.m. and he'd planned to go into town and visit the manager of an independent bookshop, hoping they'd stock his book. He should have been excited but Isabelle had put a spanner in the works.

He poured milk over the cereal and gave the bowl a jiggle to gauge how much more he needed. He liked the muesli to be just floating.

His mum came into the kitchen and took her own bowl from the cupboard. 'What was all that banging about last night? You alright?'

He didn't bother to look up. 'Just a spider, Mum. I got rid of it.'

A crash startled him. Pieces of his mum's shattered cereal bowl lay strewn across the floor.

Thomas looked up and almost slipped off his stool. His mum seemed to have shrunk, as if gravity were weighing her down, and her skin now had a greyish pallor that had aged her overnight.

He stood up. 'Mum, are you okay?'

'Yes, of course … It's just a stupid bowl.'

'No, not the bowl. You. Are you okay? You look tired.'

'I've been awake since five,' she said and rummaged in a corner cupboard. 'Couldn't get back to sleep.'

She pulled out a dustpan and brush and knelt on the floor.

'Here, let me do that.' Thomas said. He swept up the pieces and wrapped them in newspaper. His mother fetched another bowl.

'I'll have a lie-down this afternoon and see what's on telly,' she said, and tipped just a few cornflakes into a plastic bowl.

No wonder she was losing weight. He should have paid more attention. But that was just it – he hadn't looked at her properly in ages. He'd never needed to. Every part of her had always been pep and pizzazz, even in the most mundane of situations.

He remembered a film – hundreds of people walking across a bridge, but just one person drew the audience's attention. The leading lady. How was that possible? A trick of the light maybe? Depth of field? But that's what it had been like with Mum. Always in focus no matter how big the crowd. Was it because she'd been coated in fairy dust?

Whatever it was, it had gone.

Now she moved slowly and her once dazzling eyes had become dull. She was blending into the background.

Like me.

The thought was too horrible. He closed his eyes, not wanting to see. She ambled past, one hand holding her bowl, the other fiddling around in her dressing-gown pocket.

'Mum?'

'Yes … er …'

She seemed confused, as if searching for the words.

'Nothing … I'm just going into town.'

'Okay. See you later, dear. Bye bye.'

As she walked towards the lounge, a small piece of white paper fluttered from her pocket and onto the floor.

He picked it up.

On it was written a single word: *Thomas.*

CHAPTER 5

Thomas caught the bus into town, his book wrapped safely in a Sainsbury's carrier bag. He could have driven, but it was half-term and the car parks would be crowded. And he'd never enjoyed driving; the weekly shop was enough. His friends sometimes teased him, enquiring when his Ford's 300 foot service was due.

Not that bus journeys were without their stresses. Thomas had once read a book called *Cold Sunflowers* where the protagonist had trouble getting off buses. He could relate to that. He hated being the centre of attention. Ringing the bell was like saying 'Look at me', and Thomas avoided it at all costs.

Today, he needn't have worried. The bus stopped without request and he joined the queue of people waiting to alight at the Post Office.

Having navigated the unpredictable crossroads – the green man often flashed in time with the green traffic light

– he tried not to bump into fellow pedestrians, which was harder than usual because of the school children out and about. His progress was slow and accompanied by a litany of apologies.

Left or right? How did you choose?

He'd once read that people in the Middle Ages had kept to the left because most were right-handed and that left their sword arm free. But on a modern crowded pavement that advice just didn't work, so he bumbled this way and then that.

Some people were mildly amused by his clumsiness; others seemed majorly irritated. A few breezed through, pirouetting around him with a smile, somehow illuminating that moment in time. He turned and watched them, wondering if he might see the faintest flutter of wings.

He arrived outside the small independent bookstore and composed himself. In his teens, Thomas had been an avid science-fiction fan, and Blue Tiger Books had an entire basement dedicated to the genre. He'd become a regular visitor. These days, the logo looked rather flaky but it brought back happy memories and so, buoyed by the sight, he opened the quaint door and stepped inside.

Over the years, the shop had seen off competition from big names – WH Smith, Hatchards and Waterstones – all of whom undercut them outrageously. And yet Blue Tiger was still going. This was no thanks to Thomas, who preferred to buy his books online. The irony of asking the owners for help hadn't escaped him.

It was darker than he remembered, and the little light that made it through the front windows illuminated the dancing dust motes. Three tables each displayed a 'new release', though the publications were all several months old. The shelves overflowed with books of all sizes. The covers of some faced outwards; others were wedged in sideways, their spines to the back, titles invisible. Boxes of books littered the aisle and there was an unpleasant smell of damp.

The shop assistant was of around Thomas's age and sat behind the main desk, her eyes glued to a computer. He wished he had a job surrounded by books, though maybe it wasn't as much fun as he thought because every now and again the woman emitted a tiny sigh or groan, or muttered 'Oh dear, oh dear'.

Thomas waited silently for several minutes, but she paid him no attention, so he said hello.

The woman leapt up, threw her hands into the air and then to her chest, breathing raggedly.

'I'm so sorry,' he said, taking a step away from the counter. 'I didn't mean to startle you.'

'Look at me,' she said. 'I'm shaking, man.' She held her trembling hands out towards him.

The woman spoke with a soft Geordie accent. Thomas liked it. He apologised again and the woman waved it away.

'You just gave me a fright, that's all. There's been some robberies in the town.'

'In bookstores?'

'Well, no.' The woman climbed back onto her stool and brushed her hands over the front of her dress. 'But you never know, do you? Anyway, chuck, how can I help?'

'I phoned a couple of days ago about you stocking my new novel,' he said. 'I'm a local writer.'

'Hmm, yes. I think I remember.'

'This is it.' Thomas took the book out of the orange carrier-bag wrapping and placed it on the counter, thinking how unprofessional he must look. His worries were confirmed when the sales assistant tried to hide her smile.

Her fingers picked out the words on the cover. '*Angel's Delight.*'

'Yes,' Thomas said. 'It's about a girl called Angel who leads a really hard life and falls in love with a rich chap who owns the flats where she lives. He's a bit of a rotter and treats all his tenants horribly, but gradually she wins him round and they get together.' Thomas pushed the book towards her. 'There are twists and turns along the way, of course,' he added, realising he wasn't promoting it very well.

She picked it up and turned it over. While she studied the back cover, he studied her. Green cardigan over a grey cotton dress buttoned down the front. Wavy hair, auburn with a single purple streak. Her ears hung with variously sized golden hoops, and a silver stud pierced one side of her nose. Thomas wasn't sure about that; what if she had a cold? She wore little make-up, which accentuated her dark eyes.

'Can you pass my book on to the owners, see if they'll stock it?'

'Ah, well, I'm the owner, chuck.'

'Sorry. I didn't realise. There used to be a couple here.'

'They retired three of four years ago. I bought the shop. I see you're not a regular.' She laughed.

Thomas blushed. 'Well, no, not exactly.'

'Don't worry, you're not the only one.'

'I came in here a lot when I was younger. The sci-fi section downstairs was the best.'

'Ugh, don't remind me. We had a leak. It flooded the basement. We never recovered.' She closed her eyes. 'All those beautiful books.'

Thomas glanced at her left hand. No ring.

'Did you buy it with a partner?' he said, feeling a little sneaky.

The woman held his gaze, and a smile twitched at the corners of her mouth. Thomas looked down at his book.

'A business partner and life partner. Or so I thought. But he left and took his half of our money with him. Unfortunately, all the ruined stock somehow became part of my investment.' She laughed, but there was an obvious sadness in it. 'So as you can see, I'm in a pickle. Anyway, I don't know why I'm telling you all this. I just wanted to vent, I guess. You came at the wrong time. I was looking at my debts. Every month, I'm further in the red.' She shook her head. 'I don't know if it's worth you leaving your book, chuck. I can't see the shop staying open much longer.'

'Don't say that,' Thomas said. 'Blue Tiger Books has been here for as long as I can remember. It's part of the town. You can't close.'

'Who'll miss me? People like picking up books and turning the pages, but then they get the big discounts by buying from Amazon. Even you never come in, and you're a writer.'

Thomas tried to form a response, but words failed him. He took a deep breath. 'You're right. But I don't work so … so maybe I could help. It looks like it needs sorting out more than anything.'

A huge smile flash across the woman's face. 'That's kind of you. I'll be okay though. I'll read your book, promise. I'm Maria by the way.'

She held out her hand. Thomas took it in his. It was small and soft. It felt nice.

'Bye, Thomas,' she said.

'How did you—'

She pointed to his name under the book title. 'Maybe this will be the saviour of Blue Tiger Books.'

Thomas walked towards the bus stop. For once, left, right or down the middle didn't matter. Instead, he glided through the crowds.

What was that warm feeling, like the people glowing in those old porridge adverts? Not rolled oats. Something else.

Something like happiness.

CHAPTER 6

The doorbell rang.

Iris was changing the sheets in her bedroom. She tutted and sighed, and had only just reached the landing when it rang again and then once more.

Who could it be? Wait a minute … wait …

She hurried down the stairs and opened the door.

A man in a smart dark suit and striped tie stood before her.

'Morning, Mrs Blueberry. Lovely day.'

Iris looked up into the dark and cloudy sky.

'Remember me? Of course you do. Peter Lipscombe.' The man held out his hand. 'Now, I just need a couple more signatures on here, my love. Damn solicitors. Always so careful, aren't they?'

His voice was low and precise with no noticeable accent.

'What's this for?' Iris asked.

'You remember, my love. We're going to sort things out so your son doesn't have to pay inheritance tax. Forty per cent, that's what it is. Would you believe it? It's criminal, isn't it? You're going to save him *one hundred thousand pounds*.'

The man took an uninvited step into the hallway. 'May I, Mrs B? Let's spread out on the table, shall we? It's going to be such a delightful surprise for – what's his name now?'

'It's … er …'

Mr Lipscombe strode past her into the lounge. Iris hoped his shoes were as clean underneath as they were on top.

'What a nice mum you are. You know what? I'd keep it all under your hat if I were you. Just imagine him worrying about the tax and then finding you've sorted it all out. He'll be bowled over. It's all down to you, Mrs Blueberry. What a lovely surprise.'

He lifted his bulging black briefcase onto the table and pulled out a file of papers. Strange. His voice sounded so jolly but his hands were shaking.

'There now. I'll need you to sign here and here and over the page here.' As he pointed to the pencil crosses, his cufflinks glinted and a waft of aftershave found Iris's nose. 'Who are your next-door neighbours? We'll get them to witness your signature.'

Iris crossed her arms. 'They're at work.'

'Oh, it doesn't matter about that. I'll get them to sign in the office. Actually, I can sign on their behalf as long as they're alright with it. They are, aren't they? What's their name?'

Iris felt confused and pressured.

'Robert and Daphne Marchant, but—'

'Great, let me pop them down here. That would be number 33, wouldn't it?'

'Yes, but—'

Mr Lipscombe passed his pen and the document to Iris.

'Oh, don't worry about reading it, my love. It's just the standard solicitor drivel.'

'But shouldn't Robert and Daphne be here when I sign?' she said, and her voice seemed hopelessly small even to her.

'These forms always say that. It's just so solicitors can cover themselves in case there's a complication. Just put your squiggle here.' He pointed to the bottom of the page.

She put the pen down. 'Perhaps I'd better speak to my son.'

'And risk him having to pay £100,000 and spoiling the surprise? You don't want to do that, do you?'

'Well—'

'And you know EU regulations are changing from tomorrow.'

'Are they?' Iris looked up from the paper.

'Yes, that's why I came today. We won't be able to do this tomorrow. They just want to get their hands on your money. It's our last chance to stop them, Mrs B. Tell you what.' He put his hand on his chin. 'As we've had to do all this at such short notice and in such a rush, I'll reduce my charge from £1,000 to five hundred. What do you think of that?'

'Well … that's very kind but—'

'It's got to be done today though. Those damn Frenchies are making things complicated.' He retrieved the pen and held it in front of her. 'And, Mrs B,' – he paused and leant towards her – 'I didn't mention it because I'm sure you wouldn't be pulling a fast one, but there's an environmental report here that shows your home's built on top of a landfill site. Methane and carbon dioxide leaking out all over the place. House prices are dropping you know. People are hallucinating and having near-death experiences. You haven't had any have you, Mrs Blueberry?'

'No, no nothing,' Iris said.

He waggled the pen. 'That's it. Just sign here.'

His hand took hers and guided it towards the papers.

'I'm just not—'

'That's it, here we are, just above those dots.'

Iris watched the pen slowly excrete her spidery signature. She felt far away, almost in a dream.

Once, when she was a girl, she'd been freewheeling down a hill on her bike. Her friend had grabbed her arm and rocked her as they raced faster and faster out of control. She'd been terrified and wanted it to end. She'd purposely crashed her bike, grazing her elbows and knees just to make the fear go away.

She felt the same way now.

Just do it. Get it done.

'Lovely, that's all sorted then … Mrs Blueberry, are you alright?'

Iris heard his words but they were far away. She was still on her bike.

'Mrs Blueberry?'

'Yes … yes, I'm alright. But who are you? I'm so sorry but I can't remember.' Her mind was blank. It was as if she knew the beginning and the end of the maze but couldn't connect the two. Jenny, her friend had been called. And the bike had been red and green. She could even hear her mother scolding her as she'd bandaged Iris's injuries. But no matter how hard she tried, she couldn't recall who this man was.

'Don't you worry, Mrs B. It's all done now, all sorted. You can forget about it and your son doesn't have to worry about a thing. It's all done and dusted.'

The strange man bundled the papers into his briefcase, not bothering to straighten them, and made his way to the front door.

'I'll be in touch with a copy of the contract. Lovely to meet you.'

Iris watched him stride down the path towards a large shiny blue car that bleeped and flashed as he pointed his key at it. The man looked as if he was in a hurry.

She returned to the kitchen, put the kettle on and flicked through her white cards.

> *You have sold the house to Mr Lipscombe. Talk to Thomas.*

Now she remembered. Suddenly, Iris didn't feel very well. Not well at all.

CHAPTER 7

Thomas skipped up the stairs, still glowing from his encounter with Maria. It had been a while since he'd spoken to anyone other than his mother. He thought about Blue Tiger Books. Was Maria single? Could he help with the bookshop? Get it back on its feet?

Years ago, when he'd worked in town, he'd spent his lunch breaks in either a record shop or a bookshop. He'd loved music back then. Buying records had become an obsession, and opening a gated sleeve to reveal the lyrics or more pictures a drug. What did they mean? What secret information was contained within? Over the years the passion had departed. He still listened, but the tingle of anticipation was no longer there.

With books the fix was different. Not instant, more a sense of cosiness. The book was a haven, a raft when he felt like he was drowning. He'd considered studying to become a librarian but the idea had seemed less appealing after the pressure of A levels and with the offer of a paying job on the table. Still, he could always lose himself in a book, and no one thought him strange or rude for not talking or taking an interest. Books were a shield for his shyness, and he'd come to hide behind them more and more.

Imagine spending every day in a bookshop, and with Maria for company. He turned the handle and opened his bedroom door. She'd seemed so—

It was mayhem.

Clothes were strewn over the bed and floor, his table lamp was on its side and books scattered across the carpet, their pages creased and torn. The net curtains had slid down, their spring-loaded pole unable to support them. Bright-blue sky and the tops of houses from across the road now filled the upper half of the window.

Thomas gawped at the mess, closed the door behind him and leant against it in case his mother tried to come in.

'What the … what have you done? Where are you?'

There was movement under one corner of the crumpled white lace, like a miniature ghost had taken up occupancy of the windowsill. Thomas couldn't help but smile, and gently lifted the fabric.

The fairy looked forlorn, her wings were folded downwards and her hair tangled. Thomas leant in, his head only inches from hers. Isabelle's eyes were red and wet.

'What's the matter? What's wrong?'

She shut her eyes, clasped her hands tightly across her stomach, and turned away.

'Come on now. What's been going on here?' Thomas said.

She took a deep shuddering breath and mumbled, 'I was frightened, I was.'

'Why? There's nothing here to hurt you. Please, turn around so I can hear you better.'

Slowly, Isabelle faced him.

'I was frightened of by myself,' she said.

'You didn't like being alone?'

'Yes. By myself.'

'But you're always by yourself, aren't you?'

Isabelle frowned and shook her head. 'Never. I was always with Blueberry. Never by myself. I didn't like it. It was quiet, it was. Blueberry was always doing something – singing, moving, talking, laughing, dreaming. Now I only got me.'

'Well, I'm here.'

'It's not the same. I'm not warm and cosy anymore. There's no tingle in my heart.'

'Can't you get that again?'

Isabelle huffed and crossed her arms, her eyes like saucers. 'No. Because there's no Blueberry, of course,' she said.

'Maybe we can get you back with Mum, or could you go to someone else.'

'No, no. It's broken,' Isabelle said. She snivelled and wiped her nose with the back of her hand. 'We're not like you. We only feel like that with one person, we do.'

'I don't think we ever feel like that,' Thomas said.

The fairy laughed. 'You do. Not everyone has a fairy, but

people still sparkle when they're warm inside. Blueberry would sparkle without me when she saw Big Blueberry or you. She still does.'

'What do you mean?'

'She still shines when she sees you, just not as much. And Big Blueberry, well sometimes I got very cross and steamy in my head when she was with him. When he soared away, I didn't think her light would come on again.'

'Dad?' Thomas asked.

Isabelle nodded.

'Why doesn't she shine as much when she sees me now?'

'Cos *you* don't. When you was little, I'd see you running around, getting into boxes, on your two wheels, pretending you were flying like me. It was a hard job, hiding from your tiny eyes. You believed in things. Now you're so slow. No colours anymore.'

Thomas was silent. The previous evening Isabelle had asked him what he did and he'd had no answer. Now she'd said he didn't shine. He wanted to argue with her, defend himself, but she was right.

No one had ever said, 'You're older. Stop skipping, don't stroke stray cats in the street or sing-along with the radio,' but he had. Just like the day he'd decided to eat all his dinner rather than leaving the last bit. Suddenly, something had changed. No, that was wrong. It hadn't been sudden. There'd been records, gigs, big nights out, friends and fun. So what had happened? When had the world stopped being exciting? When had he sunk beneath its vibrant colours into numbness?

There'd been times when Thomas wished he were religious. How comforting a faith would be, having that warm blanket wrapped around him. If he collected something – teapots, paintings, even stamps – at least there'd be the joy and excitement of discovering something new.

There was a knock on the door.

'Thomas?'

'Come in, Mum,' he said without thinking.

Isabelle sprang towards the cupboards, a stream of golden dust fizzing behind her.

His mum pushed the door open and gawked at the catastrophe in front of her. 'What on earth's happened?'

'Just having a sort out,' he said.

'Are you alright?'

'Of course. You just make more mess to begin with, don't you? It's all okay.'

His mum shuffled her feet and looked down. 'I came to tell you … I came to tell you that …'

'Mum?'

She tutted and brushed imaginary fluff from her jumper. A lump formed in Thomas's throat as he took in her bewildered expression, her eyes exploring the room as if for the first time.

'Nothing important. I can't remember now,' she said.

'Are you alright, Mum?' He wanted to reach out, take his mother's hand, yet remained a couple of feet away, arms straight by his side.

She nodded and turned to leave.

'Mum … do you remember when dad would have a

spring clean like this' – he gestured towards the mess – 'and get everything out of his drawers? All his tools and old papers. He'd spread them out, then get bored with the whole thing and put everything back in the same place.'

Iris laughed. 'Yes. You know what? When I went through his things, I found a tiny box with an old penny in it. I'd forgotten all about it. I found it when we were on our honeymoon in Weymouth. He said it would bring us luck and had kept it. He never told me. He had every one of your baby teeth and all the Father's Day cards you made, all there, safe, rolled up with a band around them. Everything he owned told a story – the screwdriver he used to build your cot and the hammer he knocked nails into your goal posts with. When the memory faded, the sight of those things brought it back. So I don't think he got bored with his spring clean. He just didn't want to throw anything away that had a memory attached to it. It was all too precious.'

Thomas looked at his mother, lost for words. She closed the door behind her.

'Isabelle?' he hissed. 'She's gone. Where are you?'

CHAPTER 8

Iris switched on the TV. She was still warm from the happy memories and frustrated by her inability to recall anything recent. The thing she was supposed to tell Thomas fluttered close by in her head, yet remained stubbornly just out of reach.

She was using the telly's catch-up function to watch the soaps but even that was becoming increasingly problematic. Videotaping had been so much easier – just pop it in and press record. Sometimes she pressed the wrong button and deleted the programme, and somehow she'd recorded twenty-four hours of news over the top of some of Thomas's films. He probably wouldn't notice. She wouldn't ask him for help though. He was becoming impatient with her questions about TVs, phones and iPads. Best just to pretend everything was all right.

She reached under the cushion and removed her cards.

You have sold the house to Mr Lipscombe. Talk to Thomas.

Was that why she'd gone to see Thomas? If only she could remember. Tomorrow would be okay. She'd talk to him then.

Sold the house. The words transported her.

She was young, in her favourite flowery dress, bubbling so full of excitement she thought she'd burst. The smile wouldn't leave her lips as she walked hand in hand with Eric to the foundations of their first home, skipping over puddles and slipping in the mud, the breeze warm on her arms.

The wonder of that beautiful summer's day had never left her. Their first home. Always full of love. And here she was, still. They'd never moved, and she knew she never would. Would Thomas extend the legacy or sell up? She hoped he'd stay.

She looked over at Eric's empty chair. How could the presence of one other person fill a room and their absence make it so empty? She ran her fingers along the dark, cracked leather, feeling the indents, the shape of him.

I miss you so much.

She closed her eyes, and it was as if she were being turned inside out, the muscles in her chest and stomach twisting with longing and loneliness.

Why did this happen? Why was life so beautiful and so horrible? She screwed her eyes tighter and then opened them ever so slowly.

And there he sat. Eric. So strong, so handsome.

'Hello, darling,' he said, so matter-of-factly, as if he'd been sitting there all along.

'But—'

'Your hair's looking nice. Have you had it done?'

Iris patted her curls, unable to remember the last time anyone had complimented her. She felt warm and safe again. It was like having hot chocolate on a winter's day.

'I gave myself a perm,' she said.

'It looks lovely. How're you keeping?'

'Oh … not so good. I keep forgetting things,' she said, wishing more than anything that he would wrap those powerful arms around her, keep the cold at bay.

Eric chuckled. 'Everyone forgets things.'

'Not like this. I forget everything. Where are you?'

'Here, of course.'

'No, not now. Where did you go?'

He looked puzzled for a moment. 'I … I'm here.'

'You're not, darling. You left … you died.'

'I …' He looked around the room, confusion stretching his mouth taut.

'Don't worry,' Iris whispered. 'You're here now.'

She reached over. Only a moment ago there'd been nothing but cold leather. Now, she found his hand, warm to her touch.

'I think I've done something awful,' she said.

He smiled and looked into her eyes, making her heart thump and her breath catch in her throat.

'You could never do anything awful, darling.'

'But I have.' Tears threatened, deep and heavy. 'I think

I've sold the house … I might have even given it away. I thought I was helping.'

'Everything'll be all right. With you, things just seem to work out. You know they do. You've said so yourself.'

She squeezed his hand. 'I've just been lucky.'

'You always say that, but you make your own luck, I reckon.'

For a moment, everything seemed right again. When they were together, she oozed with confidence. He was her shield, her castle. With him she was free to act the fool and send arrows of laughter into the dourest of invaders, always knowing she could retreat behind the battlements.

More tears welled, happy ones this time. She mouthed *I love you* and felt giddy with it.

Thomas hurtled through the lounge door and almost fell onto the carpet, distracting her for an instant. By the time she looked back, Eric had gone. She couldn't help but gasp from the disappointment.

Thomas scanned the room, and a memory of Christmas washed over her. Hunt the thimble. Waiting outside the closed door. Thomas flushed with excitement, his mouth full of crisps, always the first in, always scouring the most inaccessible places.

'Thomas, are you alright?'

He walked around the room, lifting ornaments and peering behind furniture. 'Were you talking to someone?'

'It must have been the TV,' she said. 'Have you lost something?'

'No, just thought I heard a funny noise. I think it's these radiators.'

He knelt beside the end of one and edged towards the curtains, his back to her, then slipped something into his pocket – something golden perhaps, though she couldn't be sure – then stood up and smiled.

It was a guilty smile. Like the one he'd had that time he'd eaten three days' worth of chocolate from the Advent calendar in one go.

'Good stuff. Everything seems okay,' he said, giving the radiator a tap. 'Why are you grinning?'

Iris wanted to tell him.

It was because she remembered. And whatever was going on with her head in the present, nothing could steal her past.

CHAPTER 9

Thomas hurried up the stairs, Isabelle bundled in his dressing-gown pocket 'Don't do that again,' he said, slumping onto the bed. 'I didn't know where you'd gone.'

'I went to see Blueberry, I did. To see if she's alright.' She shielded her eyes from the bright light.

'I know, but I was worried. And Mum – I mean Blueberry – might have seen.'

Isabelle failed to supress a small smile. 'You don't needs to worry.'

'Well, I was, so just let me know where you is going – are going.'

Isabelle giggled.

'It's not funny,' Thomas said, crossing his arms.

'I shouldn't be laughing, I shouldn't. Two days ago I was hidden and happy,' she said. 'A purpose I had, with Blueberry. Now I can't even dodge a podgy human hand.'

Thomas looked at his hand. 'It's hardly podgy.'

'And have you ever looked in your pocket? It's dirty. It smells of apple core and orange peel and melted chocolate and unwashed fingers. Horrible. Never put me in there again.'

Perhaps, he reasoned, but surely the exaggerated gag was a little over the top.

* * *

The next morning Thomas woke early. Isabelle twitched and buzzed beneath his handkerchief. Her tiny body looked so fragile in the sunlight. And she'd lost her colour, like a burnt-up firework offering its final few stuttering puffs of brilliance.

A few days ago, he'd have been fretting about what to watch on Netflix. Now he was worrying about the health of a fairy.

The phone rang.

Thomas bounded down to the bottom of the stairs just as his mother lifted the receiver. Her hand trembled, and she looked at the phone as if unsure what to do with it.

'Hello. Is there anybody there?' came the tinny voice on the other end.

His mum looked around wide-eyed, and held out the phone to him.

'It's for you,' she blurted, and squeezed past him and into the lounge.

'Hello?'

'Hi. It's Maria from Blue Tiger.'

Thomas's heart raced.

'I read your book. It won't win the Booker, but some people would say that's no bad thing. I thought it was a nice, gentle romance. A display in the front window, highlighting the fact that you're a local author, might get some interest.'

'Wow, that's amazing. Brilliant.'

Maria asked him if he could drop some copies off at the store.

'Sure,' he said. 'I've got plenty. Can you sell three hundred?'

'*Three hundred?*' Maria giggled. 'Where on earth do you store them all?'

'Don't ask,' he said.

'We'll have to discuss your commission, and you said you could help me get this place sorted. I was thinking we could give it a try if your offer's still there, like.'

'I can start this afternoon if you want.'

'Perfect. Bring a photo of your books.'

The line clicked. Thomas looked at the receiver, not quite believing what had just happened. His face ached and it dawned on him why.

He'd been smiling since the moment he'd heard her voice.

* * *

Isabelle was still on his bed, though awake now.

'Where you been? I was lonely again, I was.'

'You must've heard me. I was on the phone.'

She pointed at Thomas's mobile. 'Why don't you use that?'

Thomas shrugged. 'I never hear that one. Anyway, it was the bookshop; they want to stock my book. Can you believe it? And Maria wants me to help her in the shop.'

'Maria? I don't know her, I don't.' Isabelle crossed her arms.

'I'm sure I told you – she owns the bookshop.'

'Colours you've got. You alright?' She cocked her head to one side like a puppy waiting for a treat.

'Course I am,' he said, but glanced in the mirror. He looked relaxed and content. And, yes, colourful.

'Must be your effect on me,' he said.

'I knows it,' the fairy said with a shrug.

'Anyway, what about you?'

The fairy looked down and straightened her skirt. 'I'm not feeling very well, I'm not.'

'Yes, you look pale.'

'It's what happens, it is, when a fairy loses her person.'

'We must be able to do something – get you back with my mum maybe.'

'Once it's broken, it's always broken. I can't go with anyone else either,' she said, and looked down at the bed. 'I should just go to the forest and wait with the leaves.'

'Don't be silly. You're different. You came to me,'

'I shouldn't have done. I could get into big trouble talking to you, I could.'

'Things can change. We'll think of something – I know we will.'

Isabelle nodded but her eyes told him she wasn't convinced.

Thomas looked around the bedroom for something to lighten the mood.

'Can you help me? I need to take a photograph of these for Maria.' He pointed to the books.

Isabelle flew over to the teetering pile, which swayed as she perched on top and posed, head tilted, chin resting on the back of her hands.

Thomas laughed and pretended to take a picture with an imaginary camera. 'That's more like it.'

The fairy shot up into the air.

'That's not funny,' she said, her arms crossed as she hovered above the books.

'What's wrong?'

'Shooting at me. That's how fairies fade, that is.'

Thomas thought for a moment. 'Taking photographs make you disappear, makes you separate from your person?'

'Yes.'

'I didn't know. How would I?'

'I thought you did. We thought everyone knew after Cottingley.'

'Cottingley?'

'Where the first fairies faded.'

'I don't know what you're talking about,' Thomas said.

'But you must know. All fairies know about that, we do. We found out about cameras, and peoples nearly found out about us.'

'Not ringing any bells whatsoever. Why don't you tells … tell me about it?'

'It was those two girls, Elsie and Frances. They was only little, they was, and didn't have their own fairies, so some of us living in Cottingley decided it would be alright to play with them. The silly girls borrowed their grandfather's camera, went to the bottom of the garden and took a photo of the games.' Isabelle huffed and shook her head. 'We didn't even know what a camera was in those days. A few weeks later, we couldn't believe our eyes. All the fairies were in the newspaper, dancing around with the girls. Sprites, they called us.' Isabelle shivered. 'It was awful.'

'I remember now,' Thomas said. 'They looked like paper cut-outs, they weren't real.'

'They was,' Isabelle snapped. 'Over the years, we've altered them so they look silly, but the girls caught the fairies on film, they did. All those Cottingley fairies separated from their people and faded away.'

'Why can't you hide when people take a photo?' Thomas said.

'We can. Once we understood what was going on, the queen told everyone, and it was easy to keep out of the way. We sees a camera and, whoosh, we're gone. But more and more of us are fading, and we don't know why. It's so sad.'

'Hang on a minute. The queen?'

'Yes. She doesn't do much.' She rolled her eyes and pursed her lips.

Thomas arranged his books into a tidy but casual pile, then picked up his phone. 'Okay, you better move now.' Thomas made a shooing motion.

'Why?'

'I'm taking a picture?' he said.

She looked puzzled and Thomas held up his phone.

'But that's for talking,' Isabelle said.

Thomas laughed. 'People don't talk on them much these days, but they do lots of other things, including taking pictures. See? Here's the camera.'

As the words left his mouth, the cogs fell into place.

Isabelle gasped. 'But we didn't know. We didn't know,' she said, her tiny voice cracking.

'And that's why more and more fairies are fading. Think of all the selfies people take.'

Isabelle looked confused. 'Selfies?'

He took a picture of himself and showed her.

'I wondered why people kept smiling at their phones,' Isabelle said, and landed back on the pile of books.

'This is good,' Thomas said. 'Don't you see? We've found out what's happening. Now we can do something about it.'

'But there's so many phones – everyone has one.' She covered her eyes and wept, her shoulders shuddering with each breath.

'Look, we know what's causing it. That's a start. We didn't know that five minutes ago, did we?'

Isabelle shook her head.

'Now we've got to figure out how to make things right. Can you tell the queen what we've found out?'

Thomas felt a little light-headed. First the bookshop and now this. All this excitement. All this *being involved* – it felt good.

'I can send her a message,' Isabelle said. 'But I'm feeling so weak.' She put the back of her hand on her brow, pretended to stagger and glanced sideways at him.

Thomas frowned. 'Okay … that's good. See if you can do that.' He said, then adjusted his position and took the photograph.

CHAPTER 10

Lipscombe Property Associates had been going through a bad patch. The UK housing market had virtually dried up, and a foray into foreign investment had been a disaster.

An elderly couple had contacted him wanting to sell their entire investment in a Los Cristianos holiday retreat – some ten properties – because it was 'getting too much for them'.

Over the years, Peter Lipscombe had tried to listen to the little voice in his head telling him not to be greedy, that when things looked too good to be true, they often were. But the couple had been so innocent, so desperate to shed their burden, that he'd ignored that voice. Instead, he'd offered them a reasonable price – not the best, but not rock bottom either. A fair transaction.

Peter had never been able to emulate his father's guile in the business world – the dark art of the deal. But this one had seemed like a dead cert, likely to make him more money than ever before, and would ensure the company was financially secure.

He'd been proud of himself, and had boasted of his success to his assistant, Marion, acting with ridiculous bravado when he'd told her he was onto a good thing with the old couple. 'But let me see now,' he'd said on the phone, and even winked at Marion while he was speaking, 'Los Cristianos – that's right next door to Playa de las Américas, isn't it? … Yes, I know it's the biggest resort, but British drunks often put people off. Oh and isn't there a large volcano on the island? That could lead to a tsunami further down the line. It was on the BBC. Didn't you see it?'

The couple had protested, but Peter had held steady. 'Yes, flights are cheap, but global warming will put paid to that. No one will be able to afford travel soon.'

Eventually they'd reduced the asking price, shaken hands in a coffee shop – Peter's treat – and signed the documents. They were such a nice old couple that he'd barely glanced at the papers. After all, he'd seen the photographs, and the resort looked stunning. He was going to be a millionaire.

A champagne visit to his new property made it devastatingly evident that he'd been duped. He was now the not-so-proud owner of some brick shacks on the side of a dusty mountain. The photos had been mock-ups. He'd applied for permission to build, but the Spanish authorities had refused, as apparently they had many times before. He'd attempted to contact the couple, but they seemed not to exist, and he'd found himself dealing with unsympathetic and occasionally aggressive men with harsh accents.

It wasn't just the couple who'd vanished. So had his money.

Since then, his finances and his mood had spiralled downward, and Marion had been subjected to round after round of abominable bullying. He couldn't snap out of it. Of course, it was a mask; he couldn't bear the thought of her knowing just how much trouble he was in. Why she hadn't resigned was beyond him, though the notion filled him with dread; he'd be sunk without her.

'Coffee?' he snapped.

'Yes, Mr Lipscombe.'

'Is it so hard to have a coffee ready for me by 9 a.m.?'

'No, Mr Lipscombe.'

'Well, where is it?'

'I don't know, Mr Lipscombe,' she said, and put the post on his desk.

'Any news from that nutty lady at number 35?'

'No, Mr Lipscombe. Here's the file.'

Number 35 was going to be his salvation – the owner was on her last legs, couldn't even remember who he was. Each time he visited, she looked worse than the last.

And it's not like he was doing anything illegal. She wanted him to look after the property. It was a worry for her, all that maintenance and inheritance tax. He imagined erecting a *For Sale* sign while two burly police officers wrestled the loony woman's son to the ground.

This whole affair wouldn't be his proudest moment but it would get him out of trouble, so it had to be done. There were always winners and losers in business – his father had told him that.

As he reached over for the file he nudged the mug Marion had placed on his desk. The coffee spilled onto the papers.

'For Christ's sake, Marion.'

'Sorry, Mr Lipscombe. I'll get a tissue.'

'I don't know why I keep you on, Marion, I really don't,' he said, and grimaced at his rudeness.

Dark-brown liquid dripped from the documents onto Marion's cream cardigan. She wiped the wool, creating a larger smudge, and walked towards the kitchen without another word.

Peter shook his head; he was dragging Marion down with him. She was smart, efficient and highlighted his glaring errors without belittling him. Despite missed wages and his constant criticism, she'd stuck with him. She deserved better.

He picked up the next folder on his desk, his latest project, a rundown bookshop. Interesting. He glanced up and for the briefest of moments thought he saw Marion raising two fingers beneath the long curls of her black hair.

CHAPTER 11

Thomas grabbed his coat and ran into the kitchen. His mum was talking to herself. She'd put on some red lipstick, and although still pale, she looked happier.

'Oh, you made me jump,' she said. 'Dad always used to say I jumped too easily.' She turned to the stool next to the refrigerator and smiled. 'Do you remember, Eric?'

'Mum, I've got to go. I need to get my bus. Are you okay?'

'Course I am,' she said. She turned back to Thomas and fumbled with her apron. 'I have something to tell you.'

'What is it?'

His mum sighed as she rummaged in her pocket. 'Don't worry. I'll tell you when you get home. Have a lovely time … Tommy.'

Thomas laughed. She hadn't called him that for years.

* * *

He ambled down the high street, looking more closely at the people he passed. Some were illuminated, while others appeared drab and sad, and he wondered why he'd never noticed that before. Fairies? If they were present, they were hiding.

As he walked into the bookshop, the smell of damp wrapped itself around him and dusty books piled high on the floor obscured the shelves. It was a wonder anyone could find anything. The bookshop seemed to be set up for Maria's convenience rather than the customers'.

She was sitting at the counter still engrossed in the computer screen.

Thomas closed the door quietly and tiptoed towards her. She held her chin in her hand, her fingers half-covering her mouth. The light from the monitor illuminated her face.

Thomas stopped halfway down the aisle, picked up a book and pretended to study it. He coughed and took a step forward. Maria smiled and he stumbled as his legs momentarily forgot how to work.

'Have you been drinking, man?'

'Sorry. I came straight over to show you my books.' Thomas leant over the counter and swiped through the photographs he'd taken with his phone until he found the right picture. He could feel her eyes on him, and a warm flush crept over his neck and cheeks.

'Oh my, that's a lot of books,' Maria said.

'Yes, they're just sitting in my room. Think you can sell them?'

'Well, we're a bookshop, but look around. You might have more success in Waterstones.'

'I like it here,' Thomas said. 'And you said you needed help to get things straight. Well, here I am.'

'We need to shake on a deal,' Maria said.

'I've never done this before. What do you think's fair?'

'Tell you what, you help me and I take twenty per cent. Does that cover your costs and give you a bit extra?'

Thomas did a quick and most likely inaccurate calculation. His publishers had taken him for a ride; eighty per cent would barely cover his expenses. Still, the chance of selling his book, working in the bookshop and being with Maria more than made up for it.

'Deal.'

Maria laughed. 'Don't you want to negotiate?'

Thomas shook his head and said, 'Do you want a hand now? I could make a start, get things tidy.'

'My knight in shining armour,' she said. 'Feel free.'

He started with the heap by the door. They seemed in no particular order so he began to alphabetise them by author, blowing dust off the covers as he went, removing books from the shelves and replacing them with others from the pile. By the time he'd reached the Ls, things were looking a lot tidier. He stretched and stood back to admire his work.

'What a difference,' Maria said, beaming, and handed him a steaming mug of coffee.

'Looks good, doesn't it?' Thomas said.

Maria moved closer until their shoulders were touching. A tingle danced down Thomas's arm to his fingertips.

'Thanks,' she said. 'I'd kind of given up, but seeing you working so hard and caring, well …' Her breath caught.

'I've enjoyed it. It's given me something to do.'

'What do you normally do?' she asked.

'I got made redundant a while ago. I live with my mum. My book kept me busy, but I've been lost since I finished it. I guess I gave up. But you know what? I've discovered that things change – they really do.'

'I dunno.' Maria shook her head. 'Sometimes I think things go so far you can't turn them around. The bookshop's like that.'

'It's not. I'm sure we can do something.'

Maria laughed. 'You're amazing man. You almost make me hopeful.'

'I'm not joking. It looks better already.'

'Maybe, but I've got someone interested in buying it. Wants to turn it into flats, I think.'

'But you can't. I mean … it's always been here. It's like the town hall. I always used to come here.'

'And there you have it,' Maria said. 'You *used* to come here. If I had a pound for everyone who's said that, well … I'd have five or six pounds.'

Maria laughed at her own joke but Thomas remained mute, embarrassment overwhelming him. He tried to think of something to say but nothing clever or interesting came to mind so he just shook his head.

'It might not happen,' Maria said, and nudged his shoulder. 'I'm only speaking to the guy. We might turn it around, mightn't we? Come on, buck up. It should be me who's fed up.'

'I know, but I feel I've let you down, not supporting the shop.'

'Don't be silly. When my boyfriend left, I let myself down. I just didn't have the energy. I got swamped. Truth is, I blame everyone for not buying my books, but who'd want to come in here? Look at the place. Everything's gotten on top of me.'

She folded her arms and the collar of her dress opened slightly, revealing a flushed neck. She looked sad but defiant, and Thomas thought he'd never seen anyone look so beautiful.

'What?' Maria said, and tilted her head.

Mortified that she'd caught him staring, he shook his head. 'Nothing. I was just thinking.'

'Enough. Tell me what you enjoy,' Maria said.

'I don't do much now but I used to love music. I bought loads of albums and went to gigs.'

'Really?' Maria said. 'What sort of music do you like?'

'Everything, well … I'm not keen on country. Rock's my favourite, something with a guitar solo that makes you fly, especially if you've had a bit to drink.'

'Oh, yes, I like that feeling. Do you know Marillion's stuff?'

'Yeah, Fish. And "Kayleigh", wasn't it?'

'That's their old music, which was good, but they have another singer now. He's brilliant.' Maria's face came alive as she spoke. 'They got songs to make you fly and songs to make you cry. I love 'em, I do.' She glanced sideways at him.

He felt strangely at ease, tipsy almost. Words flew from his mouth into the dusty air of the bookshop. 'You know, all my life, I've dreamt of being at a gig with someone I love. When the music reaches that point where you get tingles down your spine and you feel you're floating on the ceiling, I just want to hold them tight and sway.'

Maria looked into his eyes, her smile bright in the gloom. 'Tell you what, if we get these books sorted out, I'll take you to a Marillion gig and sway with you for as long as you want.'

Thomas laughed. 'You're on. Out of my way – I need to get cracking.' He pretended to rush over to the books.

'I want them done properly, mind. No shoddy workmanship.'

Thomas resumed his work. A few minutes later, the shop door clunked open and a man in a tailored black suit strolled inside. He looked at Thomas with such disdain, his eyes almost rolling, that Thomas took an instant dislike to him.

'Hello,' Maria said. 'Can I help you?'

'I hope so. Are you the owner? Maria …' – he looked down at his notes – 'Maria Wise?' The man spoke in a curt, authoritative tone, as if he thought himself a cut above.

'Yes, that's me. What can I do for you?'

'I've been looking forward to meeting you. I'm Peter Lipscombe. We might be of mutual benefit to one another.'

CHAPTER 12

Lipscombe followed Maria to the counter, his hand on her back as if guiding her. It gave Thomas a bad feeling, like the man was asserting his control over the situation.

Thomas hardly knew Maria, but he liked her and wanted to know more about her. Bookshops had been his happy lunchtime haunt. He felt safe in those spaces, and now he had the chance to work in one. This man could change everything with the swirl of a pen.

'Could you get us a tea?' Lipscombe said, looking directly at Thomas.

'No, Thomas doesn't work here. He's just helping me,' Maria said.

'He doesn't mind do you, Tom?'

'It's Thomas,' he said, his voice no more than a breathy whisper.

'Pardon me. Look, where's the kitchen, Maria? Show Tom,' Lipscombe said.

'It's just round there.' She pointed. 'But as I said, Thomas doesn't work here.'

'He doesn't mind. Get one for yourself, Tom. You look like you need a break.'

Maria mouthed *Sorry* and shook her head.

Thomas put down the book he was holding and walked towards the kitchen. What had Lipscombe meant? *You look like you need a break*. What had he meant by that?

He glanced in the mirror above the sink as he filled the kettle. Same old face, hair a little straggly but not too bad, a bit of stubble. Maybe he should've shaved; it made him look rather pale. Damn it, why hadn't he taken more care?

The kettle overflowed and water splashed on the floor.

'Shit,' he hissed.

'Everything alright in there?' Maria called out.

'Yes, just coming.' He mopped up the water and peeked through to the counter. They were standing close together, shoulders virtually touching. Maria pointed at the monitor and giggled with every word the interloper said.

Thomas felt heat rising to his face and had to summon all his reserve to avoid slamming the cups on to the counter.

'Thank you,' Lipscombe said without looking up.

'The books look amazing,' Maria said. 'Want to sit with us for a bit?'

Mr Lipscombe stared directly at Thomas, his mouth taut. He shook his head so slightly that Thomas wondered whether it had really moved.

'No, I need to get cracking. I'll give you a ring.'

Thomas walked down the aisle past his sorted books.

He had to admit, they did look good. Maria called out another thank-you, and he turned. But her attention was already back on the computer.

* * *

'Are you alright? I'm just watching telly,' his mum called from the lounge.

'Yes, Mum. I've got stuff to do,' he snapped, and thumped up the stairs and into his room.

Isabelle hovered over a pile of books. 'You shouldn't be talking to Blueberry like that, you shouldn't.'

'I know. She just gets on my nerves sometimes.'

'She loves you, she does.'

Thomas threw his phone on the bed. 'She says stupid things.'

'Blueberry's old. She forgets.'

'Yeah, I know. I'm just fed up today.'

Isabelle crossed her arms. 'Fed up you are, when this fairy's fading?'

'Oh.' Thomas sighed. 'Yes, I'm sorry. Any news?'

'I've told the queen about the phones,' Isabelle said. 'She couldn't believe it. She might be able to help me too. I need to see her, I do, but I just feel so floppy.'

Isabelle settled on the bed, and Thomas knelt on the floor so he was at eye level with her. She was paler, and her wings had slackened and no longer shimmered. The shower of golden dust that always followed her was now sparse and came only sporadically.

'What are we going to do then?' Thomas said.

'I don't know, I'll think of something.' Isabelle shifted

her weight from one foot to the other. 'What about you? Why are you so grumpy?'

'Don't ask … actually, do ask. So there was this man in a suit. He was incredibly rude and treated me like I was a little kid. He's trying to buy the shop. It's such a lovely place. It's been there forever, and Maria, she just seemed to be swept along by his stupid small talk.'

'Who's Maria?'

'I told you – you're worse than my mum. She's the owner. She's had a hard time keeping that shop going all by herself and it's not making any money.'

'Sounds like it would be a good idea to sell it, it would.'

'No,' Thomas snapped. 'No, it wouldn't. I can help her. We can make it lovely again.'

Isabelle frowned. 'Red you've gone. Why's that?'

'I haven't.' He touched his face, which felt hot, and glanced in the mirror. A pink blush was growing over his cheeks. Thomas folded his arms. 'I'm just cross, that's all.'

Isabelle laughed. 'You look like you did when you was little, you do.'

Thomas put his arms by his side, scratched his head, then folded them again.

'You're in a fluster, like Big Blueberry when he first arrived.'

'Dad? What happened?'

'Well, he came to visit and I watched him while she got ready. He was up and down, sitting on the sofa, then pacing around the room. It was funny – he couldn't talk. He'd brought some flowers, he had, but didn't give them to her until she asked if they were for her.' Isabelle smiled and twirled in the air. 'The next day we went to his house. We was all going out for a meal. It was cold and dark so we went inside. It was lovely and warm and he led us to the front room and waited for Blueberry to go in first. You should have heard her gasp. The room was full of flickering candles – on the mantelpiece, the chairs, the table, the floor. I never sees something so pretty. Like a million glow-worms it was. He put a record on the music player and they danced slowly round and round the room. I was laughing because she was laughing. But only inside – a happy happy feeling, laughing inside. Have you had that?'

Thomas shook his head. 'I don't think so; maybe when I was little.'

'No, you've been grey for ages,' she said.

'I have not!' Thomas said.

'You have – I told you before. I haven't seen you bothered about anything, I haven't. You don't get angry, just annoyed at silly things, like with your mum. Well …' – she smirked – 'until you got home today.'

'What do you mean?'

Isabelle lay on the bed and giggled as gold fizzed from her wings and onto the duvet. 'You was all hot and bothered today. I think there's more to it than just a nasty man in a suit, I does. Like when you say "Maria" your eyes go wobbly.'

'They don't.'

'They do. I tell you, they do. Anyway, you can't see your eyes.'

'I can in the mirror.'

'That's not the same, is it? Say "Maria" and look in the mirror.'

'No. I'm not playing that game.'

'Say "Maria".'

Thomas sighed, and looked in the mirror. 'Maria.'

Isabelle laughed. 'There, your eyes went wobbly.'

'I didn't see them do any such thing.'

'You didn't look properly, you didn't.' She was laughing so hard she could hardly speak.

Thomas gave an exaggerated huff and opened his laptop. Yet try as he might, he couldn't stop smiling.

The fairy hovered by his shoulder as he typed two words into the browser: *Marillion songs*.

CHAPTER 13

Iris watched Thomas as he bounded down the garden path. It had been a while since she'd seen such a spring in his step. He tended to trudge, shoulders stooped as though the world were weighing him down. Not today, though. Today he moved with purpose.

The sun was high and the flowers in her garden were coming out. Red, black and gold tulips formed tiny fireballs in the borders.

'Remember Amsterdam?'

A familiar voice. She turned. Eric was sitting on the stool.

'I do,' she said. 'It was lovely. Especially the flower market where we got those.' She pointed through the window and smiled as the tulip stems bent towards her in the breeze, bowing to her.

'And the waterways,' Eric said. 'Don't forget them. That lovely boat trip we had.' Eric chuckled. 'Remember the space cakes?'

'That was your fault. We should never have visited Anne Frank's house after eating those.'

'It wasn't one of our best ideas, was it? Why did everything seem so funny?'

'Space cakes, that's why.' Iris laughed. 'It's a wonder we didn't get chucked out.'

'I love you,' he said.

The words had come without warning, and Iris took a tiny step backwards, moved by their power.

'I … you stopped telling me,' she said.

'I took things for granted. I should never have done that.'

Iris wiped her eyes. 'You have no idea how much I miss you. My life's been so empty.' She gulped, her breath a wheeze. 'And now I can't remember anything and there seems to be a hole where my heart used to be. I'm nothing now.'

'Oh, my darling, please don't say that. To us you're everything.'

'You're not here, and Thomas … oh, I don't know what's wrong with him. As for me, look at these.' She ran into the lounge, lifted the sofa cushion and pulled out the wodge of cards.

You have a son called Thomas.

Your husband died – his name was Eric.

'I can remember that one,' she said.

You must pay the papers on Saturday.

Take your tablets at 6 p.m.

Check the gas is off.

'Cards rule my life. Look at this one.'

You have sold the house to Mr Lipscombe. Talk to Thomas.

'What's that mean? I don't know what I've done.' She threw the cards onto the worktop. 'I don't want to tell Thomas. He'll be cross.'

'You know you must though, darling.' Eric spoke softly. 'I'm sure it will be all right. It always is with you.'

'That was before,' she said. 'You were always my lighthouse, showing me the way, but there's something else. I can't explain it. I worry all the time now. Nothing's easy anymore.'

Eric laughed. 'Welcome to the club. That's how most people feel. I still don't know how you used to do it. You breezed through everything.'

'It was always easy when you were with me.'

'You can do it, I know you can. The first thing you have to do is tell Thomas. He'll be cross for sure,' Eric chuckled, and his eyes stared into the distance. 'Remember how he huffed at having his hair cut and wouldn't go out until it grew? He was stubborn, wasn't he?' He returned his gaze to Iris. 'But you have to do it – then you'll feel better.'

'It sounds easy but I keep forgetting. I can't remember what I've done and what I haven't.'

'Thomas will sort it. He's a good boy.'

'I don't think he likes me anymore.' Iris looked down at her dress, not wanting to meet her husband's eyes.

'Don't be silly, of course he does. You're just squashed together in a small semi – you're bound to get on each other's nerves sometimes.'

'Are we? I don't get fed up with him,' Iris said, and brushed her hands over her apron.

'You're his mum, that's your job.' Eric laughed and didn't speak for a few moments. 'I'm not here, am I?' His voice cracked as he said the words.

'No,' Iris whispered.

'I want to hold you. Why can't I hold you?'

'You died, Eric.' Iris felt the tears welling, and Eric's outline became just a smudge of colour. 'You left me alone. I didn't like you for a long time.' The words, so deeply buried, were wrenched into the world. 'And you never said you loved me, not for years. Not for years and years … and then you couldn't.'

'I've always loved you. I love your smile, I love your voice, your hair, your body … I loved the breeze you made as you hurtled past me, towards your next big idea.'

'Why didn't you say?' Her voice was tiny, like a small child's.

'I told you, I took it all for granted.'

'That's not it.'

Eric reached out one hand, but as it moved away from his body it became translucent. He sighed. 'All those parties. You were there, leading the dance, and I was in the corner, so proud of you but longing to be by your side.' He leant forward. 'You were always so in control, so perfect. I just felt silly. You were the strong one.'

'No! You were the strong one. I could do nothing without you. Why don't you know that?' She was crying now. 'And you were always at my side, you idiot. When you were at work, when I was at Mum's, whenever we were apart you were always here. *Here.*' She patted her chest. 'It's so easy, isn't it? To think things'll never change. To not say what we should've said because we think there'll always be time to say it.' Her breath came in tiny stutters. 'Then you went away and I couldn't tell you.'

'Tell me what?'

'That I love you. You're my world.'

'That's silly. I know that.'

'But I didn't *tell* you.'

'You didn't need to, my love. I knew by the look in your eyes, your smile, the way you rested against me at the bus stop, and how you did that sideways glance as you spoke.'

'And you would do that little nod. You see? I need you,' she said.

'I know it's hard but you'll be fine. You have Thomas.'

'But I keep forgetting.'

'We need a plan; we need to get you to remember.'

'But how?'

There was a knock at the door.

Iris tutted and went to the front door. The postman handed her several letters. An official-looking one was inscribed with the words *Lipscombe Property Associates* in curly blue script.

'I just need you to sign for this one,' he said. 'Registered mail.'

Iris used her finger to scrawl her name on his machine.

What on earth was wrong with paper and pen? These days, everything seemed harder.

She returned to the kitchen and ripped open the envelope.

'Careful, you'll cut yourself,' Eric said. 'I hate paper cuts.'

'You always say that.'

She pulled out the letter and read it aloud.

Dear Mrs Blueberry,

Further to our discussion of the 14th, I am pleased to confirm that after considrable considration we have decided to include your house as part of our equity release scheme as a result you can rest asured you will no longer have the responsibility for the maintenance of your property (subject to a £500 excess) and in return on your deth or should you decide to move into a care home (wich ever is sooner,) your property will become the property of Lipscombe Property Associates t he bonus here is that if you did the later you will not have to sell your house to pay for the care home fees.

Should you not whish to proced with our agreement you have 21 days from the date of this letter to let me no? If I we do not here from you by that time I will assume your ascent to the mater it has been a pleasure to do business with you as always.

As always your busness is our pleasur.

Kindest regards,
    Peter Lipscombe

Iris turned to Eric and held the letter up. 'What do you think?'

'Well, if that letter's anything to go on, I'm sure Thomas will find something that bloody Lipscombe Property Associates has done wrong. Look at the spelling mistakes and the way it's written. The man must be a moron.'

'Eric!'

'Well, it's ridiculous. I've never seen anything like it.'

'Now I have this' – she waved the letter – 'perhaps I could go down there and speak to them.'

'No, my love. You must talk to Thomas. Let him do it.'

'He'll be cross. I want to sort it out myself.'

'Iris, you've always been the most stubborn person I know. You get a bee in your bonnet and off you go, taking everyone with you. But you're not like you were; you're not young anymore for a kick-off.'

'I know, but I can do this. I know I can.'

'Iris, please don't.'

'I made this mess – now I'm going to sort it. By myself.'

Iris took the letter into the lounge, bundled it up with her cards and hid it under the sofa.

When she returned to the kitchen, Eric had gone.

CHAPTER 14

The weekend had been very pleasant indeed, and Peter whistled a jaunty tune as he unlocked the door to the office. He'd secured the old woman's house and made some headway with Blue Tiger Books. Things were on the up.

The bookshop was in a worse state of affairs than he'd imagined – run down and shabby, books piled higgledy-piggledy in semi darkness. But the owner seemed full of life. Pretty too. She didn't so much walk as glide, like a monarch. Yes, that was it – there was something regal about the way she moved. As she'd pulled up a chair by her computer and gone through the accounts and floor plans with him, she'd reminded him of Marion.

The shop had been losing money for several years. Its remaining as a bookshop seemed hopeless, but as a property ripe for development, Peter reckoned there was money to be made. For one thing, it was a good size. There was a large basement, the shop itself, living quarters and storage space two floors up. If he could buy it for a knockdown price and secure planning permission for several luxury flats, the profit would be astronomical.

And his problems would be over.

Their first meeting had gone well. Maria had seemed confident and in control, but it was obvious she needed him. She'd been extremely friendly, laughing at all his jokes and nudging his shoulder as they'd looked at the screen.

The downcast figure who'd been standing by the stack of books was another matter and could be a problem. Maria had said he didn't work for her, but the last thing Peter needed was some disgruntled employee with a contract to be paid off. He made a mental note to find out more.

And there was something else about the man.

Tom or whatever his name was had almost slammed Peter's teacup on the counter, spilling some of the liquid onto the desk. The tinge of red on his cheeks had given away his annoyance. And several times he'd sneaked tiny but significant glances at Maria when she wasn't looking. Then, when Peter had brushed shoulders with Maria and she'd laughed at something dull he'd said, Tom had definitely got the hump.

He'd known other people like Tom – polite and hopeless. Never won anything. They'd rather leave a situation feeling aggrieved but worthy than confront it. True to form, the man had turned tail and left. A dignified exit. A dignified defeat.

Just a few files poked from Peter's in-tray. Next to those was an empty coaster where a steaming mug of coffee should have been.

'Marion!'

'Yes, Mr Lipscombe.'

'Is it really too hard to have a coffee on my desk when I get into the office? What do I pay you for?'

'Yes, Mr Lipscombe. It's just that you don't always get in at the same time, and I thought that if I wait until you're actually in, the coffee'll be hot for you.'

'Marion, we've spoken about this before, have we not? I don't pay you to think. I pay you to do what I ask.' He poked the air with each word. 'Now get me a coffee … please.'

'Yes, Mr Lipscombe.'

'Did you send that letter I wrote to the batty lady by registered post?'

'Yes, Mr Lipscombe, but I wish you'd let me write your correspondence for you, like you used to.'

'Yes, and you'll be running the business soon, won't you, Marion? I'm quite capable of writing a bloody letter.'

Peter's chest began to thump and he felt hot as memories of school and failure surfaced. He took a deep breath. 'It was a bloody risk sending it, but we're watertight now. Let's hope it just ends up in the bin or' – Peter laughed – 'she puts it on some toast. Now, coffee.'

Marion returned with a mug and placed it on his desk. 'Mr Lipscombe, I'm not sure it's right what we're doing to that woman.'

'Which is why you don't get paid to think. All this legal stuff is way above your head. Just stick to what you know and make use of that O level … what was it in?'

'Which one? I got ten—'

'Use that cookery O level to make us both a nice sandwich and make sure my coffee arrives on time. Let me worry about the rest.'

He regretted the vicious words as soon as they were out and stared down at the steaming coffee.

'But, Mr Lipscombe, it doesn't seem right to me.'

'Marion, we're in dire straits. We're doing her a big favour. No maintenance charges until she's dead.'

'But she has to give up her home.'

Peter could have sworn she'd almost stamped her foot.

'Small price to pay for peace of mind, I'd say.'

Marion walked back to her desk as the office door opened. Peter leapt up from his chair.

'Mrs Blueberry! How lovely to see you.'

Her eyes, red-rimmed, either from the wind or from crying, flashed around the room until they fell upon Peter. She was bundled up in a short, green anorak and dark trousers, and in one hand she clutched a screwed-up envelope. She seemed so fragile that Peter wondered whether the slightest breeze might blow her over; she struggled even to keep the door open long enough to get inside.

He took the elderly woman's arm and led her to a seat.

'Come over here, my love, and sit down. Marion, get Mrs Blueberry a nice cup of tea, please. Sugar, Mrs B? Now what can we do for you today?' He patted Iris's hand and removed the envelope.

'Well ...' Her voice caught, and she rocked in the chair, head moving from side to side. 'I wanted to ask you about this letter.'

'What letter's that now, Mrs Blueberry?'

She looked down at her empty hands and turned them over. 'But … I …'

Marion placed a mug on the desk.

'There, look a nice cup of tea. That's all, thank you, Marion.' He gestured for her to leave them.

'Mr Lipscombe, do you think we should phone for someone?' Marion asked.

'That will be *all*, thank you, Marion.'

Peter patted Mrs Blueberry's arm with one hand and passed the letter to Marion behind his back with the other, mouthing *Get rid of this.*

'Now, my dear, what's all this about a letter?'

'Yes …yes … I have it here somewhere, it's … let me just look.' She slipped a small bag off her shoulder and fumbled with the clasp.

Peter reached over. 'Here, let me,' he said, and clicked it open.

'I know it's here somewhere,' Mrs Blueberry muttered as she rummaged through her belongings.

Several white cards dropped onto the floor. Peter picked them up and looked through them. 'What are these now?'

Thomas's phone number is 0709 567132.

Pay bills on the 3rd.

The bus home is number 65. Try to count eleven stops.

'Oh, nothing. They just help me remember sometimes.' She held out her hand.

'Now don't let your tea get cold, Mrs B,' Peter said, and pointed at the cup. While she was distracted he pocketed a card.

'Any sign of the letter, my love?'

'No. I don't know what I've done with it.'

'Oh dear. I'm sure it wasn't important, otherwise you would've looked after it, wouldn't you?'

'But it was important, I know it was – that's why I'm here. I think.' Iris took a sip of tea.

'Well, I wonder what it could have been about,' Peter said.

Iris screwed her eyes shut and frowned. 'It's the house. I remember now.' She tried to stand. 'It's the house. I don't want to sell it.'

'Now, now sit yourself down. Selling the house?' Peter said softly, and glanced at Marion, who was watching intently, hands on her hips. 'You're not selling the house, Mrs B. Don't you remember? We're making things easier for your son. None of that nasty inheritance tax. Thousands of pounds he'd have to pay. And no more worry for you either. How old's your house? Forty, maybe fifty years?'

Iris nodded.

'What happens if the drains collapse, or you get a hole in the roof? What will you do then? By putting it all in the hands of Lipscombe Property Associates, you'll have none of that worry ever again. That makes sense, doesn't it?'

'Well, yes, but I'm not sure. I should talk to Thomas.'

Peter laughed. 'And spoil the surprise? Imagine how happy he'll be. One minute he's thinking, *Where do I find all the money?* and the next he finds out his lovely mum's taken care of everything. You're a star, that's what you are.'

Marion glared at him.

'Well …' Iris bit her lip and shook her head. 'Are you sure?'

'Of course. We're professionals. Look at all these awards.' He pointed to the wall where several framed certificates hung.

Iris stared at her hands.

'Now, I'm glad that's put your mind at rest.' He stood up. 'On one of your cards it said the number 65 is the bus that gets you home. Is that right?'

'Yes,' the frail woman mumbled, still looking down at her lap.

Peter took her hand and helped her stand. 'There you go – ups-a-daisy.' He guided her towards the door. 'You'll be all right getting home, will you? Course you will. Bye bye now. It was lovely to see you again. Give my regards to that lucky son of yours.'

Mrs Blueberry turned, her eyes full of tears. He swallowed hard, placed a hand on her back and guided her onto the street. 'That's it. I think your bus stop's down there on the right, isn't it?'

She shuffled forward with such tiny steps that she barely made any progress. Peter nipped back inside the office and closed the door. Marion shook her head.

'What?' he said, both annoyed and ashamed.

Marion said nothing, just turned her back on him.

Peter pulled out the card that had fallen from Mrs Blueberry's bag and read it again.

You have sold the house to Mr Lipscombe. Talk to Thomas.

CHAPTER 15

Thomas had never thought he'd spend the weekend wishing it away but he couldn't wait to get back to Blue Tiger. He was determined to impress Maria and hoped there'd been no more contact from Lipscombe. There was still so much to do – he wanted to finish sorting the shelves and have a good look around the basement to assess the flood damage, his plan was to reopen that part of the shop. He hadn't spoken to Maria about it, but felt sure his idea would be a success.

The first time he'd discovered the tiny basement staircase, it was like finding a secret passage to a world of sci-fi treasures; he'd felt like an explorer. No other bookshop in town had gathered a collection quite like it, and over the following weeks he'd spent his lunchtimes choosing between Clarke and Heinlein, Asimov and Dick. Little white postcards had been pinned to the shelves – detailing the staff's favourite books. Thomas had loved taking a chance on a new read, especially when an employee called Thufir Hawat had recommended it.

Today, Maria was at her desk. And with a customer too. Maybe his spring cleaning was working.

The man paid for his book, bade them a cheery good-morning and left.

'Well,' Thomas said. 'A customer. Whatever next.'

'Cheeky,' Maria said, and punched his shoulder playfully. 'How was your weekend?'

Good question. It had been a strange one.

His mum had seemed agitated. She'd spent her time doing odd jobs but finished none of them. The duster remained on the windowsill, the tray of compost half-used and her new trousers shortened in just one leg.

'What's wrong, Mum? Got stuff on your mind?' Thomas had asked.

'Nothing dear. It'll all be fine on Monday.'

He'd asked her what was happening on Monday but the question had confused her and she'd shaken her head, looked at the empty leather chair and said, 'Monday? I don't know about Monday. Whatever day it is, it'll be fine, won't it, darling?'

Again he'd pondered how often he'd taken for granted her effortless energy, regardless of whether she was gardening, cooking or planning a party. Now life itself seemed a struggle. Losing Isabelle would account for her lack of sparkle, but there was something else. She seemed distracted and troubled of late. He'd thought about talking to her, but it felt weird talking to his mum about her worries. She was the strong one, the grown-up, the one who'd always given him advice.

Then there was Isabelle.

She'd seemed forlorn, sitting on a pile of books as he tidied his bedroom.

'Thank you,' she'd said quietly.

'What have I done?' Thomas had asked.

'Well, you could have sold me for scientific research, you could. Or given me to the newspapers, swatted me, or just run away. I don't know.'

'I suppose so, but I like to help, and part of that's because of you. You make your own luck, Dad always used to say. Mum enjoys looking after people. That's rubbed off.'

Isabelle had laughed. 'She was always like that. I didn't do it.'

'But you gave her the confidence.'

'Yes, that was me,' she'd said, and glowed.

'You gave her wings.' He'd smiled at her and perched on the edge of the bed. 'Why do some people have fairies?'

Isabelle had been quiet for a long time.

'I don't know,' she'd finally admitted. 'We're just there. We don't get a choice. I think it's like some people have blue eyes instead of green.'

'So it's just luck then?'

'As I said, I don't know. When Iris was born, so was I. It's like the sun rising each morning – it just happens.'

Thomas jumped. Maria was tapping his shoulder.

'Earth to Thomas … I said how was your weekend?'

'Sorry. Miles away. It was okay, thanks. So, were you busy?'

'Yup. I think your tidying's helped. I've put a couple of spots in over there. Look.' She pointed towards the front of the shop.

Thomas followed her finger. It was undoubtedly brighter, and the lights illuminated a table laden with newly arranged books.

'That's where we'll put *Angel's Delight*,' Maria said.

'Oh, God, I don't think I'm ready for that,' Thomas said, and took a step backwards.

Maria laughed. 'Have confidence – you're a writer.'

'That's true but … well, it doesn't seem like a proper book.'

'Hey' – she glared at him – 'if that's what *you* think, and you're the author, how do you expect anyone else to see it differently? C'mon, man, have some backbone.'

She was right, of course, but he'd lost his confidence. Asking Blue Tiger to feature it had been the last desperate throw of the dice, and now, incredibly, Maria was willing to display his novel, to sell it to actual people … like a proper book. It was unbelievable. But all he could think about was whether it was good enough. Would people like it or hate it? He couldn't bear the thought of criticism. It was a cliché, but *Angel's Delight* was his baby and now he was about to send it into the world. Perhaps it would be better just to call the whole thing off.

'Thomas …' Marie's soft Geordie accent broke the silence. 'Why so thoughtful today?'

'Sorry, I'm not quite with it … so I was thinking – would you mind if I took a look in the basement? It would give you more space for your books and you could open it for meetings and—'

Maria shook her head. 'No, don't worry about that.'

'But it would give the shop a bit extra, something Waterstones hasn't—.'

'It'll never work,' she said. She was no longer smiling.

'I'm sure I could do some—.'

'Thomas, just leave it, man.'

She looked so sad in that moment that Thomas had to avert his eyes. He spent the rest of the morning jazzing up the window display and setting up genre-specific tables, from cooking to computers, and detectives to dance. He marked up a chalkboard with white and pink script advertising their book of the week and adjusted one of the spotlights to draw customers' attention to it. Finally, he vacuumed the dust off the floor. Maria came down the aisle holding a cup of coffee. Her mouth formed an O.

'It looks amazing. Absolutely fantastic!'

Thomas couldn't stop himself from grinning.

'It looks like a new shop, it's wonderful.' Maria walked around the new displays.

He allowed himself to lap up the praise. And why not? It was good. Now, the shelves were neat, and the store seemed to have a natural flow that would move the customer from one enticing table to the next.

'I've been listening to Marillion,' he said.

She chuckled. 'You have a good memory. What did you think?'

'I like them, though they have so many records it's going to take me an age to listen to everything.'

'Start with *Marbles*,' Maria said. 'That album got me through my break-up. I didn't come out of the house for three months. Everyone in that band felt like a friend by the end.'

'Your break-up?'

'With my partner. Actually with the shop and my life too.' She sighed. 'I'm sorry I was snappy but I can't face the basement. That's when he said it was over – after the flood. He couldn't take it anymore. I can understand that, but I still can't work out the suddenness of it all. We were a team, did everything together. Then it was just me. And to top it all, he left me with all the debt. Why would he do that?'

'Did you speak to him?'

'We never spoke another word to each other. I was too upset. The solicitor sorted it out. I signed everything.' She shrugged. 'And then a month or two later he got married.'

'Married? Do you think—'

'I don't like to think about that, although I have. I've thought about everything, including aliens.' She laughed.

'Well, I don't want to push you, but it could be a new start. We could get this bookshop buzzing. What do you reckon? Give me a week?'

'You're on fire, man. When you first came in here you were a little mouse. Okay, give it a go if you think it's worth it.' She looked at the floor. 'You should know that I'm probably going to sell anyway, so it could all be for nothing.'

'Maria. Really?'

'I haven't decided for sure, but that guy who came in has made me a decent offer … well, an offer.'

'I didn't like the look of him.' Thomas said. 'You should be careful.'

She smirked. 'I'd never have guessed.'

Thomas felt the blood rush to his cheeks. 'All I'm saying is, if it's too good to be true, it most likely is.'

He walked towards the tiny staircase, felt Maria's eyes on him and straightened his posture, trying to effect a cool nonchalance. Unfortunately his feet had other ideas and he nearly tripped on the carpet.

'Careful!' Maria called out, her voice full of mischief and delight.

* * *

A single neon strip flickered as it warmed up, and Thomas wondered if Maria had let out some of her anger in the basement. Books were scattered over the floor as if they'd been thrown, their covers ripped and twisted. All were sci-fi classics and he recognised many of the titles as he flipped them over with his foot.

It was worse than he'd imagined, not least because of the smell … like a hundred cats had peed in the same spot. The carpet was still wet, but the mildew covering the books wasn't helping. The whole lot would need to be removed and destroyed, perhaps even the shelving too.

Had he promised too much? Maybe, but if he couldn't fix the basement, Maria would sell.

Damn it, why was he so hopeless? His job, his girlfriend, his attempt at watercolours, playing the guitar. Everything he tried was doomed to failure.

One book was open in a V shape, its spine in the air, and Thomas remembered lining books up like that as a child, creating a tunnel and running his train track through it.

He'd lie on his stomach, his chin resting on the floor, and watch the train appear out of the dark. His whole life had been ahead of him back then.

He kicked the book and it spiralled towards the shelving. On the carpet was a small soggy square of white. He picked up the card and ran his finger along the smudged words.

Flowers for Algernon by Daniel Keyes

Following their experiments on the lab mouse, Algernon, university researchers turn Charlie into a genius. Algernon's new intelligence fades, and he dies, and Charlie realises the same fate awaits him.

I think *Flowers for Algernon* is heartbreaking and brilliant. The idea behind it is perfect, and horribly disturbing. An all-time classic.

Thufir Hawat

Thomas placed the little card reverently on the bookshelf and smoothed the sodden edges. Maria's words came to mind: *C'mon, man, have some backbone.*

He would sort out this basement even if it bloody killed him.

CHAPTER 16

Mr Lipscombe was a bully. No doubt about it. Marion had been disgusted by how he'd spoken to that old lady, and once again, she'd let him get away with it.

Why was she so loyal to him? Why not just tell him to stop? Better still, why didn't she just tell him to get stuffed?

She wasn't frightened of him. True, she didn't want to lose her job but there were plenty of others. She had skills, office-management experience, and ten bloody GCSEs, for God's sake.

When he'd first taken over the business from his father, everything had been perfect. They'd worked together as a team; he was good at talking to people, a natural salesman, and could bring in work with little effort. Marion was the organiser; she could run the office without thinking and turn his dictation and rambling notes into presentable documents.

Those early days had been so happy. Red wine on Friday afternoons and cream cakes on birthdays.

These days she rarely got a thank-you and spent most of her time answering the phone, filing and buying his shopping, which was usually seven microwave meals a week.

Tenerife.

That's what had started it, she was sure of it.

Mr Lipscombe hadn't talked about it, but he'd been different ever since that trip – rude and irritable.

And he'd taken over her duties as though he'd lost confidence in her. All the accounts had been moved, and he'd started paying the bills and writing his disastrous letters. Consequently, business had dried up. It was as if he wanted to do everything himself, as if only he could get them out of the mess. And yet he was going about things the wrong way. Together they were strong, but he was blind to her ideas and ever more desperate in his dealings. He looked a mess too, his stubble growing in proportion to his despair.

Mr Lipscombe closed the door behind poor old Mrs Blueberry and Marion couldn't bear to even look at him. She strode across the room and picked up the woman's barely drunk mug of tea.

'What?' Mr Lipscombe said.

Marion sighed. 'If you don't know, I'm not going to tell you.'

'You're worried about Mrs Batty? We've done everything right. It's all legit.'

'It isn't, you know it isn't. Why can't you see that? It's

wrong. Everything's wrong. And it's getting worse and so are you and I … don't want to be part of it anymore.'

She was close to tears and, not wanting him to see her upset, grabbed her coat and hurried past him. 'I'm taking an early lunch.'

'Marion …'

She slammed the door shut, took a breath and began walking, with no idea where she was heading.

Unable to hold back the tears, she leant against a wall and began to sob. An elderly man stopped and asked her gently if she was all right.

'Just boyfriend trouble,' she said, grateful for his kindness.

She wiped her eyes and shook her head. Not far ahead a group of cyclists were circling a single figure wearing a short, green anorak.

Marion began to run.

She was no athlete, but she gathered speed, dodging some people and knocking into others.

The four boys riding around the frail old lady chanted. 'Crazy bitch, crazy bitch, she's just a crazy bitch.'

Marion forced her way inside the circle and held Mrs Blueberry.

'Bog off, you little bastards,' she yelled, spit flying from her mouth. It felt so good to be shouting. 'You should be ashamed of yourselves. She could be your grandmother.'

The boys laughed, but stood on their pedals and rode away.

'Come on,' she said. 'Let me take you home.'

The old woman's head darted from side to side, and

she looked up at Marion with terrified eyes. 'I don't know where I live. I've forgotten.'

In one hand she clasped a white card so tightly that the skin was turning white. Marion tried to prise her fingers open but she only looked more frightened.

Then Marion remembered the letter.

She'd stuffed it in her pocket as soon as Mr Lipscombe had handed it to her. She pulled it out, straightened the creases, and there was the address.

Yes! She punched the air.

'Don't worry. I know where you live,' she said.

* * *

Mrs Blueberry rested her head on the car window and didn't say a word for the entire journey. The letter Marion had read was undoubtedly part of the problem. Which meant she could make things right – show the letter to Mrs Blueberry's son and put an end to this nightmare.

She drove into a small cul-de-sac. Mrs Blueberry's house was a semi with a trimmed lawn and beautifully kept flowerbeds.

'Who's the gardener?' Marion asked.

Mrs Blueberry laughed. 'That's me,' she said. 'My son Thomas doesn't enjoy gardening. Eric does, though.'

'Who's Eric?'

Mrs Blueberry didn't respond, just fumbled with her key in the lock. Marion helped her.

'There you are. You're safe and sound at home. Do you mind if I come in?' Marion said. 'I can make you a nice cup of tea.'

Mrs Blueberry nodded and led her into the kitchen. The fridge door was covered in a mosaic of magnets. She moved one and smiled. Dorset. She'd been there.

They sat in the lounge and sipped their tea, Marion opposite Mrs Blueberry.

'Thank you so much,' the old woman said, and tears pooled in her eyes.

Marion reached over and patted her hand. 'It's okay, you're home.'

'You saved me. What were those boys doing?'

'Just being little brats.'

'But I'm not a witch. Why did they say that?'

'Of course you're not. They were just being nasty kids. Look, why don't you put your feet up?'

Mrs Blueberry nodded and stretched her stockinged legs out on a stool in front of her, one hand in Marion's, the other holding her cup. They sat like that for a while until Mrs Blueberry seemed relaxed and settled, and Marion decided it was safe to leave.

'I have to go now. Talk to your son about the house. Don't forget.'

She strolled into the hallway and put on her coat. The front door opened and a voice called, 'Home, Mum. You okay?'

Marion said hello, and the young man almost jumped out of his skin.

'Sorry, I didn't mean to startle you,' Marion said, and offered her hand. 'It's Thomas, isn't it?'

'Yes … who are you?' He looked at her warily.

'I helped your mum this morning. She was lost.'

Thomas shook his head and removed his shoes. 'Lost?'

'I don't think your mum's very well. Can we talk?' Marion nodded towards the kitchen. He led the way and pushed the door to.

'Is that you, Thomas?' Mrs Blueberry called out.

'I'll be through in a minute, Mum.'

'She was in town,' Marion said. 'In a terrible state. She couldn't find her bus. A group of boys were circling her on their bikes and chanting. It was horrible. No one was doing anything to help.'

'What … I don't get it. She didn't say she was going out. She could have come with me. What was she doing in town?'

This was the time to hand over the letter, yet Marion hesitated. If Mr Lipscombe found out she'd betrayed him it would certainly be the end of the business. And despite everything, she wasn't quite ready to give up. Surely there was still a spark of hope for them. If Mrs Blueberry told her son about the house, Mr Lipscombe need never know what Marion had done.

'How do you know Mum?'

The tone of his voice was defensive.

'I don't know her,' Marion said moving into the hallway. 'I met her earlier at my office. Listen I have to go, but you need to talk to her. She's got something to tell you.'

Thomas took a step forward, then quickly hopped onto one foot. Panic washed over his face, and he seemed distracted. 'Yes, okay. Well, I don't know your name, but thank you.'

'It's Marion,' she said, and pushed past him out of the front door, the crumpled letter still deep in her pocket.

CHAPTER 17

As soon as the door was shut, Thomas looked down. He'd trodden on something and a sixth sense told him what it was.

Isabelle lay on the carpet.

And so did an upturned drawing pin.

His mother had dropped it the previous evening and despite a thorough hands-and-knees search, they'd failed to find it.

The pinprick in his socked foot had ensured he'd hopped away before bearing his weight down on the floor but the fairy wasn't moving. One wing lay trapped beneath her. The other projected from her side, bent in the middle, flapping limply in the draft from beneath the front door.

'Thomas, who was that lady?' his mother called from the lounge. 'She was very nice.'

'I don't know, Mum. I've just got to do something. Hang on a minute.'

He tore a cardboard strip from a cornflakes packet and slid it under the fairy's body, like a miniature stretcher, then took her upstairs and laid her on the bed.

She still hadn't moved. Thomas held his breath and prodded her tiny body with his finger, once, then twice.

Isabelle twitched. She was alive!

Thomas found a cotton bud in the bathroom and doused it with cold water, then gently wiped her face with it.

Her eyelids flickered open.

'Isabelle! I thought I'd killed you.'

She shook her head. 'You nearly did, what with those great big feet of yours.'

Thomas laughed. 'That's the first time anyone's called my feet big.'

'It's not funny,' she said, and attempted to flutter her wings. One twitched a couple of times and fell limp. She propped herself up on her elbows. 'But it's not your fault. I didn't feel well before you squished me.'

'What happened?'

'When that lady was about to leave, all my strength just disappeared, it did, and I couldn't flutter. Before that I'd felt well again.'

'What were you doing downstairs?'

'I wanted to explore,' Isabelle said, and beamed excitedly. 'I didn't like it to begin with – it felt so open and dangerous. But then I saw things … the dripping tap sending ripples across the washing-up bowl, and the red wood of the stool where Eric used to sit and watch Blueberry cook. There were dark lines across the seat, there were. I could almost see where his legs rested year after year, wearing away the wood. It was lovely.' Isabelle leant forward and whispered, 'And then I looked outside. And, oh my, the colours! They made me dizzy. All those flowers –yellow, white and red. And the grass – it's so green.'

Thomas smiled. 'I suppose I just take it for granted.'

'I loved being with Blueberry. I wouldn't change it, and I want to go back, but I felt so free. Your dad used to say, "We look but we don't see." Do you remember? Hunt the thimble? I never looked but, Thomas, the sky, have you seen it?'

Isabelle was talking so quickly it was difficult to understand her.

He hesitated. 'Well, yes.'

'It's so blue and big' – she stretched her arms wide – 'and the clouds and the way they float? I had to hold on to the kitchen curtains just to stop myself falling over, I did.' She slumped back down on the bed. 'Now it's like I know something bad's going to happen and I can't do anything about it.'

'We'll sort it. Have you spoken to the queen again? She said she could help, didn't she?'

Isabelle looked away. 'I'm too tired.'

'Okay, first things first. We need to fix your wing.'

Isabelle shivered.

'Look, bear with me. I've never done this before,' Thomas said, and considered how ridiculous those words were. 'Look at me – I'm about to mend a fairy's wing. Like that's a normal, and everyday thing. I've never been near a sparrow's wing, let alone a frigging fairy's.'

'That's a naughty word, and Blueberry wouldn't like it.' Isabelle put her hand over her mouth and stifled a giggle.

Thomas rummaged along one of the shelves and found a matchstick and some sticky tape.

'Okay, lie on your tummy.' He held the match against the gossamer-thin wing, worried the tape would be too much. Then again, what choice did he have? 'Hold still.'

Isabelle buried her face in the bed, and Thomas gently taped the match to the wing.

'We'll soak your wing before we take the tape off. That way, there'll be no pulling.' Despite his best efforts to speak with confidence, his voice shook a little. 'Okay finished. Now get some rest. You've had a nasty shock.'

'Thank you.' Isabelle's voice was small, and she was trying not to cry. 'Thomas, I didn't like you very much at first, but now I do.'

He smiled. 'Thanks … I think.'

'You're getting colours again,' she said. 'Not many, but they're brightening every day, they are. Especially when you come back from that Tiger place.'

Isabelle yawned and rolled onto her side, her knees pulled into her chest, the broken wing propped awkwardly.

'Sleep well,' Thomas said.

'I will,' she replied, her breath already heavy.

* * *

Thomas could hear his mother's voice as he tripped down the stairs, and figured she must be on the phone.

'I think it's all done. I sorted it,' she said. There was silence, and then, 'There's no card, look. Yes, I thought so too, but it must be all right. No … I'm not going to tell him, there's nothing to tell. He's a worrier. He takes after you.' She laughed.

Thomas entered the lounge. His mum was staring at the leather chair in the corner of the room. There was no phone.

'You alright, Mum?'

His mother started and turned to face him. She looked around the room, eyes wide, hands wringing.

'Mum what's wrong? Who were you talking to?'

'There's nothing wrong, er … dear,' she said, and patted her hair into place. 'I wasn't talking to anyone. Honestly, I'm fine. Just a bit tired.'

'Who was that Marion woman?'

'Oh, I don't know. Just someone I met in town. She gave me a lift home.' Iris reached for the remote control.

Thomas felt himself getting cross. 'You can't have some woman who you've never met giving you a lift home. She said you weren't well.'

'I just felt tired, and she was very kind.' She pointed the remote at the TV, and Fiona Bruce joined the conversation.

'Mum talk to me. What about those boys on bikes?'

'I … I don't remember … they were just boys being boys … Thomas? Yes?' She seemed pleased. 'Thomas, don't go on so. I'm fine.'

'But that woman said I have to ask you something. I can't understand why you're talking to a stranger and not me. I know for a fact you've not been yourself, Mum. And there's a good reason for it.'

'Oh, Thomas, don't be silly. Everything's all right. It's

all sorted. You worry too much, like your dad. Everything works out with me, you know it does.

'That was before you lost Isa—'

Thomas fell silent. His mum turned towards him, her eyes shining.

'Pardon?'

'I mean you were younger then. Now you might need my help with things. That's all.' Thomas said, looking away.

A shadow seemed to fall across her face as she slumped in the seat. Thomas looked out of the patio doors to check the sky. The sun was still blazing yellow.

'Mum?' he whispered.

But she was lost in the telly. Jacobs Manchester was introducing his game show *If Fishes Were Wishes.*

CHAPTER 18

'Marion, are you alright?'

'Yes, Mr Lipscombe,' she replied, without looking up from her computer.

'But you haven't spoken to me all week,' he said, moving towards her.

'I've got nothing to say. I'm just getting on with my work.'

Her silence was unusual. If anything, her frequent chatter irritated him. She'd talk about anything – paintings, politics, what she had for tea, EastEnders, her cat - which he secretly did like to hear about. But now that the office was so quiet, he missed it. He missed Marion.

'But—'

'Mr Lipscombe, I work here.'

The sharp interruption stopped him in his tracks.

'I do my job and, as you keep pointing out, you don't pay me to do anything else. We don't have to be friends.

You're my boss. I'll do what you say within reason, but the way you treated Mrs Blueberry just wasn't right.'

'Don't be so silly. I've told you it's all above board. She's signed the papers.'

'You forced her to. You lied to her – a poor old lady who doesn't know what she's doing.'

Peter threw a file onto his desk. 'That's where you were on Monday afternoon, isn't it? I knew it – you were with her.'

'Yes, I was. I saw the poor woman in town and took her home. She was lost, in a terrible state.' Marion stood and faced him. She looked close to tears.

'You had no business,' he said, raising his voice. 'She's a client – that's the end of it.'

'Yes, exactly. SHE'S – A – CLIENT,' she said, as if she were talking to a child. 'Years ago, you looked after your clients, prided yourself on excellent customer service. Word of mouth – that's how we'd get on, you said. And we did … we were doing so well and people loved you and then it all changed with Tenerife. Why won't you talk about that? I don't like it here anymore. What we do is horrible. You've become horrible.' She wiped away a tear.

'Marion, you don't understand.'

'Don't understand what? That we're crooks? That one day we'll have the TV cameras here and both end up in prison?'

The phone rang. Marion grabbed it.

'Lipscombe Property Associates,' she said, her voice still trembling. She held the phone towards him and looked away. 'It's for you.'

'Who is it?'

'I don't know. I think it's the Eastern European gentleman who often rings.'

'Tell him to ring back,' Peter hissed.

Marion spoke into the phone, her voice muffled. Then she released a small gasp.

'He wants to talk to you. Now. He's very insistent.' She held the receiver towards him again, but now she looked concerned rather than angry.

'Okay, I'll deal with this. You might as well head off home.'

She handed over the phone but seemed reluctant to leave.

'Thank you, Marion,' he said, and nodded towards the door.

She sighed, put on her coat and slipped out of the office without another word, leaving him feeling alone and vulnerable.

'How can I help?' he said, trying to keep his voice steady.

'Ah, Mr Lipscombe, how very nice that you should take the time to talk to me.' The man spoke softly with an accent.

'Sorry. Things have been a little hectic here.' Peter almost fell onto the desk, his legs like jelly.

'Wonderful news. So our little arrangement is drawing to a conclusion, yes?'

'Well ... soon. In a couple of weeks it'll be signed over. I'll take possession when the old lady goes into a home. Then you can buy it from me and sell at a good profit. I've also found a bookshop, too. It's perfect. You can renovate it into flats; pay all the tradesmen in cash. It'll be worth a fortune.'

'Interesting, but we're in a hurry, Mr Lipscombe. You know that. You said nothing about care homes.'

Peter laughed nervously. 'Well, it's that or she dies. Whichever is first.'

'I see. We didn't expect a delay. But as you say, she is old, and old people have accidents, don't they? So perhaps we won't have to wait so long.'

Peter didn't like that inference one bit.

'Pardon? What do you mean?'

'No need to worry, Mr Lipscombe. Follow the plan – acquire the properties, then purchase them from yourself on our behalf with the cash. I assume it's safe.'

Peter looked at the locked cupboard. 'Yes, it's safe but—'

'Mr Lipscombe, there isn't a problem is there?'

'No, no, of course not, but this will be the end, won't it? I think I'll have more than paid you back,' he said, trying to sound assertive.

Silence.

'Hello?' Peter's heart thumped so hard he could barely breathe.

Glass shattered to the left of the door, spewing tiny shards over the tables and floor. A red brick – dirty and cobwebbed – bounced off his desk and landed at his feet. He jumped down, crouched on the floor, and peered out of the window.

The voice on the other end of the phone returned, breathless, furious. 'I will tell you when you have paid the debt. Do you understand, Mr Lipscombe?'

Peter nodded.

'Do you understand?' the voice hissed.

'Yes ... Yes.'

'Good. This is what you are going to do. Purchase the bookshop and inform me when you have signed for the house. Leave the rest to us.'

'But I don't know about the bookshop. I'm just negotiating with the owner at the moment.'

'It sounds perfect. I would be very very disappointed if it didn't come our way. Do you understand?'

'Yes,' Peter whispered.

The phone clicked, leaving him with only the dial tone.

He wiped his clammy palms down the front of his shirt, gulped in air and closed his eyes. What a mess he'd got himself into. The question was, how was he going to get out of it?

The foreign investment overwhelmed him whenever he thought about it. Which was nearly always.

Night-time was the worst, the glowing digits on his alarm clock changing as if in slow motion as he counted the hours until morning. He hadn't had a good night's sleep since returning to the UK. Images of the barren land and broken buildings tortured him. Coffee had become his safety net, but he'd cut back when he'd noticed the tremble in his hands. Not a good image.

He'd put everything into Tenerife. Of course, now he knew he'd been an idiot, but it had seemed like the chance of a lifetime. Speculate to accumulate, his father had said.

And what had he been left with? A worthless investment, a business facing ruin, and no money with which to buy anything that would enable him to recoup his losses. And he was in arrears with the bank – borrowed beyond his means. And they wanted their money back too.

Just when there'd seemed to be no way out, Seth Ozil had offered him a lifeline.

They'd met at The Bakers Arms – a pirate's den, where all the colourful and less-than-honest characters gathered, a pub he'd often passed but never dared enter. The men sitting outside always appeared either drunk or drugged. That day had been no different.

Inside, it was as if someone had switched off the sunlight. Dust hung like fog and bulbs flickered beneath grimy shades, casting yellow circles onto the floor.

Lipscombe had ordered a beer and sat at a table pitted with graffiti knifed into the wood. He'd waited alone for half an hour, then gone to the toilets.

An enormous man with a shaven head covered in tattoos had been sitting on a stool by the sink, cutting a large brown block of cannabis into smaller pieces.

'What you after?' he'd said.

'Nothing,' Peter had replied. 'Just a pee.'

'Hurry the fuck up.'

Peter unzipped but had felt the man's stare behind him and been unable to go. He'd washed his hands and caught the man rolling his eyes as he'd fumbled with the door.

Back at his table, he'd found a refreshed pint glass and a well-dressed man in the seat opposite his own.

'Mr Lipscombe, how lovely to meet you.'

The man's accent had sounded exotic but somehow sinister. He'd introduced himself as Seth Ozil, said he had a proposition, and gestured to the empty chair. The white Ralph Lauren insignia had stood out against the man's close-fitting black sweater, as had the muscles flexing beneath his sleeve. Peter had thought him a perfect parody of style and wealth – the stubble dusting his tanned face, the immaculately cut dark hair, the sunglasses perched on the top of his head – but the cold blue eyes had been humourless and he'd shivered involuntarily.

A sixth sense – the one he should have listened to during the Tenerife fiasco – had told him to leave, but he'd sat, and taken a sip of his pint.

'I have a problem,' the man had said, 'and I understand you do too. If we put our two problems together, neither of us will have one.'

'I … I don't—'

'You need money,' the man said. 'We have lots but we can't do much with it. It needs to be in the system. It needs to be' – he'd hesitated, and leant back in his seat – 'cleaned.'

Peter had gawped like a fish, then muttered, 'Sorry, I'm not sure how I'd do that.'

The man had sighed and explained. They'd provide him with cash deposits. Peter would pay off his loan instalments. The money would then be in the system. It was a win–win. All he had to do was purchase properties and sell them to Ozil at a reduced price. If they needed renovation, all the better. Ozil would inject more money into the system through the payment of tradesmen.

He'd laughed then, and said, 'Who doesn't like cash in hand? We then sell at a profit and the money returns to our accounts, legitimate and clean. All you have to do is bury our payments in your books. That shouldn't be too hard, should it? Just add some fat to any income you receive.'

Peter had wanted to know where the man's money came from. Was it illegal? He could be arrested.

But Ozil waved the matter away. 'That is of no concern to you.'

'But—'

'Mr Lipscombe,' Ozil said, 'I rarely repeat myself. I will do it once, because we're getting to know each other. The source of the money is of no concern to you. I hope that is clear.'

His stare had been so cold and hard that Peter had to look away.

'I know about Tenerife. You are facing financial ruin, probably within a month if you don't get an injection of cash. Quite simply, I am offering you a chance to save your business, well, your grandfather's business.'

Peter shuddered at the memory of that meeting. What an idiot he'd been. He banged his fist against the desk drawer, leaving a dent in the grey metal.

He sat then for a while, breathing deeply, trying to calm himself.

Greedy, that's what he was. Just plain greedy. Yes, he'd wanted to help the old couple, but he'd known there was a tidy profit to be made. And Ozil had played him for all he was worth with his parting comment: "And you can make a lot of money at the same time."

Read him like a book. It was that which had swayed him.

Peter stood up and straightened his tie. He needed to ring the glaziers but somehow it seemed too much. All he wanted to do was go home and sleep. He fumbled with the lock on the old stationery cupboard. The door opened with a small creak. Inside were ten large suitcases. He opened the nearest one, battered and blue with *Happy Holidays* written along the front.

It was full to bursting with bundles of ten, twenty and fifty-pound notes.

Peter began to cry.

CHAPTER 19

Thomas had started with the books. Throwing them away felt like the worst possible sacrilege. *Rendezvous with Rama, Stranger in a Stranger Land, I, Robot* … all books were special but these came with memories. He'd forgotten lots of them, but then the title or a picture would trigger something and he'd end up daydreaming about the railway station, an early-morning commute to London, and an hour to himself with a novel.

Speed had been the solution. He'd gathered armfuls and shoved them into black plastic bags, all the while averting his eyes. Like a surgeon averse to the sight of blood.

The next job had been the carpet.

He'd never noticed how horrible it was – plain, light green, practical. He'd pulled the corner and to his surprise it had lifted easily. Beneath it, he'd discovered beautiful wooden floorboards that needed nothing but a clean. Thomas had set about the task with alacrity.

Those two weeks, despite worrying about his mother and Isabelle, had been amongst Thomas's happiest.

Maria would come down the stairs on the hour, bringing a welcome drink and sometimes a cake. He'd realised then that he was the type of person who responded to the carrot rather than the stick; the tiniest compliment from Maria would see him increasing his efforts, working tirelessly to please her. Her acclaim was a drug he wanted more of.

He'd glance at the staircase, willing Maria to come down, craving her company and the lilt of her Geordie accent.

'Thomas, here's a thought for the day,' she'd said. 'Did you know there's only ever been one sunrise and it just goes round and round the earth. Has done for millions of years.'

He was quiet for a moment and then smiled, 'That's true isn't it.' He said watching as she cut two different cakes in half so they could have a piece of each.

It didn't matter what she did – the way she ate her cake, how she carried herself, the way she dressed – she was just cool, like she wasn't trying but it worked all the same.

After that, he'd tackled the shelving. Again, the quality had amazed him – solid wood, not modern chipboard and veneer. Once he'd washed away the dust and mould, he marvelled at how the grain showed through, different shades twisting in elegant simplicity.

With a little help from a Mediterranean Breeze diffuser, the damp odour had dissipated. Now, two weeks on, only one final job remained. The far wall was obscured with a high pile of flattened cardboard and other junk, all covered in thick and sticky cobwebs and littered with mouse droppings.

Thomas worked from the top and threw the boxes into the skip. To his amazement there, in front of him, was the crest of a small brick archway and beyond, another room.

Of course! He remembered now. It had always been empty and unused. It was a decent size, too – perfect for book launches and poetry readings. Or they could hire it out for group meetings. He was unable to contain his elation, like Carter discovering Tutankhamen's tomb.

'Maria,' he shouted. 'You've got to see this.'

'Okay, two ticks, chuck.'

The stairs creaked and footsteps heralded her arrival.

'Look,' he said, and pointed towards the extra room.

Behind Maria, a pair of shiny black pointed shoes descended the stairs.

Lipscombe.

'Will you look at that?' Maria said. 'I'd forgotten all about it. It's amazing.' There was a song to her voice, a happiness. 'Oh, Thomas, you've worked so hard, but, well ….' She gestured with her hand seemingly for the creep Lipscombe's benefit.

'It looks very good,' Lipscombe said. 'I'm not sure if I can increase my offer though, if that's what you're after.' He laughed in a confident, manly baritone. Thomas hated him.

'No, of course not,' Maria said.

Thomas watched in horror as she took Lipscombe's arm and led him about the basement.

'I'm just surprised. I'd forgotten all about this room.

Look at the floor and the bookshelves – they're … they're beautiful.'

'You're right. I think we could allow you to remove them during the renovation.'

'Wouldn't you want to use the floorboards?'

'No, I think we'll gut the place and start again. Believe it or not, that's often the cheapest way.'

'So you won't be keeping the bookshop?' Thomas said, wanting to emphasise Lipscombe's plans, just in case Maria hadn't grasped them.

Lipscombe turned, his mouth taut, and for a moment, the confidence had gone. Instead, Thomas saw something else: desperation.

'No, we won't. There's a need for more housing in the town centre, and this is the perfect building.'

'You said there was a chance of opening a shop on the ground floor though,' Maria said.

'There was … there is. We'll see what we can do.'

Lipscombe glared at Thomas. A bead of sweat trickled down his temple.

'It would be a shame to close it. It's part of the town. There's been a bookshop here for as long as I can remember,' Thomas said, enjoying the man's discomfort.

'Yes, I know. Thank you for that. Who are you? Have we met?' Lipscombe raised his eyebrows.

'I'm sorry,' Maria said. 'This is Thomas. He's been lending me a hand.'

'I see, just a volunteer then.' He turned his back on Thomas. 'Maria, if I can be so bold … I don't think it's a good idea to waste your time, or for that matter Thomas's, with all this renovation work. You told me about your partner – won't this just dredge up those awful memories?' He put a hand on her arm and looked straight into her eyes.

So she'd told him about her ex. They'd obviously got to know each other. Thomas's ears started pounding.

'I don't mind,' he said.

Lipscombe's head spun around, and he glared.

It's okay,' Maria said. 'I'd like to remember Blue Tiger as it was before I sell. Plus, I haven't one hundred per cent decided I even want to.'

'That's all right, Maria. Take your time. I have to warn you though, my clients won't keep this fabulous offer on the table for too much longer. In fact, I'm visiting another property later on today. Just bear that in mind.' Lipscombe looked at his watch. 'Right, must make tracks. Lovely to meet you again.' He shook Maria's hand and turned. 'Don't work too hard, Tom,'

Then he raced up the stairs, his black shoes slapping so hard against the wooden treads that the shelving shook.

'Well, there we are,' Maria said, and started to climb the stairs.

'Don't sell it,' Thomas said so quietly that he was sure Maria couldn't have heard him.

But she turned, her brown eyes easily finding his. Lost in her smile, a happy dizziness overwhelmed him.

'You okay?' she said.

Thomas looked around the room. 'Yes. I just think you could make this shop work again. I really do. The basement gives you a load more sales space, and just look at that extra room, you could hire it out.' Thomas stopped for a moment, then grinned.

'What?'

'A coffee shop. It could be a coffee shop. Waterstones do it – why not you?'

'Jesus, man, when you get a bee in your bonnet you go for it, don't you? A month ago I was in despair. Now I've got two blokes offering me the world.' She stretched out her hands. 'A coffee shop in here?'

'I don't know what's got into me. I'm not usually like this,' Thomas said. 'It's just life's been so … so bloody grey. Yes, that's the word, like John Major on *Spitting Image*, you know?'

Maria looked blank.

'Forget it. The thing is, before, nothing mattered. Nothing. I couldn't have cared less about anything. And now I do. I think this place can be special, and I can help make that happen.' He pulled out the white card he'd found when he first visited the basement, and twisted the corners. Maria came over and traced her fingers over the words.

'What a pretentious, opinionated prick.'

'What? No! I loved Thufir Hawat's recommendations. I always looked forward to reading the next one.'

'You did?' Maria said, looking up, her eyes drowning him again. 'Thufir was me.'

CHAPTER 20

It had been a week since Lipscombe's visit and Maria hadn't mentioned selling the shop once. Surely that was a good sign. And the bookshop itself was going from strength to strength. More people were browsing and there'd even been a queue at the till. Maria talked about taking on a part-timer.

Isabelle was asleep on the bed. Thomas tucked some cotton wool around her and she opened her eyes.

'You looked cold,' he said, and sighed.

'I'm okay.'

'You're not though – look at you. You lie there all day. Your wing's getting better but you're not. I can tell. You're skinny. Your face, Isabelle – it's just bone.' He wiped his mouth. 'Please tell me what I can do. I'm out of my depth here. Out of ideas.'

'Ah,' she said. 'He does care for me.'

'Shut up, Isabelle. It isn't funny.'

'Where have you been, the Tiger shop? Let me see your eyes?' She sat up. 'Yep, wobbly again.'

'Stop it. I'm not joking. What can we do? You look so poorly.'

'I don't know,' Isabelle replied. She lay back down and closed her eyes. 'I think your mum's ill, Thomas. I didn't see it before, but I really think she is.'

'Don't change the subject. It's just old age, just forgetfulness. Sometimes even I end up in the kitchen and don't have a clue why I'm there.'

'Do you remember playing What's the Time, Mr Wolf?'

Thomas nodded.

'You'd take a step closer to Blueberry, then freeze. Then you'd take another. I was always willing her to turn at the right time to catch you. But she'd let you get to within arm's length and you'd nearly wet yourself with excitement, you would.' Isabelle laughed.

'I didn't,' Thomas said.

'Then a dash and a grab and we'd all snuggle together.'

'I remember,' he whispered.

'This is a game of Mr Wolf, Thomas. Time has sneaked up on Blueberry. She can never win, never turn around to stop it.' She sat up again, shook her head and folded her arms. 'We should have noticed. I was too close, and you were still being the baby. Iris was the strong one.'

The fairy was right. His mum hadn't been her usual self. He'd tried to ignore it, hoping it would go away.

'And that lady who came,' Isabelle continued. 'Marion? She had something to tell us, she did. I know she did!'

'Okay, okay. I'll speak to Mum. Promise. But what about

you? You're getting worse. You've lost your colour. You're asleep when I leave and asleep when I get home. I need to do something. Do you have doctors? Vets? I dunno.'

Isabelle laughed. 'Vets? You're cheeky, you are. We're just the same as our people – their doctors help us, they do.'

'But you haven't got a person, Isabelle. What happens then?'

'I don't know,' she mumbled.

She raised her arm, and Thomas glimpsed the bedsheet through the delicate skin.

'Put it down,' he said. 'I don't like it.'

'I know, it makes me shake too. I'm fading, I am.'

Thomas held his head in his hands. 'That's my point. So what should I do?'

'I need to see the queen, I do. I know some fairies who've got better when they've faded. They went to see her. She must know how to save me, and she did say she'd help.' Isabelle winced and lay back down on the bed, holding her stomach. 'But I can't go,' she whispered. 'I'm feeling so weak and now my wing's broken. Thomas, you'll have to visit her. I've told her about the phones so she owes me a favour.'

'Me? How do I do that? Will she even see me? Won't you get into trouble for telling me about her? What about—'

'I can't think of another way, can you? I can tell her you're coming. Maybe she can look out for you.'

'How will I find her?' Thomas said.

'You'll find her. Just search for Jacobs Manchester.'

'Jacobs Manchester? The TV star?'

'No, Jacobs Manchester who runs the chip shop down the road. Yes, of course the TV star.'

'But—'

'It's the only way.'

CHAPTER 21

Marion was alone at her desk again. Since the office window had been smashed she'd barely seen a whisker of Mr Lipscombe.

'It's just kids,' he'd insisted, but his voice had caught in his throat and he shielded his face with his hand, feigning interest in some old paperwork.

She'd taken several phone calls from the man with the accent, but he'd left no message. Marion wasn't sure if it was her imagination, but as the weeks went by, and his calls were unreturned, the man's voice became quieter yet more sinister. It was nothing she could put her finger on, but she felt threatened, as if she were being held responsible for Mr Lipscombe's absence.

The office was quiet without him, and although she didn't miss his moods, she missed him. At least she'd had company. At home it was always quiet. She had been so proud when she'd bought her flat and moved out of her parents' place. A new beginning.

She'd had so many plans. She'd hit the clubs, stay out late, bring home boys, find the perfect partner, lose weight. She'd be a new woman. But the reality had turned out differently, and she was lonely.

To go out you needed friends, and she'd always been a loner at school. Everyone said she was the nicest person they'd ever met, but she was quiet – could never think of the right words to say at the right time. And so she'd remained silent. Friendship groups had developed, but she'd always been outside their perimeter.

The freedom she'd looked forward to had required more than a little courage. There was nothing worse than standing in a noisy club alone, pretending to wait for someone, trying not to meet anyone's eye and keep that 'I'm having a whale of a time' smile on her face. Coffee shops were easier. She could read a book or look at her phone. But time moved so unbelievably slowly and after a while she'd just stopped going out.

She'd redecorated her flat, covered many of the walls with original art pieces – something to collect and organise. But she longed for someone to share it with other than the TV and her cat, Deirdre Reynolds.

So yes, she missed Mr Lipscombe and was worried by his absences. Over the last few weeks he'd worn a persistent sheen on his brow, and his complexion had become almost ghostly. Dark bags under his eyes matched the stubble that had become too long to be designer.

But now here he was. The phone rang just as he walked

through the office door. Marion was about to answer but he held up a hand.

'I'll get this.'

He held the phone to his ear and stared at his other hand, which trembled.

'Hello? … Hello?' he said.

Marion moved to a far desk where she knew a phone was linked to Mr Lipscombe's.

He'd had his own secretary in the early days – an attractive and efficient blonde who'd taken all her boss's calls on this shared line. He'd let her go six months later, claiming there wasn't enough work for the three of them. The decision had surprised Marion. The other woman had been much better fitted to the image of an up-and-coming property agency. The phone, however, had remained.

She lifted the receiver and listened.

'Mr Lipscombe,' said the Eastern European voice, 'is the house yours now? It's a very simple question.'

Marion looked over at Mr Lipscombe. He cradled his head in his hand, and his eyes were closed.

'By the end of the day it will technically be ours. But we can't do anything with it until the old lady no longer lives there. So it could be a while.'

'Yes, of course. But, as I said to you before, she is old. Accidents happen, don't they?'

'I'm not sure what you mean by that.'

Her boss tried to make his voice sound authoritative but his strained expression spoke volumes.

'Just stating a fact. The lady is old … yes?'

Mr Lipscombe nodded.

'So let us hope we don't have to wait too long. I trust negotiations on the bookshop are progressing well.'

'Not really. I'm no further forward, I'm afraid. I need to meet with the owner again. She seems to be having second thoughts.'

'I see.'

There was a long silence that even Marion found uncomfortable.

'You must get on top of this. Surely you need no further encouragement. I passed your house yesterday when you didn't answer my calls. Number 37, isn't it? Lovely house, an enormous bay window. Is that your cat, the big ginger one? Loves sitting outside.'

'You leave my bloody cat alone,' Mr Lipscombe hissed.

He had a cat? He'd never mentioned that, though he'd often asked about hers, even during the past few horrible months.

'Just remember,' the caller said, 'this is no game. You should not have signed up if you couldn't deliver. Did you think we would make payments to you for nothing?'

'I didn't know it was going to be like this,' he whispered.

'Well, now you do. Get used to it.' The caller laughed. 'The only way you exit is in a hearse.'

Marion gasped and put her hand over her mouth. Mr Lipscombe looked up at her.

'You need to clean our money. Then, and only then we will all be happy. You'll be rich too. It's dog eat dog. You must be the rottweiler, not the poodle.'

Marion gawped at Mr Lipscombe but he only shook his head.

'I have to go,' her boss said.

'Just confirm. The papers are in order and after midnight the house is yours, and by definition mine.'

'Confirmed. Tomorrow it's done.'

'Good. Don't be so elusive. I can visit you at home if you would prefer. You have ten days to acquire the bookshop. Goodbye.'

The phone clicked quiet but Mr Lipscombe continued to clench the receiver to his ear.

Marion went towards him and whispered, 'What on earth's happened?'

His head jerked upwards, and he put down the phone.

'Nothing to worry about. I've told you before, Marion, I make the decisions.'

'I was on the phone. I heard everything.' Marion said, more forcefully and louder than she'd intended. 'Who was that? What have you got us involved in?'

'It's just business. I needed an injection of—'

'It's Tenerife, isn't it?'

'These people are just new investors, that's all.'

'Don't be so bloody stupid, and don't treat me like a fool. He sounded dangerous. He threatened you. Don't you understand? I'm scared. What the hell's going on?'

'You shouldn't have been listening. Everything's alright.' He stood and walked into the kitchen. 'Get me the Blueberry files, please.'

'Get them yourself. I'm going out.' She grabbed her coat and covered her face with her hand so he wouldn't see her tears.

'Marion,' he shouted and took a step towards her,

reaching for her arm. 'Where are you going? Come here. We can talk about this.'

For a moment, the urge to comfort him was overwhelming. He looked so forlorn, eyes beseeching her, his only ally.

'Where are you going?' he said again, quieter this time, more resigned, as if he already knew the answer.

'I'm going to warn that poor old lady,' Marion said, her voice catching in her throat.

'But you don't understand. Please don't—'

She closed the door behind her, cutting him off, and began to run.

She'd bought the old-style Volkswagen Beetle soon after she'd moved into her new flat. It was dark purple, and although the years had taken away its shine, Marion still loved it. Like her flat, it was a place of sanctuary. Unlike her flat, it had never broken its promise of freedom.

She grabbed the steering wheel, her fingers white with the effort, and sobbed.

What do I do?

She remembered the caller's icy threat to Mr Lipscombe: *The only way you exit is in a hearse.* But it wasn't just about him, was it. What had he said? *Accidents happen, don't they?*

Marion made up her mind. She should have done this before and spoken to Mrs Blueberry's son. She needed to warn them both.

She started the car and blinked away her tears. Mrs Blueberry's house was a twenty-minute drive – a straight route if she followed the New London Road.

As she passed each side street, and there were many,

the urge to turn around tugged at her. She didn't want to be disloyal to Mr Lipscombe but God knew where it would end otherwise. It might even be too late. A chill inched down her spine. What had he done, the idiot?

The house looked quiet. All the windows were closed and there was no car in the drive.

She knocked on the door and a few minutes later, Mrs Blueberry opened it. Marion said hello, and reminded the woman how they'd met.

'Um, yes, I remember,' Mrs Blueberry said, but there was no recognition in her eyes. Her arms hung loose at her sides and she looked over Marion's shoulder, as if searching for someone else.

'Is your son in?' Marion asked.

'Yes, I'll just get him for you,' she said and climbed heavily up the stairs, pulling on the white wooden banister.

'Thomas? Thomas, your friend's here,' she called.

'I'm not actually your son's friend,' Marion said, poking her head through the doorway.

Mrs Blueberry took no notice, just called out once more, then came back downstairs and made her way into the lounge.

The hallway was full of knick-knacks – some on the floor, others on a small table surrounding a lamp, yet more perched on a tiny shelf above the radiator. A copper fairy with blue-green wings hung on a tarnished gold chain from the wall. It spun in the breeze, taking Marion back to happier times for a moment.

Familiar music from a TV game show drifted into the hallway. Marion took a tentative step inside.

'Mrs Blueberry?'

She peered into the lounge. Mrs Blueberry was sitting on the settee, smiling, engrossed in the programme.

The music built to a crescendo. '*Now here's your host …*'

Marion's eyes were drawn to the vase of flowers on the dining table. Strewn over the decorative lace cloth were a dozen small white cards. Marion moved closer.

'*The one and only …*'

She picked up the nearest card.

'*If fishes were wishes …*'

The writing was spidery and hard to decipher but she could just make out the words:

> *Thomas, your son, has gone to London. He will be away for a few days. Ready meals are in the fridge.*

'*… Mr Jacobs Manchester.*'

The applause from the TV became manic and Marion walked back to the front door. The fairy caught her eye again, and she cradled it in her fingers. *Damn it.*

CHAPTER 22

Thomas couldn't help it; the train journey to London still excited him. There'd been regular family trips to the city when he was young – London Zoo, Madame Tussauds, the museums and St Paul's – and he experienced the same thrill as he boarded the carriage now.

He sat in an aisle seat, hoping he wouldn't have to share when the train got busier. A book or headphones? He opted for music and searched for another Marillion album, determined to impress Maria.

The rocking soothed him as the world raced by, he closed his eyes and thought about his mum. He'd been too close to notice; it was Marion who'd forced him to see. It was more than just losing Isabelle, that was clear now. The word 'dementia' gnawed at him. His mum was his rock, the grown-up, and he didn't feel ready to be the one in charge.

Sometimes, late at night, warm under the covers and cloaked by the darkness, he'd draw his knees to his chest.

For just a few moments, he was a child again, dependent and vulnerable, all his worldly experience gone. In that space, he was no longer corporal, just thought, cocooned by his childhood. He couldn't explain how it worked, only that it did, and that it was perfect and beautiful.

Now it was time for a change of the guard. He had to take the reins. *They're changing the guard at Buckingham Palace.* He smiled, remembering the words from the book, the turn of each page, the feel of his dad's firm chest against his head.

And Maria … she was so different to anyone else he'd known, pushing the boundaries even down to the way she dressed – a perfect palette of the unusual.

Thomas had once tried to paint in the modernist style after going to a Kandinsky exhibition. He'd been so sure it would be easy, but his paintings had been dull and lacked depth. Maria was like Kandinsky; she knew how to make colour work.

She was beautiful too, but not through clever make-up. Her beauty ran deeper. Perhaps it was grounded in her confidence. Nothing seemed to phase her; she could talk to anyone about anything, and she made you want to listen, but was interested in doing the listening too. Thomas was used to keeping his ideas to himself, and at first she'd had to prise the words from him. But the more time he'd spent at the shop, debating books and life, the easier it had become. As if she'd liberated him.

Maria had a fairy, he was sure of it.

* * *

The large white building looked like a seventies office block. Only this one had the words *Elstree Studios* boldly displayed across the fascia.

A security guard nodded as he entered the building, and a smartly dressed receptionist smiled in his direction.

'I'd like to see Jacobs Manchester, please,' he said.

'Are you here for the show? You're rather late. I'll just check you off the list and then we'll take you through.'

'No, I—'

'Name?' she said, lifting a clipboard.

'Thomas Blueberry but—'

'What a great name – now, let me see.' She ran her finger down the column of names, then went back to the top and did it again.

'I can't see your name on the list. Have you got our letter on you by any chance?'

'Well, no, you see I'm not going to the show. I just want to see Mr Manchester.'

Damn. This wasn't going very well. He should have come up with a better plan.

'In that case, I'm sorry. Mr Manchester *never* sees members of the public.' She put the clipboard down and looked at him sympathetically. Thomas got the feeling she'd dealt with plenty of lovesick fans in her time.

'Could I make an appointment?' he asked.

'I'm sorry, Thomas,' she said quietly. 'It won't do any good. He just doesn't see ordinary people.' She patted his hand and glanced towards the security guard, who took a step closer.

'But I really need to see him. It's for a friend of mine. She's dying.'

'Is she a fan then?'

'Oh, yes. It's her last wish. It would really help. Perhaps just a message? She watches *If Fishes Were Wishes* every afternoon. You wouldn't think a tiny little tumour on the brain would be so awful, would you?' He thought of Holden Caulfield in *Catcher in the Rye*.

'Oh dear, that's awful,' she said, and picked up the clipboard again.

Thomas had another idea.

'Maybe I could let the newspapers know what a nice man Mr Manchester is.'

He could almost see the cogs turning as the receptionist considered the alternative story the newspapers would run – how Jacobs Manchester hadn't been prepared to send a message to a dying woman.

She looked at her list again and said, 'We have a few spaces for this afternoon's show. I could fit you in and perhaps Mr Manchester will talk to you afterwards, though I can't promise anything.'

'No, of course not, but that would be wonderful. Thank you very much' – he looked at the woman's name badge – 'Lucy.'

She led him along a narrow corridor and across a parking lot full of discarded props. Laughter erupted from the nearby building and Lucy heaved open a door and beckoned him through into a huge studio.

Two security guards nodded as they passed, and Thomas took his seat and mouthed a thank-you to Lucy.

The warm-up comedian left the stage and an excited murmur rippled through the audience.

In front of the seating area, a large tank of crystal-clear water filled the breadth of the room. Hundreds of colourful metal fish had been anchored to the bottom by various lengths of cord. Two boats – one yellow, one red – were tied to a jetty that doubled as a stage.

The studio went dark, and the audience fell silent. A fanfare blared through the speakers, and Thomas jumped. Spotlights swirled around the room, transforming it from practical to magical, and settled on the jetty. Through a haze of dry ice, Jacobs Manchester appeared, waving to the crowd and making heart signs with his hands. Light bounced off his sparkling jacket and onto the audience as he turned on the spot, hands high in the air. His luxuriant dark hair – perhaps a tad too long, Thomas thought – wafted as he kicked his legs in time with the beat, and tapped pointed and polished red crocodile skin shoes.

'If fishes were wishes …' the announcer said with a touch of an American accent, and the applause became deafening as he introduced the star.

The next two hours passed in a blur. For the first part of the show, two people sat in each boat, one answering questions while the other fished. If they caught a fish they won a prize. If they got it wrong, a glamorous assistant placed a bucket of water beside their boat. The opponents could either continue fishing or dump the water into their competitors' boat. Teams had to decide how many buckets to let build up before they stopped fishing because each fish caught contained a prize.

The game was over when either boat sank.

The winning boat today was the red one. It held a

photogenic young couple who beat a rather staid, portly and shocked mother and son, who lost despite appearing to be several buckets ahead throughout the contest.

Jacobs Manchester's role involved ridiculing the contestants and goading the audience. He seemed to relish both tasks.

Thomas knew there was always a musical interlude, but was still floored when Adele took the stage. After a breathtaking performance, Jacobs Manchester appeared once more through the smoke and introduced part two.

A spotlight fell onto a single boat containing the victorious couple from the first half.

'Duncan and Jemima,' he said, his arms raised, 'all that stands between you and half a million pounds are' – the audience joined in – 'six questions, two whales and one perfect storm.'

The applause exploded.

'Are you ready to play?'

The young couple nodded manically and waved to friends.

'Ok, for every question you get right you can pull up a fishing line and catch a prize. You can bail out of your boat at any time, in which case you can keep whatever prizes you've won. If the boat sinks before you bail out, you lose all the prizes. If you answer the 6th and final question, you can choose a golden rod one of which will have caught a fish worth half a million pounds. Choose the wrong one and the boat sinks. Is that clear?'

They both nodded, still waving.

Jacobs stood back, mimicked a fisherman casting off,

and together with the audience chanted, 'Let's fish for a wish.'

A powerful wind machine whipped up the water, and the two contestants grabbed the side of the boat to steady themselves. The studio lights faded and lightning flashed across the blackened ceiling. Dramatic music faded and a throbbing pulse took over, speeding up as more questions were answered. Two enormous whales appeared and spurted water from their blowholes into the boat.

Jacobs Manchester's voice boomed questions from the PA. Every time they got one right, they chose a fishing rod and reeled in a fish with information about a prize. Question five landed the star prize, a car. The couple huddled together, shouting above the storm, water crashing down on them, and decided to abandon ship, much to the annoyance of the booing audience.

Soaking wet but still waving and grinning, they bounced onto the jetty. Jacobs Manchester ran through the loot they'd won. All the time, he kept his distance, taking a step back if the contestants got too close.

'Until next time when we'll wish for a fish,' he said.

Then, with a final wave, he retreated from the stage. The house lights came on, and the enchantment of the past two hours was gone.

The still-excited audience headed for the exits. Thomas decided to chance his arm and repeated the story about his dying friend to a security guard. The man disappeared for a few minutes. Then, to Thomas's amazement, he appeared by the water tank and beckoned.

Jacobs Manchester was waiting.

He looked smaller off stage, his presence somehow diminished, not least because his make-up was beginning to run in the little rivulets of perspiration. And yet Thomas still felt star-struck and tongue-tied. He extended his hand. The star did not shake it.

'Hello, I'm *the* Jacobs Manchester,' he said. 'I know how wonderful it is to meet me. Lots of people can't talk, so don't worry.' He waved his hand as if absolving Thomas's muteness. 'Now, a little bird told me your friend has a nasty tumour. Is that right? Hmm? Hmm?' He nodded, eyes half-closed. 'Right, let's see what we can do … If fishes were wishes, what would you wish for, hmm?' He clasped his hands together. 'We know, don't we? Yes, yes, you'd wish for that tumour to disappear, wouldn't you? Hmm? Well, now you can, I've said so. So there you are.' He opened his arms, Christ-like. 'Did you hear? I've said so – me, Jacobs Manchester.'

He took one of the coloured fish from the show and held it towards Thomas.

'Here's the fish. Wish on the fish. Touch it.'

Thomas tentatively reached forward.

'Go ahead. Not too close. Now wish on the fish. Do it in your head if you can't speak. That's it – wish on the fish. Well done. There we are.'

He passed the fish to a runner and turned.

'Lovely to meet you.'

'But … Mr Manchester, I—'

'This will heal her soon. Just you wait and see. Bye bye.'

The star walked off with his assistant, saying, 'That's it, write it down. Contact the papers. They love it, don't they?

It's all about what you believe in, isn't it? And they believe in the fish.' He laughed. 'Do you think it's got powers? I do, and I should know. I've got powers too, you know.'

'I know, Mr Manchester, you've said so before,' the assistant mumbled.

'Mr Man—'

A burly security guard stepped from the side and blocked Thomas's path.

'This way, sir,' he said, pointing towards the exit.

'But I just need to—'

'This way, sir.'

The guard gently but firmly clasped the top of Thomas's arm and guided him to the door.

The twilight surprised Thomas. The artificial glow of the studio had made him think it was earlier. Like when he used to go to a matinee with his mum and it would be dark by the time the film was over. The change disorientated him now, just as it had then.

What now? He'd come to London to meet Jacobs Manchester's fairy, it was literally a matter of life and death.

Instead, he'd wished on a bloody fish.

CHAPTER 23

The hotel was typical budget accommodation. Rows of doors lined endless narrow corridors. Thomas slid his key card into 275 and the green light flashed. At least that had worked.

He flopped onto the double bed, piled the pillows behind him and channel-surfed.

He'd always enjoyed his work trips to Leeds and Manchester – the freedom to do what he wanted, eat what he liked. Tonight, though, the buzz had abandoned him. Would his mum see the food in the fridge? Would she stay indoors? He'd left her to fend for herself, and for what? To search for Jacobs Manchester's fairy? Foolish didn't even begin to describe his actions, though he had to admit, he'd enjoyed the show. And Jacobs Manchester certainly knew how to whip his audience into a frenzy.

He closed his eyes, and let the canned laughter on the TV wash over him …

* * *

Darkness had replaced the evening gloom when he came to. The TV had switched into standby. Disorientated, Thomas reached behind and fumbled for the light switch on the headboard.

A bleak yellow light leached from the lamp and illuminated the bed.

And what was hovering two inches from his nose …

Thomas lurched backwards and banged his head hard on the wall.

A fairy? *Another one?*

'Shh,' she said, and put a finger to her lips. 'I've been waiting ages for you to wake, you lazy bastard.'

'What? Hang on … you can't swear.'

'The fuck I can't.'

As she spun in the air, golden dust spilled beneath her, onto the floor, the table and the bed.

Thomas rubbed his eyes. Had she flipped him the finger?

'But you're a fairy … are you the queen?'

'Yah de yah de yah. It's so boring. Yes, I'm Queen Cortina but I'm not a bloody fairy. I'm an angel,' she said, fluttering her eyelashes and offering him an exaggerated smile.

She settled onto the table and folded her arms, posing in a long blue dress that flowed around her like an ocean, then flicked the tresses of her long, dark hair.

'So what've you got to tell me? Don't just sit there, gawping with your fat mouth. You won't believe the risk I've taken to be here. If anyone finds out I'm meeting you they'll banished me. Isabelle. What a bitch she is.'

'Isabelle? What's she done? She's not well, you know. That's why I'm here.'

'She's such a goody two shoes. I expect she's been doing her bloody baby talk with you,' she said, and then added, 'she has.' The laugh that followed was full of spite.

'I ... we need your help. Isabelle thought you'd know why she's fading and how we can stop it.'

'She hasn't got a person, that's why. She knows that.'

'Yes, I know – she used to be my mum's fairy.'

'Angel.'

'Okay, angel. But how can I help her now she's got no one? She said you've helped other fairies. There must be something I can do. I can't let her die.'

'Blah blah blah. I've just told you what's wrong with her.'

'I know what's wrong. I want to know how to make her better.'

'So you know what's making her ill?'

'Yes.'

'So what will make her well, do you think?'

'I don't know.'

'You humans really are thick. No wonder you're fucking up the planet – you know, the place you live in the vacuum of space?' Cortina shook her head.

'I don't think you should swear like that. What will the other fairies think?'

'What will the other fairies think?' she repeated in a high, mocking voice. 'Do you think I care? I'm stuck here with Jacobs bloody Manchester. Have you ever seen such a prick? It's all down to me, everything he's done. I've loads of names in my address book. He's filed under T.'

'T?'

She laughed. 'T for tosser.'

'But he's your person. Surely you must like your person.'

'Why?'

'Well, because you're a fairy.'

'Ang—'

'Angel. Aren't you supposed to have a special bond? Isabelle was with my mum all her life.'

'Isabelle ... she's old school. She thinks she has to stay with her person till death do us part. Sod that.'

'Hang on, you mean you can move around?' Thomas sat up and leant towards her.

'Course we can – if we fancy it. That's how she'll stop fading. Find someone else. What's his name? The drug baron in Mexico?'

'El Chapo?'

'Yes, him. He wouldn't have been anything without his angel. She helped him build his empire and escape from prison loads of times. But as soon as he got banged up for good, she moved on. She's not going to spend the rest of her life in a prison cell.'

'B-But you can't help a drug lord! You're supposed to be nice, do good things and help people who deserve it!'

'Oh, yeah, like Tinker Bell. Have you seen the cocks we have to deal with now? DJs, hedge-fund managers, reality fucking stars with egos as big as a planet. It's not like Bruce Forsyth anymore, you know.'

'Did he have an angel then?'

'Yes, of course he did, stupid. But he deserved it. He had some talent. Now all they have to do is stick a few pictures on Instagram, whatever that is, and with our help, they become influencers, whatever those are. They actually think they're doing some good and have an opinion that's worth listening to.' Her face had turned beetroot red, and she was shouting. 'Why yellow's in this year, why this dog is a must-have, why that handbag is to die for, why this luxury hotel – which paid them to visit in the first place – is actually rather nice. Veritable Gandhis, aren't they? Arseholes.'

'Well, I dunno, people want different things now, don't they? Why do you stay if you don't like it?'

'We have to help our people; it's what we do. Some are nice, some are idiots. You can't choose your family, can you?' She fluttered in front of him. 'Well, we can, but most of us stick it out with the tosspots we're given. But why I stay with Jacobs, I don't know.'

'Why do you?'

'I just said I don't know.' She sighed. 'I guess I feel sorry for him. He's had a hard life. Do you know how he got his name?'

Thomas shook his head. 'I thought he made it up.'

'His parents lived up north and liked eating cream crackers. They couldn't be bothered with him as a child, sometimes left him for days, even went on holiday without him, poor little kid. So I helped him. But I didn't help him to become a prime prick; he's done that all by himself. Trouble is, people do well and don't realise it's us who got them there, and then they become prima donnas, throwing their weight around, treating people like shit. Sometimes we get fed up and move on. And guess what happens?'

Thomas shrugged.

'It's a quick fall from grace. Think of anyone?'

Thomas thought for a moment. 'George Best?'

'Yep.'

Thomas was disappointed. So much for natural talent. Never mind – he wasn't here to fret about a footballer. He was here for Isabelle.

'So if Isabelle could find someone else she'd be okay?'

'Yes. She knows that. I don't know what she's playing at. Anyway, I've been here long enough. What have you got to tell me? Isabelle said you had a secret.'

At first, Thomas was confused. Then it clicked.

'I thought Isabelle had already told you. It's cell phones. They have cameras on them. That's why so many of you are fading.'

'What are you talking about?'

'Cameras. They make you lose your person.'

The queen peered at him intently, then burst out laughing.

'Are you a total idiot?'

'Look.' He held his phone up. 'You didn't realise mobile phones had cameras on them.'

She mimicked him again, then said, 'Do you think we're totally stupid? We watch you twenty-four seven. You think we don't know what selfies are?'

'I don't understand ... Isabelle said ... What about the Cottingley fairies? The girls who took the picture of sprites dancing in the garden. She said that's when you first discovered what cameras did.'

'What are you talking about? They were paper cut-outs. Everyone knows that?'

'But—'

Thomas stared at Cortina. She stared back.

He threw his jumper over her.

'What the—'

'Shh, we've got company,' Thomas hissed.

In his peripheral vision, he saw two golden shapes dart out of the darkness beyond and through the half-open window. If he hadn't been used to seeing Isabelle flit around in his bedroom, he'd never have noticed.

He tried to remain nonchalant. He switched on the television, plumped the pillows, lay back on the bed, and crossed his arms behind his head. While he stared ahead at the flickering picture, he tried to track the fairies' paths out of the corner of his eye.

They were systematic, working their way around the room.

Searching.

His heart thumped hard in his chest and he pretended to yawn and stretch, then turned on his side and reached for a newspaper. The fairies darted toward his jumper and hovered over it. Thomas almost didn't dare breathe in case a ragged wheeze gave him away.

Though it seemed like an hour, moments later they moved on.

Thomas remained rigid, squinting at the small black print. The fairies circled the bed once more, then zipped across the room and out of the window.

Only once he was sure they'd gone did he reach forward and lift his jumper. A shower of gold fell from it.

'Fucking bitch – that fucking shit-faced little turd.'

The tirade continued for another minute or so, and despite the tension, Thomas smiled.

'She set me up. She tried to get me caught talking to a person. I would've lost the crown, the sneaky little bitch. And what are you smiling at?'

'I just never imagined in my wildest dreams I'd rescue a foul-mouthed fairy queen.'

'Angel – I'm a bloody angel.'

Thomas laughed.

'It's no laughing matter. She set us up. She wants to be queen.'

Thomas slumped back into the pillows. Cortina was right. Isabelle had used him, lied to him. And what about his mum? Had Isabelle in fact abandoned her?

'I don't know what to do anymore,' he said.

'Go back and tell the little bitch it didn't work.'

'But what about my mum? Why would Isabelle leave her?' His eyes blurred with tears. 'She's not well.'

'Coz she's a mercenary fuckwit, that's why,' Cortina said, her tiny fists clenched into balls.

Thomas remained silent. She flitted around his head and then landed on his outstretched hand.

'She thinks she's better than everyone else does prim and proper Isabelle.' She met his eyes for an instant, then looked away. 'I hate her, and you should too after what she's done to your mum.'

Thomas was inclined to agree.

CHAPTER 24

Peter parked his beloved metallic-blue Mercedes E class outside the bookshop. His father had driven a Rover, said they were unbeatable, and Peter had followed his father's advice, until Lipscombe Property Associates had become his. He'd wanted something to match his new executive position, to make a statement, and what could be better than a Mercedes? The cost had been prohibitive so he'd leased one. So what if the car would never be his? The impact was just the same.

A Rover would still get him around town and use far less petrol, but Peter felt empowered behind the Merc's wheel, and when he drove to a meeting in it, he walked into the negotiations with just a little more confidence.

The door shut with a satisfying and expensive clunk. He strode along the pavement, determined to get the bookshop signed over. And what was wrong with that?

He was offering a decent price. Bloody Marion – she made him feel guilty about everything.

But it was a new day, and things were looking a lot more positive. The old lady's house was now part of his portfolio, the deadline for second thoughts having passed. Whatever Marion had intended to do, she must have thought better of it.

Blue Tiger Books was looking good, he had to admit – the new lighting, the colourful blackboard promoting the book of the week, tables stacked with books of different genres. All the dust-filled nooks and crannies had been cleaned and books that had been piled on the floor were now arranged neatly on the shelves. The mountains of empty cardboard boxes littering the aisles had been removed, too. A ramshackle charity shop had turned into a cool indie store.

This was now a place to be seen. And given the number of customers milling about, he wasn't alone in thinking so.

His first thought was to congratulate Maria, tell her what a wonderful job she'd done.

She looked up and waved. He half-raised a hand, delighted that she'd seen him. Then, like rain spoiling a summer's day, he remembered the purpose of his visit. He lowered his hand and strode over to the counter.

She looked around, and called out, 'Becky, can you cover?'

A young girl, maybe a student, looked up from the pile of books she was stacking.

'You won't believe how busy I've been. Becks has been a saviour. Let's go to the basement.'

He followed her down the narrow stairs. There was

power in the way she moved – not physical. Something else, a blithe confidence.

'What do you think?' she said.

She'd painted the walls white, the floorboards were clean and polished, and the shelves heaved, full with books. It took his breath away.

'And look through here,' she said, pointing to the other room.

It too was white, which made it look larger. Maria had arranged several posters on the wall. 'I thought I could display local artists' work, and Thomas said it would make a great coffee shop – nothing fancy, just somewhere for people to sit, read and relax.'

'Thomas?' he said.

'You know, the chap who's been helping me.'

'Ah, yes.'

If that idiot hadn't got involved this would have been a doddle. Now he wasn't so sure.

'The store looks lovely,' he said. 'But your account books don't.'

Maria looked down, and Peter felt ashamed.

'No,' she whispered. 'But people are shopping here again. We had our best day ever yesterday. I've been here all weekend. Working every night to get it right. Thomas inspired me. He believed in the shop. More than I did.'

Bloody Thomas.

'You've done a superb job and I don't want to put a dampener on things, but you're in so much debt it'll take you ages to clear it. Didn't we agree the best way forward is to sell up?'

'We did. But it looks so nice now, and there's always been a bookshop here. I just feel I'm letting down all the previous owners and betraying the town.'

'Don't be silly. Sometimes you have to look out for number one. This money will set you up, give you a bit of breathing space, and I don't think my backers would be averse to keeping the bookstore open.'

'Really? Do you really think they would?' she said.

'I know so,' he replied, and thought how easy it was to lie.

It hadn't crossed his mind until now. He had been lying to Marion for months, and he'd hated it, but she'd been too close to see the truth. The old lady had been easy because she was doolally. But Maria was different – intelligent and confident. It should have been harder to lie to her. She shouldn't have been so easily taken in. But it wasn't, and she had. And now the deceptions just slipped off his tongue without his even having to think about it.

'I'm sure when they see how nice the bookshop is and hear about the history, they'll keep it going. You know what?' He looked directly at her. 'They might even need someone to run it.'

She put her hand to her mouth. 'Really? That'd be weird, wouldn't it?'

'Course not.'

'I don't know. I don't want to waste your time. I've fallen back in love with the shop.'

'Well, it would be a win–win if you could manage the store and have all your debt cleared, wouldn't it?'

'Well …'

'You needn't make your mind up now. Why don't I take you to dinner? Somewhere special but quiet. We can talk shop while we're relaxing. Business and pleasure, what a great mix, eh?'

Peter knew he was talking too quickly, that he sounded desperate, but he couldn't stop himself.

'I can bring all the paperwork and talk you through it. What do you say? No one's going to twist your arm, and you've seen my valuations. I've got to tell you though, my clients are keen to get a foothold in the town. If it's not your shop it'll be another, so the offer won't last much longer.' He stepped back and shrugged. 'I'm just trying to tell you how it is, not force you into a corner. I just want you to know.'

Maria sighed, and Peter's phone buzzed. He checked the caller ID and leant on the counter to steady himself, waiting for the nausea to subside.

'You okay?' said Maria, frowning.

'Yes. It's just hot in here. I need some fresh air.' The phone continued to buzz. 'Look, you've nothing to lose, and what's more, you get a free meal.' He laughed, but it sounded forced. 'Here's my card, text me. Say seven thirty? I have to take this call.'

Peter stumbled up the stairs and out of the shop, and answered his phone. For what seemed like ages there was nothing but white noise. Seth Ozil's accented voice broke the silence like a hammer blow.

'Ah, Mr Lipscombe, I thought you were avoiding me again.'

Peter leant against the bookshop window and pulled

air into his lungs. 'No, no … of course not.'

'Good. I am glad to hear that. What progress have you made? Is the house ours?'

'The deadline's passed, but it's not ours until the old lady vacates.'

'Leave that to us. And the bookshop?'

'I don't—'

'And the bookshop?'

Peter sighed. 'I've just been talking to the owner. I'm taking her out for dinner tomorrow to finalise things.'

'To finalise things … I'm pleased. It seems you have done the deal.'

'Well not—'

'Is it done?' Ozil snapped.

'Not quite.'

'I'm told the shop is thriving, Mr Lipscombe. It's not the rundown shell you described.'

'It was … it's just … I don't know what's happened to it.'

'That's unfortunate, Mr Lipscombe. You know I set my heart on it.'

'It's still possible. I know I can convince her.'

'Where are you meeting?'

'Luigi's.'

'I know the owner well. I'll talk to him. You will have the downstairs room. I will send you some company to help you concentrate on the matter in hand rather than the pretty girl. How does that sound?'

Peter raised his voice and tried to sound assertive. 'I don't need company. I'll sort it.'

'I'm sorry, Mr Lipscombe.' Ozil spoke so softly that

Peter pressed the phone closer to his ear. 'You lost the luxury of deciding the minute you misled me.'

'I didn't—'

'Please don't interrupt. You will have company tomorrow. You will sign the documents. I am not making requests, I am making statements. Is that clear?'

'I don't know if she wants to sell now.' The words scuttled from Peter's mouth on a single quick breath.

'The power of persuasion, Mr Lipscombe, the power of persuasion. Let us hope it is your persuasion rather than mine that does the trick. It's always so much nicer to use the carrot rather than the stick, don't you agree?'

The phone went dead.

Peter staggered along the pavement to his car, occasionally stopping to catch his breath. The click of the door opening usually brightened his mood.

Not today.

CHAPTER 25

The journey to the office was miserable. The cold, grey concrete surroundings depressed Marion, and she longed to see some flowers to brighten her mood.

That she'd even taken that journey was baffling. She'd never walked out of anywhere before, and now she'd done it twice in just a few weeks.

Yet here she was again. The quietness still struck her as strange. In the early days, Mr Lipscombe had always been the first in, and she'd be welcomed by the aroma of freshly brewed coffee. The office had felt like a second home, a warm sanctuary from her lonely life, and she'd looked forward to going to work. Yes, Mr Lipscombe was her boss, but she'd felt they were friends too. Now everything had changed, as if she didn't belong.

The flickering lights somehow added to the gloom rather than diminishing it. She wandered around the desks, running her finger along the wooden tops, trying to capture what had once been. She thought about the man who'd telephoned and the threat. Mr Lipscombe had been ashen-faced when he'd put the receiver down.

She reached his desk. Should she …? It had never crossed her mind to look through his files. She'd always waited for his return, even when a customer had a query. It had been an unwritten protocol they'd adopted from the start.

Now, though, she was tempted.

She glanced at the door, pushed her guilt to one side, and began to rifle through the files.

And couldn't believe what she was looking at.

Aside from just a few small ongoing pieces of work, the bulging folders were stuffed with blank sheets of paper. They had almost no work, and the decline had been hidden from her for months. Why hadn't he told her? Why was it a secret? They'd been a team, hadn't they?

She tried a drawer. It was locked. She tugged but it wouldn't yield so she moved on to the next and pulled hard. It sprang open so fast that she lost her balance. The plastic tray careened out, scattering pencils, pens and paperclips over the floor.

'Oh, for—'

Nestled in a piece of Blu Tack was a small key that she recognised instantly. It opened the stationery cupboard. Over the past few months Mr Lipscombe hadn't let her near it, and all the office supplies had inexplicably been moved to the kitchen.

Like a fugitive, she stole over to the cupboard door, not wanting to open it but knowing she would.

She slipped the key in the lock.

'Don't.'

Marion jumped and dropped the key.

Mr Lipscombe stood in the doorway, the spring-hinged door pressing up against him, as if battling with his attempt at entry. He looked frail and lost.

'Why not?' The assertiveness in her own voice echoing around the empty office shocked Marion. She felt close to tears. 'I think—'

'Marion, we've spoken about this before. I don't pay you to think.'

'You used to,' she said. 'I'm sick and tired of the way you treat me, the way you talk to me.'

'You don't understand,' he said, and took a step towards her.

'Just keep away from me. I want to know what's going on.'

She picked up the key and slipped it back in the lock.

'Don't, Marion,' he whispered. 'Please.'

There was such sorrow in his eyes, but something else, too. Fear?

She opened the cupboard, heard her boss's footsteps behind her, but she was already opening the suitcase.

She flipped the lid, and fell backwards into his arms.

'What have you done?' she screamed, and began to pummel his chest with both hands. 'Let me go.'

He held her tightly, forcing her flailing arms to her sides. 'Shh, please don't.'

'What do you mean? Don't what? Where did that come from?'

'I didn't want you to see it. It was the only way to save the business. I … I didn't want to let you down.'

'Let me down? We've been a team. I love working here. Love working with you. At least I used to.'

Her ragged breathing calmed and she relaxed into his arms.

'I lost everything in Tenerife,' he said. 'Everything my grandfather built, everything we've worked for. It's because I was greedy, and I didn't want you to think less of me.'

'Any less than I do now?' she spat.

His arms loosened and he let her go.

'I know,' he said quietly.

'And this?' she said, pointing at the money in the suitcase. 'What's it for? Why have you got it?'

'They said they'd pay the bank if I laundered their money through the accounts.'

'What is it? Drug money? For God's sake, what have you done, you bloody idiot?'

'I don't know what to do anymore. Please don't say anything. If they find out you know … they're not nice people, Marion.'

'We could have worked hard, got more clients. We could have done it together. There's nothing in your files, no new leads, nothing.'

'I know. The debt was too much though. I just didn't know where to start.'

'You could have started with me. I've never let you down.'

'I know. I thought I could sort it.'

'So the old lady's house will be theirs?'

'Yes, and I'm hoping the bookshop will clear my debts.'

'But you can't be sure, can you? They might come back the day after it's sold.'

He nodded. 'You're right. They could.'

'And what about Mrs Blueberry's house?'

'It's still hers, but …'

'What?' Marion's fists balled.

'Nothing. Did you warn her?'

'No, her son was in London. Tell me. I don't want any more secrets.'

'I think they might do something to her.'

This was like being in a room with no doors. And they needed help to get out. 'I'm going to call the police,' she said, and moved towards the closest phone.

'And tell them what? That you have a feeling about something? We have no proof. And what about the stationery cupboard full of cash?'

Who was this man? She felt hot and the room seemed to close around her. She clung to the desk, waiting for the sensation to pass. 'What're you going to do?' she mumbled.

'I'm meeting the bookshop woman tonight. She'll let us have it, and that will be the end.'

'So you're going to stitch someone else up, or worse. It has to stop. It won't be the end, you know it won't.'

'I have to try. There's no other choice.'

'You idiot, you bloody idiot. I hate you.' Spit flew from her mouth in time with her words. She wanted them to wound him. Wanted him to understand the bitterness of his betrayal. 'There's always another choice. There's a choice now for you not to hurt anyone else.'

'It's just bricks and mortar. She wants to sell the bookshop anyway.'

'And what about Mrs Blueberry?'

'She's old and—'

'Listen to yourself. What's got into you? Who are you?' Her chest was tight and she could barely see what she was doing. Without thinking she began her end of day routine - locking the cabinets until she could bear it no more.

'I can't do this. I can't' Marion strode towards the door, her fists so tight that her nails dug into her palms.

'Wait, don't go … please. I don't know what to do. Marion, how do I make it right?'

'I don't know either. I don't want to be here with you though,' she said, and marched out of the office and down the street. Towards what she wasn't sure. Was she putting danger behind her or walking towards a cliff edge? Leaving wouldn't put the clock back.

She turned and started to walk back. She'd hear him out. Maybe they could find a solution.

Mr Lipscombe was locking up. He looked in her direction, raised a single hand in the air. She raised her own in reply. Then he turned and hurried off in the opposite direction.

It began to rain.

CHAPTER 26

'Boo,' Eric said, as Iris put the dishes away.

'Oh! You made me jump.'

Eric laughed. 'Isn't that what ghosts do?'

'Don't say that,' she said, and hung her tea towel on the line by the boiler.

'I'm sorry. It was meant to be funny.'

'It's not. I miss you too much. Where have you been?'

'I don't know. I think it all depends on you.'

She rubbed her apron and avoided his eyes. 'I want you here all the time.'

Eric smiled. 'I love the way you do that.'

'What?'

'Brush your apron.'

'What do you mean?'

'You always do it when you're thinking about something else. What were you thinking about?'

'You,' she said, and felt herself blush. 'Do you know the

last time anyone hugged me, the last time I felt another person's arms around me?'

Eric shook his head.

'The day you died,' she whispered. 'I read in the paper that people in solitary confinement long for touch. I feel like that.'

'What about Thomas?'

'You know Thomas. He's not a hugger.'

'But he used to be, didn't he? I wonder what happened?'

'I don't know. He got sad and it sucked the happiness out of him. Mind you, he's had a spring in his step lately,' she said.

'And some lead in his pencil,' Eric said, and chuckled.

'Eric!' But she laughed too.

'What's that on the table?' Eric asked, pointing.

'It's a message from Thomas.'

'Have you read it?'

'Yes, of course I have.'

'What's it say?'

Iris sighed. 'I can't remember.'

'Read it now.'

Iris picked up the note. 'It says he's gone to London for a couple of days and food is in the fridge.'

'Have you eaten?'

'No.'

'Right, open the fridge and get something you fancy. Light the oven and put it in, then set the timer.'

Iris did as she was told. 'Thank you.'

Eric moved towards her. 'Have you remembered what happened at Lipscombe's?'

'I don't want to talk about it.'

'Iris.'

'Well, I must have sorted it, mustn't I? I've been through all my cards. There's nothing.'

'Something's not right though, is it?'

'Eric, please stop. I can't remember.' She shook her head. 'There was a lady. I think she looked after me. She was nice. She said I had to tell Thomas something.'

'Iris, think.'

'It's no good, my mind's a blank. There's just a hole there. I can remember holding your hand in the Bluebell Woods, watching you roll on the floor, unable to breathe because you were laughing so much at *Fawlty Towers*. I can remember every single one of our holidays, but I can't remember yesterday.' She sniffed and wiped her nose.

'Shh, my love. Shh. It'll be alright.'

'Don't talk about it anymore, please.'

Eric shimmered. 'You look lovely today. Is that a new dress?'

'Yes, I got it in the sale. Seventy per cent off – only £12.00. It's a bargain.'

'It looks so beautiful on you.'

Iris looked deeply into her husband's eyes until she could bear it no more, then closed her own and drowned for a moment in memories.

CHAPTER 27

Thomas had slept fitfully, Isabelle's betrayal weighing heavily on his mind.

She'd taken him in, hook, line and sinker.

Thinking back, it had been obvious she didn't like the queen. And so she'd used him to oust her – like some Machiavellian plot. If she were capable of that, might she have been driven enough to leave his mother?

He'd wanted to go home that night and confront her, but Cortina had persuaded him to stay, promising a meeting with Jacobs Manchester the following evening.

Thomas had never been impressed by celebrity, yet the man had dazzled during his show and the chance to meet him was too good to miss. It might also be an opportunity to tout his book to someone famous. A recommendation would do wonders for sales.

He spent the morning in London, poking around the huge Waterstones store in Piccadilly, making mental notes about the promotional ideas Blue Tiger might poach – bundles, buy one get one half price, fun books at the checkout for impulse buys. Book signings too – Eric Clapton was at a table piled high with his new memoir, and a long queue of hopefuls stretched from one end of the store to the other. They wouldn't get Eric Clapton at Blue Tiger, but they could offer a space to local authors.

In the afternoon, he queued for the London Eye. It was something he'd wanted to do since it opened, and it didn't disappoint. The Houses of Parliament, Big Ben, Westminster Abbey, St. Paul's … the landmarks always made him happy; it was like coming home. And viewing them from on high gave him a buzz that buoyed him.

Anything was possible.

He called Maria, left a message and stretched out on the bed. Five minutes later, his mobile rang.

'Hello, chuck. How's the big city?'

'It's great. I've been on the London Eye, and guess what?'

'You're seeing the queen tonight,' she said.

'Better than that. I'm meeting Jacobs Manchester.'

'Get away, you daft bugger. I love him! How did you wangle that?'

'It's a long story. I'll tell you when I get back.'

'You're a strange onion. I gotta dash myself.'

'You off somewhere nice?'

'Maybe. I'm out to dinner with that Lipscombe guy. Going to talk to me about selling, like.'

It was as though a white fog had smothered him.

'You still there?' Maria said.

'Yes …' He couldn't help it – a raging jealousy began to bubble and burn in his chest. 'Well, I'd better get cracking then. You have a good evening.'

'I don't have to go just yet. We can chat for a bit.'

'I need a shower. I've got to get my skates on,' he said, trying to stop his voice from shaking. 'Have a lovely time. See you soon.'

'Okay. Bye, chuck,' she said, and he could hear the puzzlement in her voice.

He hung up and then punched the pillow hard. 'Damn it.' Why did he always just accept things? Why couldn't he have said something, told her how he felt? Why was he always so bloody meek?

There was no knowing what that smooth-talking idiot would do. It wasn't just the possibility of losing the bookshop; it was her, Maria. Lipscombe would wheedle his way into her house for coffee, and then what? Thomas's imagination went into overdrive, delivering multiple possibilities, each one just as seedy as the other, each one like a splinter in his heart.

He ate dinner in the hotel restaurant but tasted nothing. As for meeting Jacobs Manchester, his appetite for that had dissipated too. He traipsed to the bar anyway. Cortina had said she would bring him in at eight and it was now five to. Thomas got himself a pint and sat in the corner out of the way.

By nine, he'd downed a second pint, and his mood had soured even further. He hated being late for anything. He'd once read a short story by Harlan Ellison in which every minute you were late reduced your lifespan by the same amount of time. It was an excellent idea. And even if Jacobs Manchester's time was more precious than his own, an hour was ridiculous.

He bought another pint and sipped it slowly, stewing. Thirty minutes later, he'd had enough and decided to get some fresh air.

London was so different to his home town; all the stores were still open regardless of what they were selling – fruit and veg, newspapers, dry cleaning, fast food. The three pints had mellowed Thomas, and he felt safe despite the handful of drunks and drug addicts hunched in dim doorways.

He turned into a side street, aiming to double back on himself. It was dark and he was drawn to the lights of a small public house nestled amongst the residential buildings. Several people were milling around outside in the gloom. Thomas looked down, avoiding eye contact with them, and was confronted by a pair of highly polished red shoes.

He looked up. The man was staring at him. He wore a shapeless, dirty parka, and his thick-framed glasses seemed too big for his face. Light reflected off his bald head as though he were in a spotlight.

Jacobs Manchester.

Thomas moved towards him and Manchester looked down at his beer then over his shoulder, as if searching for an escape.

'Hi,' Thomas said. 'I was at your show yesterday.'

'Shh,' Manchester said, and glanced around. 'I know, I recognise you.'

'Sorry,' Thomas whispered. 'I thought I was going to meet you at the hotel.'

'What the fuck are you talking about?'

'At eight. Your fair— We were supposed to meet at the hotel.'

'Are you a fucking stalker? You're the tumour troublemaker, aren't you?'

'No. I … Well, yes … I got mixed up. You look so different.'

'Yes, I'm a bloody mess, aren't I? Hmm? But at least I can get out.'

'I really enjoyed the show,' Thomas said.

'Yah de yah de yah. Please don't talk to me about that pile of shit. I went to drama school, but you know that, don't you? You've read about it. Know everything about me, I expect.'

'No, I don't … but I know you had a hard upbringing and your parents called you Jacobs after the cream crackers.'

Manchester's head shot up and he glared at Thomas, disgust twisting his face. Thomas took a step backwards.

'What are you on? Jacobs is a family name, goes back to the eleventh century. My Father was a lord. Bloody Wikipedia. Someone's been tampering with it again.'

Thomas was speechless and returned to familiar ground. 'You certainly got the audience going.'

'A dead trout could get that lot going. Hmm? Once they get in the studio, they're like a bundle of toddlers with a bag of sugar stuck on their faces.'

'So you wear a wig?'

'No, it's all done with lights and mirrors. Look, what do you want anyway?'

'I just saw you and thought I'd say hello. Sorry.'

'Okay, well now you've said it, so sod off.'

Remembering his book sales, Thomas persisted. 'Would you like a drink?'

'And spend another second with you? I don't think so. Bye bye,' he said, and dismissed Thomas with a wave of his hand.

'I've written a book.'

'Oh, God help me. Just when I thought things couldn't get any worse.' He drained the last of his beer and looked at his empty glass. 'Okay, I could do with a laugh. The real ale.' He gave his glass to Thomas.

Thomas felt excited. He squeezed past several people and entered the pub. It was a popular place, not a seat unoccupied. His three previous pints had worked their way through, so the first stop had to be the toilets.

It was a small room with three urinals and one cubicle. The light flashed on as he entered. Motion sensors. Clever.

He took the far urinal and rested his head on the wall, enjoying the sensation of relief.

'Hello,' a tiny voice said in his ear.

Thomas jumped, spraying his leg. The fairy queen flew in front of his face.

'Christ! You can't come in here. It's the gents!'

'I've seen it all before,' she said, looking down.

Thomas turned, this time sprinkling his shoes.

'Not much to see there anyway,' she said, and laughed.

'It's average actually,' he hissed.

'Is it though?' Cortina said.

'Yes. Anyway, you promised to bring him to the hotel.'

'Best laid plans and all that.'

'He's horrible,' Thomas said.

'See what I mean? See what I have to put up with?'

'But he's *really* horrible. You should leave.'

'I know but I have to stick with him after his childhood.'

'He said his dad's a lord.'

'He says that to everyone. It's just a cover story.'

'He seemed pretty adamant. I'm going to tell him about my book. You got any advice, anything to avoid?'

'Yes, don't show him. He'll rip it to pieces. Literally.'

She laughed again, and the light flicked off, leaving the room in darkness. Thomas waved his hand around and after several attempts the brightness returned, but the fairy had gone.

He pushed back through the crowd, bought two pints and went back outside. An SUV was coming slowly down the road towards the pub, engine purring. It pulled up alongside the drinkers and one of the blacked-out windows lowered. Conversation ceased, glasses half-raised, framed in the moment. Thomas expected to see a head emerge and ask for directions.

Instead, the barrel of a small handgun appeared.

Someone screamed.

Thomas dived behind a table, knocking it sideways into Manchester.

The crack shocked the air. Tyres spun on tarmac sending dust and smoke into the night sky, and the car screeched away.

For a moment there was silence. Then a collective murmur built, and people began to sob and scream. Some were on their hands and knees, others crouched. Everyone looked about nervously.

Thomas lifted chairs and tables, searching for Manchester, and found him face down on the pavement.

Lifeless.

CHAPTER 28

Every movement felt near impossible, as if Peter's brain had been replaced by a slab of concrete that lurched every time he willed it into action.

Pull yourself together.

Tonight was vital. He had to persuade the bookshop owner to sell. His life, let alone his livelihood, depended on it.

It took him twenty minutes to get home. Maxwell the Third climbed onto his lap and kneaded his thighs until he found the perfect spot to settle.

'It's no good getting comfy. I've got to go out,' Peter said as the cat's back pressed into the stroke of his fingers.

Maxwell's two predecessors had been equally adored and spoilt. All three cats had been named after Peter's grandfather. Would he have approved? Probably. The man had been warm and loving, unlike his father. And yet it was his father's approval he'd always sought, never fully appreciating that the acceptance he'd craved had been there in the shape of the older man all along.

School had been hard. Dread had accompanied Peter through the tall green gates every day. What today would be diagnosed as dyslexia had been dismissed as stupidity by his teachers, and he'd worked alone in class. Still, he'd had friends and been popular – a rebel but never a lout.

Following a poor set of exam results, Peter's father had decided that friends were a distraction; hard work would solve his son's shortcomings.

He'd been sent to a private school, where the teachers had similarly regarded him as the school simpleton. But there'd been no friends to dilute the hurt, and no academic support. He'd not understood that the letters only danced on the page for him.

Peter's frustration had found physical outlets, and after two broken windows and one broken nose he'd been expelled. His father had been ashamed of having produced so hopeless a son, and hidden him away to avoid the embarrassment.

And so Peter would sneak out of his bedroom, across town, and over to Grandpa's house. It was a space in which love, comfort and hope thrived. Grandpa never judged. And when things didn't go to plan, he'd say, 'If you never try, you never know.'

Lipscombe Property Associates had been his grandfather's creation and Peter was sure it had been the old man's influence that had led his father to hand over the reins ten years ago. It had also been his grandfather who'd recruited Marion.

The funeral had been the worst moment of Peter's life. As the curtains had closed across the coffin, he'd told the old man how much he loved him, said it out loud. His father had turned away shaking is head, ashamed once more.

So naming all his cats Maxwell seemed perfectly apt, as in their own way they gave Lipscombe the same special feeling his granddad had.

* * *

The blue Boss suit was formal, if a little dated but a black polo shirt took the edge off. His briefcase was a burden, but he needed it for the paperwork.

Luigi's was on a small side street in the centre of town. He'd been there a couple of times with Marion – once for the office Christmas dinner and once on a balmy summer's evening to celebrate securing a large investment.

A young waitress in a black tee shirt and jeans greeted him in Italian. She crossed off his name in the diary with a battered ballpoint and glanced towards the kitchen. A man – the manager, Peter assumed – nodded.

'This way,' she said, and led him down a spiral staircase to a basement with twelve tables, all empty save for the four men whispering at the one in the corner.

Lipscombe remembered Ozil's words: *I will send you some company to help you concentrate on the matter in hand rather than the pretty girl.*

But this lot just looked like a bunch of businessmen on a night out.

Lipscombe ordered a bottle of Chablis.

If he closed his eyes, he could almost touch that summer's night again … They'd sat by a window, opened so wide it was almost like being outside, and watched the passers-by. When darkness had fallen, so had the rain, huge warm drops splashing the dry dusty pavement, scattering revellers and wetting the white tablecloths. It had been thrilling, and they'd laughed, begging the waiter to leave the window open a little longer.

Peter had wanted with all his heart to reach over and cover Marion's hand with his own. Why hadn't he? Because he'd been a coward. Because he hadn't dared risk the rejection. Because if he failed, their working relationship would be over.

If you never try, you never know.

'Hello.'

Peter opened his eyes, feeling foolish, and stood quickly as the waitress pulled Maria's chair away from the table.

She looked beautiful, bohemian. A knee-length dress just covered the top of black suede boots. She'd complemented it with a long burgundy silk jacket with a dark floral pattern. Her hair hung in loose, shaggy curls, and black kohl framed her eyes.

He mumbled a greeting and thanked her for coming.

'I wasn't going to miss a free meal, pet,' she said and laughed, but there was unease beneath the surface of her jocularity.

They ordered their food and spoke about nothing in particular until the Chablis took effect.

'So is there a Mrs Lipscombe?' Maria asked.

'No, I've always been single. Work comes first.'

'You know what they say – all work and no play, man.'

Peter nodded. 'I know.'

'And no one on their death bed wishes they'd spent more time in the office.'

Lipscombe laughed. 'That's easier said than done. If I hadn't spent more time in the office, I would've ended up on my death bed a lot sooner.'

'Touché, Monsieur Pussycat,' she said.

'I used to love Tom and Jerry.'

'Me too. So there's no one special?'

Peter smiled. 'Why? Are you on the hunt?'

'Get away with you. No, I'm just curious.'

'There's a girl in my office.' Peter didn't know what had made him say it, only that in this moment, the wine warming him, he felt safe, tucked away from the real world. Here anything was possible, even Marion. 'She's worked with me for years. She's really nice but, I dunno, it just doesn't seem right.'

'Why not, you daft bugger? Faint heart never won fair lady.'

'What are you, a book of quotations?' Peter said. 'But you're right. I need more balls.'

'You seem to have plenty of balls,' Maria said. 'Sometimes they're a little too big.'

'What do you mean?' Peter said.

'You were horrible to my helper.' She took a sip of wine, as if steeling herself. 'I'm sorry, but you came over as a bit of a jerk. He's a nice bloke and deserved better.'

'Well ... apologies. I've had a lot on my mind. Do you like him?'

Maria blushed. 'No, I—'

'What's his name?'

'Thomas.'

Peter grinned.

'What?' Maria said, going redder.

'Well, I suppose he's cute.'

'Cute? That's not something I thought I'd hear you say.'

They ate their meal in comfortable silence, then ordered coffee.

As Maria stirred cream into her cup, Peter pulled the papers out of his briefcase

'Thought I'd got away with it. This has been so nice,' she said.

'I didn't want to spoil the whole evening talking about business,' Peter said, and felt the muscles in his jaw tightening.

'Just the end of it then,' she said quietly.

'I'm sorry. It's just that I've got clients waiting on this.' He placed the document in front of Maria. 'You know that's why we came.'

'I know but—'

'All you have to do is sign and it's all done. Easy. I think it's a fair price, don't you?'

Peter glanced over at the businessmen. They were still chatting and sipping brandy, and seemed oblivious to the conversation.

'Three weeks ago I would've bitten your hand off, but … I'm just enjoying it again.' She sat back in her chair and looked at him. 'It feels like when we first opened. There's a buzz about the place again. I love talking to customers about books, and they ask for recommendations, like they trust me. I've been so down and sad, and now things seem bright again.'

It was as if the air had been sucked from the room, and Peter found it difficult to get his breath. *Stay calm*, he thought. *Desperation's a salesman's worst companion.*

'But with this money you can buy something smaller, more modern. It will be a new start.' A bead of sweat trickled down Peter's cheek and he wiped it away with a serviette, then licked his lips, trying to lubricate their sudden dryness.

'Are you okay?' Maria asked.

'Yes.' Peter felt incredibly hot. He thought about removing his jacket, but decided against it; the polo shirt would show the perspiration in his armpits and betray his panic.

'I know you're right, and I know what you say makes sense,' Maria said. 'But I don't want anything new. There's been a bookshop there for years. I know it sounds stupid but I feel like I'm its guardian. If I walk away I let the shop down.'

Peter laughed but it sounded hollow. 'You can't ruin your life for the sake of an old shop,' he said. 'Being noble won't put food on the table.'

'But you wouldn't believe the takings we've had over the past few days; they've been brilliant. People like indie. And just imagine if we got a coffee shop.'

'That's just because you've changed a few things. Look at that clothes shop on the corner. When it opened it had queues out the door; now it's always empty.'

'You're probably right, but I want to give it another go. I don't want to be plagued by what-ifs.'

'Please sign,' Peter whispered, and pushed the papers towards Maria.

'Pardon?'

'You don't understand.'

'What do you mean? I don't want to sell any more.' Maria stood. 'I'm sorry I mucked you about.'

'Sit down, please. Let's just talk, see if we can come to another arrangement.'

'I won't change my mind. I want to give the bookshop another go. I don't want to sell it.'

To Peter's horror, the four businessmen stood as one and moved towards them.

'Sit down. Now,' he hissed, reaching for Maria's hand.

'I'm going. You're frightening me,' she said, and slipped one arm into the sleeve of her jacket.

Two of the men positioned themselves either side of her.

'Sit down,' one of them said, his accent strong and strange.

Peter looked at Maria. She shook her head and turned towards the stairs. Both men calmly reached forward and took her upper arms. She tried to shake them off, but they held her fast, fat fingers white against her coat.

The two other men stood behind Peter. He half-rose from his seat but a hand on his shoulder pushed him down. He looked at the waitress, hoping she would help, but she scurried up the stairs.

'What's going on?' Maria said as she sat, and shook the men's hands off.

She looked terrified, and Peter wished he could reassure her, but he remained mute.

The two men behind Maria were smart and tough-looking – tailored jackets over pectoral-hugging white shirts, short, dark and immaculately cut hair. Maybe there was a dress code for this type of person. Only the dark glasses were absent.

'These are the papers?' the taller man said, pointing to the documents on the table.

'Yes.'

'Good. Please.' He made a signature sign to his companion, who passed him a pen.

'You will sign these now,' he said to Maria.

'I don't want to sell my shop. I've changed my mind.' Maria said. She was close to tears and taking small faltering breaths through her nose. Peter looked down at his lap avoiding her accusing eyes.

'You will sign the papers now.' The man opened the document and held the pen in front of her. 'Now,' he said, quieter this time but with more menace.

'I won't. You can't make me.'

'If you don't put your name to this document in the next ten seconds, I've been instructed to be more persuasive. I'm happy to demonstrate on this gentleman.' He nodded towards Lipscombe. 'After, I will burn your property to the ground and then I will take a trip to Norfolk to see your parents. Yes? There will be a fire at their house, and they will burn with it. You will be alive, well, just enough to hear all about it. Am I making myself, what do you say, crystal clear?'

He raised his eyebrows, as if expecting an answer.

'You are thinking this can't be happening, that you'll go to the police. Let me tell you now, before they have time to investigate, our job here will be done and we will be gone. Bye bye.'

The tall man nodded.

Peter's head was on the table, his arm wrenched high up his back, his wrist bent inwards. He screamed, spit flying onto the tablecloth.

The man laughed. 'There we are, a little taster, and no blood.'

Peter's arm was pushed further up his back. His shoulder and wrist merged into a wall of agony and his ears whooshed with such a white noise that he no longer heard his cries.

It stopped.

Maria had lifted the pen. She was sobbing and could barely hold it in her trembling hand. The shorter man pointed to the bottom of the page. She looked at Peter and he tried to shake his head but his arm was twisted upwards again.

Dyslexia had made school life hard for him, but his stature had come in handy. He'd once run fifty yards during a rugby match – with six other boys clinging to him.

And now, with Maria sobbing in front of him, all the fear, all the impotence, turned to rage.

He pushed the table forward, ignoring the searing pain in his arm. Maria fell backwards, and the table passed over her and rammed into the stomachs of the guards, felling them. They landed on their backs, writhing like muscular beetles.

'Run,' he shouted.

She leapt up and sprinted past him and up the stairs. The man holding Peter moved to block her path but Peter stuck out his leg and sent him crashing into some chairs.

As Maria reached the top and disappeared from view, he felt a blow to the back of his head. He fell to the floor and curled into a ball. A boot landed in his chest, hard and sharp, knocking the air out of him.

He heard heavy breathing and an inhuman moan and, with horror, realised the sound was his own.

'That's enough.'

The voice was familiar.

Seth Ozil.

'Pick him up.'

Hands looped under his armpits and dragged him to a table. The bruised muscles in his belly objected to being stretched upright and a groan escaped him.

'Mr Lipscombe.' Ozil moved closer and brushed the dust from Peter's suit. 'There, there,' he said softly. 'You have nothing to fear from me. I warned you there would be consequences though.'

'I tried, I did try.' Peter sputtered, shame washing over him.

'I know you did. I so wanted that bookshop. It would have been perfect. The renovations, cash payments to labourers. We could have cleaned so much money. But it seems it's not to be. Though we may have another go. I don't know.'

'She didn't want to sell.'

Ozil patted his hand. 'I know, I know. You did your best.'

'I did.'

Tears of relief threatened. Ozil knew that he'd tried. Thank God.

'But … remember how at school the teachers punished you if you didn't do something right?'

'Not if you did your best,' Peter replied quickly, looking up, snot running from his nose.

'But what if your best isn't good enough, Mr Lipscombe? How do you ever get better? At my school it was only the task that counted. I was a skinny boy.' He smiled and tensed, his shoulder muscles bulging. The men laughed. 'I know, I've changed. We had to climb ropes and touch the ceiling. The other boys did it with ease, but I failed over and over. I tried until I was exhausted, never gave up. I did my best. But the master, far from congratulating my efforts, set the other boys upon me. They beat me for ten minutes. A week later, I was not the first to touch the ceiling, but nor was I the last. I had improved my best. We need to improve upon your best, Mr Lipscombe.'

Ozil nodded to the men.

'No, no, no wait please I …'

The first punch left him breathless, and he buckled and crumpled to the floor. A kick to his forehead snapped his head backwards.

'Avoid the face,' he heard Ozil say through the fog of pain, 'and keep him alive. When you're finished, go to this address. It must look like an accident. She's old, the stairs are steep. Understand?'

CHAPTER 29

Peter hauled himself onto his hands and knees. Blood, saliva and snot dripped onto the floor. His head swam, and he focused on a picture of Frank Sinatra on the far wall.

An arm wrapped around his waist and guided him to a nearby chair. It was the waitress who'd shown him and Maria to their table.

He took a deep breath and wished he hadn't. Pain lanced through his ribs and lower back.

Ignore it. No time.

He fumbled his mobile from his top pocket and dialled.

'Need … need you to do something,' he said, the words slurred.

'Mr Lipscombe, are you alright? You sound drunk,' Marion said.

'No, I'll explain later. It's urgent. Go to Mrs Blueberry's. Get her out of her house. Please … It's not safe.'

'I don't understand.'

'Please. It could mean life or death. Get her. Don't take no for an answer.' He gagged as another hot sheet of pain assaulted his chest. 'You need to trust me. I know I've done everything wrong, but this is a chance to make amends.'

'Where are you?' Marion said.

Peter took a moment to compose himself. 'In town. I'm … I'm not well.'

'I knew it. Something's wrong, isn't—.'

'Marion, it's okay. Just get Mrs Blueberry away from her house. I'll phone you later.'

He lowered his mobile and looked at the screen. He was about to press the red disconnect button when he saw the call time increasing second by second. She was still there.

'Marion?'

'Yes?' Her voice was tiny in his ear.

He thought about everything they'd shared over the years, the togetherness he'd taken for granted and so often belittled, and searched for a few words of gratitude.

'Marion I—'

'I know,' she whispered.

'Thanks,' he replied and swallowed hard. 'Be careful.'

He stood. The room spun and he used both hands on the table to steady himself. The waitress helped him up the stone stairs.

Outside, the cool breeze took his breath away and reminded him that he was still alive.

* * *

A furry head nudged him and purred. Peter opened his eyes and nuzzled his face against Maxwell the Third's chest. The softness and smell of home made him feel safe but tearful.

The cat squirmed from his arms, jumped to the floor, and clattered through the cat flap.

Peter tried to sit up but his head swam and an intense pain in his side made him gasp. He lay back down and waited for the nausea to subside, then rolled off the settee and onto the laminate floor. From there he inched to the bathroom on his knees and pulled himself to standing in front of the mirror.

His left eye was black, blood had dried under his nose and both lips were swollen and cut. Ozil had told his goons to avoid the face. Peter wondered what he'd have looked like if the instruction hadn't been heeded.

They'd ripped the lapel of his suit, and dark-red blotches stained the front of his polo shirt. He ran his fingers through his hair. It was sticky and tangled. He felt a large lump on the top of his head and winced.

He rinsed his face with cold water, tottered back to the sofa and closed his eyes …

* * *

The landline trilled, shocking Peter out of his doze.

Let it ring.

The trill persisted until the answer machine clicked in. Somehow the silence seemed just as loud.

Again the phone rang, and Peter froze. Marion? Or …

In that moment, he hated himself. Was he really willing to risk ignoring a friend for fear it might be a foe? A glance down at his body relieved him of some of the shame. He was a mess.

He got up, took a deep breath and picked up the receiver.

'Mr Lipscombe.' The accent was unmistakable. 'How are you? I trust my companions persuaded you that we can always better our best.' Ozil laughed.

Peter tried not to make a sound – not even a breath.

'By tomorrow morning,' Ozil continued, 'the circumstances will have changed in our favour. I will call at the office and pick up the papers for the house. Make sure they're ready.'

Peter remained stubbornly mute.

'No hard feelings, I hope, Mr Lipscombe … Mr Lipscombe?' There was just a little uncertainty in Ozil's voice. 'I know you're listening. We will need another suitable property to replace the bookshop … How's your cat, by the way?'

'Touch my cat and I'll kill you.'

Ozil laughed. 'Ah, there you are. I hope my men weren't too rough with you.'

'They nearly killed me.'

'Come, come. I'm sure you exaggerate.'

Damn him. Ozil spoke as though he were batting away an annoying fly.

'They broke my ribs, you bastard.'

'Well, that's hardly a near-death experience, is it now? But, yes, I'm sure it's painful. Think of it as a little reminder.'

'You're a monster. You should be locked away.'

'I'm sure I don't need to remind you that we are both,

how do you say it? In the same boat. You too would go to prison for a very long time for your part in our little venture.' He paused. 'Have the papers ready. It's always a pleasure doing business with you. And your cat says meow, meow … oh, he's gone very quiet. The cat must have got his tongue, eh?' Ozil laughed cruelly.

Peter began to hurl a litany of profanity down the line, then threw the telephone across the room. It crashed into the far wall and knocked over a vase, spraying broken glass over the floor.

He sank to his knees, curled himself into a ball and sobbed, uncontrolled and gasping.

Something nudged the back of his head. Something oh so soft …

Maxwell the Third padded over his shoulder and into his arms.

.

CHAPTER 30

It was her favourite night – a double bill of Corrie and one episode of EastEnders. An hour and a half of other people's lives.

Iris looked across at the armchair; he was there, ready as always.

'I don't know why you like the soaps so much,' she said.

'Ah, there you are. You nearly missed the start.' Eric smiled and reached across to her. 'And it's your fault. I never watched them when I was at work, did I?'

'You weren't home in time.'

'True. They've got depressing though. Even Corrie. That used to be funny.'

'I know. I don't like them so much these days. There's enough sadness on the news.'

'Have you remembered about the house yet?'

Iris looked away and folded her arms. 'Oh, Eric, I've told you. Stop going on.'

'We need to remember, Iris. You need to talk to Thomas.'

'I'm sure it's all sorted. Shh now, let's watch.'

They sat in warm, easy silence.

Every now and again Iris would glance across at her husband, engrossed in the story, his mouth moving slightly with the dialogue.

Watching the soaps had become a ritual, something they both looked forward to. Him with a whisky in his hand, sitting in his favourite armchair; her sipping sherry on the sofa. She hadn't had a sherry for ages.

The credits scrolled and Iris got up. 'I'm going to get some soup and soldiers.'

'That won't fill you up. Thomas put food in the fridge,' Eric replied, shaking his head.

'I know, I'm just not hungry.'

It was getting dark and Iris peered through the window as the last of the dog walkers headed for home.

She switched on the light and caught her reflection in the window pane. She'd lost weight, her arms little more than bones. She touched her hair. It needed colouring. How had she forgotten to do that? She turned in profile and straightened her back, like the young girl she'd been, so full of life and energy. It was a pity people only saw this frail shell of an old lady, a false reflection of what she was like on the inside – full of life and possibilities.

A garage door rumbled. Ron next door probably.

Iris took her snack into the lounge and flicked through the channels.

'So what're we watching now?' Eric said.

The lights flickered out and it took a moment for Iris's eyes to adjust to the dark.

The solar lights from the garden shone through the patio doors – pulsing blue, green and red.

'It's the fuse, isn't it?' she said. Why did these things always happen when she was by herself?

'I expect so,' he replied.

'I said we should've got that fixed.'

'Don't worry. You remember – I showed you what to do. You need to go to the garage, get the fuse and thread the wire through.'

'Yes, but if we had a new box, I'd just have to flick a switch.'

'Write it down. Get Thomas to sort it. But you have to do it this way for now.'

Iris stood and brushed the creases from her apron. Thomas had shown her how the torch worked on her mobile, but she could never remember. Instead, she felt her way along the sideboard and hallway to the front door.

Outside, the street lamps illuminated the front garden, and Iris easily made her way to the garage. The swing door clanked open, and she found the torch Eric had left just for this purpose.

Please make it work.

She flicked the switch and a shaft of light highlighted the dust swirling in the night air. Iris swung the beam around to reassure herself that the garage was empty.

It was. She put the stepladder up against the wall under the fuse box and stepped onto the first rung. The ladder slid to the left, and she hopped off and adjusted it. Footsteps on the drive made her turn but there was nothing save a dark car parked across the road, just its sidelights on and a figure partially visible through the window.

He seemed to be staring at her. She'd never seen the car before and felt self-conscious. What if she fell and he saw her? It would be embarrassing.

Come on. Just do it. Like going to the dentist or the doctor – it would soon be over.

The muscles in her calves trembled as she climbed the ladder. She opened the box, blew on the dust, and pressed the fuses to see if one had dislodged. At the end of the row, there was a gap. She checked again. One of the brown Bakelite fuses was missing.

Iris shone the torch over the floor, stretching the shadows. Maybe it had fallen out when she'd opened the box.

The floor was bare.

Eric had once smashed a fuse when he'd dropped it. He'd kept extra ones in the spare bedroom ever since.

She made her way across the front garden, and she was sure she heard footsteps again under the pattering rain.

The front door clicked shut. She swung the torch towards it.

The breeze?

Iris was sure she'd shut the door when she'd left the house.

The strange car was still there, sidelights on. The man was staring down the road. Slowly he turned, and his eyes met hers. Iris gasped and almost stumbled, her heart quickening.

Calm down. You're being silly.

The front door opened easily, and she stepped inside. It felt alien, somehow, though she couldn't put her finger on why. She checked the lounge, waving the torch about quickly.

'Eric,' she whispered.

There was no reply.

The kitchen felt all wrong – not the place she remembered, full of the smell of warm cakes, meat pies and roasted vegetables.

The ceiling creaked.

She stood still, barely breathing. Iris had lived in her house for so long she was familiar with all its sounds. When Thomas had been younger, she'd known which squeaking stair or floorboard to avoid in case the noise woke him.

The noise above her sounded like one of those boards.

But Thomas was in London. And if she phoned the police to alert them about an empty house, they'd cart her off to a care home for sure – a scatty old lady unable to look after herself.

She knew what would solve the problem – the fuse and the light.

She began climbing the stairs, holding the wooden banister with one hand and shining the torch upwards towards the landing with the other. She stepped slowly and carefully, placing both feet on each tread before moving to the next.

Two thirds of the way up, there was a crash, like a vase smashing. The artificial flowers on her bedside table?

Someone cursed, she was sure of it.

Iris froze, clutching the banister, holding her breath.

A banging on the front door made her jump. She wobbled and dropped the torch, which rattled down the stairs, light bouncing in every direction until it hit the floor and darkness consumed the house.

Someone was in her bedroom.

And someone else was at the front door.

She chanced the door, descending the stairs as quickly as she dared, twice nearly losing her footing.

Another thud came from upstairs, followed by muttering, and for once she was pleased she hadn't got around to decluttering her bedroom.

She reached the front door, took a deep breath and pulled it open.

Standing there in a blue anorak, her hair matted, was the young woman who'd helped her in town. Marion?

The woman grabbed her arm and dragged her down the garden path.

'What are you doing?' Iris said. 'Let go.'

'Please, Mrs Blueberry, you have to trust me. Come with me. It's not safe here.'

'But why? What's going on?'

'I'll explain later, I promise.'

There was desperation in Marion's voice. Iris dug her heels into the wet paving stones, pulled her arm away and turned to look at the woman. The rain was falling faster now, but the fear etched into the woman's face was clear as day.

Please come, Marion mouthed.

Iris looked across the road. The strange man was standing by his car, his dark jacket shining in the rain. He looked uneasy.

It was enough.

She laced her arm through Marion's and began to jog. Rain lashed over her face and her wool jumper was sodden against her skin. They ran – for minutes or maybe an hour, Iris wasn't sure – until Marion gestured to a car.

Iris couldn't stop herself from smiling – Thomas's favourite film.

Herbie to the Rescue.

CHAPTER 31

In the distance, but getting louder, sirens wailed. Thomas looked at Jacobs Manchester's prone form. Was he …?

The TV star groaned, rolled over, and clambered to his feet. 'I need to get the fuck out of here,' Jacobs said, slurring each word, though whether it was because of the shock or the beer, Thomas couldn't tell. 'If I'm found here, it'll be all over the bloody papers.' Manchester brushed the dust from his jeans and then leant forward, his hands on his knees. He was so white that Thomas wondered if he was about to be sick.

The journey was slow and meandering to the Tube station. A few people in the carriage looked at them and whispered, and Thomas felt self-conscious, thinking something was wrong with his appearance, until he remembered he was sitting next to one of the most famous people on TV.

Outside the apartment block, Manchester unlocked

a panel to the side of the gates and placed his thumb on a small scanner. The gate glided open silently. And expensively, Thomas decided.

A concierge leapt up and bounded over to them in the hallway.

'Mr Manchester! What on earth's happened? Are you all right, sir? Let me call the doctor for you.'

'Thank you, George, I'm fine. I'm indebted to Thomas here. We're going to my room.'

They got out of the lift at the sixth floor and went into Manchester's apartment. Thomas gasped. The open-plan apartment was enormous, beautifully furnished and immaculately decorated. Manchester gestured towards the lounge area and disappeared through a door. He returned a few minutes later, his face clean and creamed, and a voluminous black wig now crowning his head. He crashed onto a huge settee at least twice his size and motioned for Thomas to take the leather chair opposite.

As soon as Thomas sat, a gentle vibration began, and he jumped forward.

'Enjoy it. Relax. Hmm?'

Thomas eased himself down, and let the chair rock the stress of the evening out of his body.

'Electrical impulses, massage gadgets and aromatic oils. Take a sniff. Cost a fortune but it's bloody good, isn't it?'

Thomas nodded, pushing his back deeper into the chair.

'Whisky? I need a whisky.' Manchester strode towards a well-stocked bar. 'TV on.'

A vast screen filling one wall flickered. The reporter was live at the pub. The caption scrolling across the bottom of the screen read: *Terrorist Attack at London Pub*.

'Thank God for that. 'TV off.'

'It didn't seem like a terrorist attack, not that I know what a terrorist attack is like.' Thomas managed a small laugh.

'It wasn't a terrorist attack,' Manchester said.

'How do you know?'

'It was meant for me.' Manchester turned away and Thomas thought he saw his shoulders shake 'And you, oh fuck, *you* saved my life. I am indebted to a scummy member of the public.' He laughed.

'What – why – who would do that?'

Jacobs returned to the sofa and handed Thomas a whisky.

'There's a saying, isn't there? Be nice to people on your way up coz you'll meet the same people on the way down. Well, I'm not on the way down but I've upset a few people on the way up, that's for sure. And some of my friends are a little, shall we say, unsavoury. People might use me to get at them. Anyway' – he raised his glass – 'I owe you one, hmm?'

Thomas felt his mouth opening and heat rise to his cheeks. It was now or never. 'I've written a book.'

'Oh God, no, not your fucking book. Anything but that.' Manchester laughed. 'Send it to me. I'll see what I can do.'

'Brilliant thanks that's … that's … well, just brilliant. I need to pop to the toilet?'

'Right down the bottom on the right.'

Thomas ambled through the apartment, on the way a group of black-and-white photographs on a small table caught his eye: A man and woman standing halfway up some impressive stairs. Two boys playing with toy cars in the mud. The same group smartly dressed at a wedding.

Everything in the bathroom was automatic. A wave of the hand worked the lights, the taps and the flush. Thomas tried everything out several times then stood in front of the toilet bowl.

A small voice made him jump. Again.

'Please stop doing that. And please. I'm in the toilet.'

'Well, aren't you the fucking hero?'

'You shouldn't keep swearing either. It's just not right,' Thomas hissed.

'He does – why can't I?'

'Because you're the fairy queen.'

'Ang—'

'Angel. Whatever. Angels aren't supposed to swear. They're up there with God, aren't they?'

She laughed. 'Oh, yes, you just need to sing me a sodden hymn. That'll make everything right.'

Thomas washed his hands. 'What's going on anyway? Who'd want to shoot him?'

'Hmm, I don't know if I should tell you.'

'What do you mean? I just saved his life.'

'Well …' She flew closer to his ear, a conspirator. 'He has a brother. He's older, looked after him when they were little. Only trouble is, he's London's number-one drug baron!' She giggled and flew high above him, showering him with gold.

'What?' He stepped backwards so he could see her better. 'You're joking.'

'Nope, and the number-one drug baron has lots of enemies. And what better way to get to the number-one drug baron than killing, or at least scaring the shit out of, his baby brother?'

Thomas shook his head. 'What on earth's happening with my life?'

'I know. Angels, celebrities and now drug barons. Who'd have thought it? We owe you one – don't forget.'

'He's going to help me with my book,' Thomas said, drying his hands. When he looked up, Cortina had gone.

Over the next two hours, Jacobs – yes, they were on first-name terms now – was generous with his whisky and with his stories, except when Thomas asked him about the photographs, at which point Jacobs changed the subject. Then Thomas retired to the spare room and slept deeply and dreamlessly until the sun woke him through the open curtains.

He got dressed and found a note stuck to the fridge door.

Gone to work. Eat what you can find.
JM.

P.S. Do I have to read your fucking book?

* * *

The 11.15 pulled into the station, and as he made his way home, reality hit him hard and heavy. What was he going to say to Isabelle, who'd used him to get to Jacobs and the queen? What was he going to do about his mum? And Maria. How the hell could she have gone out with that total idiot Lipscombe? She'd probably sold the bookshop by now, too.

'Mum, I'm home.'

Silence.

Normally *Homes Under the Hammer* or *Escape to the Sun* would be blaring from the TV at this time of day. A bowl of what looked like mushroom soup and two toast soldiers sat on the table in the lounge.

He checked in the kitchen. She wasn't there either.

A chill slithered down Thomas's spine.

He climbed the stairs, took a deep breath and opened his mother's bedroom door.

The relief at finding the room empty was replaced almost immediately by worry.

A table lay on its side, dried flowers scattered over the carpet.

Where was she?

And where was Isabelle?

CHAPTER 32

The phone rang and Thomas bolted downstairs, puffing as he lifted it to his ear.

'It's Marion. I helped your mum in town that time.'

'Oh, yes, I remember. Look, I'm sorry, I need to go. I don't know where my mum is.'

'She's with me.'

'What? How come—?'

'She's at my flat. It's a long story, but she was in danger.'

'What do you mean?'

'People want your house and while your mum's there they can't have it.' She sounded close to tears.

'What's her house got to do with it?'

'She's signed it over to my boss, Mr Lipscombe. Last night there were two men and—'

'Mr Lipscombe! He's your boss?' Thomas felt his heart gallop.

'Yes.'

'Lipscombe? I don't get it. What's going on?' He was shouting now.

'Your mum's safe. She's with me. Let's meet up and I can explain.'

'I need to go to the police.'

'Please don't. Not yet anyway. My boss is caught up in it. I think they might kill him.'

'What on earth are you talking about? This is Essex, and not the dodgy part either.'

'It's not funny. I mean it.'

Marion gulped and the phone went quiet for a few seconds. 'This is real, and I d-don't know what to do.'

'Okay, how about the coffee shop in the precinct?'

'No. Somewhere bigger where we can talk without being overheard.'

They arranged to meet at Secondsite at two o'clock.

Thomas leant against the front door and closed his eyes. What had happened to his life? A month ago he was watching Netflix. Everything was humdrum and now …

'Isabelle.'

He took the stairs two at a time.

She was lying on his bed, curled up in the cotton wool.

She opened her eyes, sat up and stretched, then groaned and lay back on the bed, her wrist applied dramatically to her forehead.

'I'm fading fast, I am,' she said, her voice tiny and shaky.

'You can cut that out straight away. I know all about you. You lied to me. You just wanted to get rid of the queen.'

'I didn't, I didn't, I—'

'Stop talking like a baby. Everything you've said has been a lie. You wanted them to catch the queen talking to me, to disgrace her, didn't you?'

Isabelle folded her arms, her lips straight and thin.

'You used me. Tell the truth.'

Isabelle was silent, then took a deep breath. 'Yes ... yes, alright, I did. She doesn't deserve to be a queen. She's horrible. She's got no manners or morals.'

Thomas laughed. 'And you have?'

'I did have. Cortina swears and drinks and ... she has no dignity. She's from the gutter. I'm good. I've always done my best. Someone like me should be queen.'

'And all that crap about mobile phones and cameras – you made me look a complete fool.'

Isabelle laughed. 'Well, you deserved it if you thought fairies were that stupid.'

'It would be funny' – Thomas raised his voice – 'if it wasn't just a cover for you to leave my mum. You're horrible. Have you seen the state she's in? It's all your fault.'

'*Excuse me?*' Isabelle yelled. 'Have *you* seen the state she's in? You never even realised she was ill. And I never left your mother. I would never leave her. She was my world.' Isabelle began to cry.

'You did though, didn't you? Just because you wanted to be the queen. You're so selfish.'

'NO. She rejected *me.*'

Thomas took a step backwards. 'What?'

'She left me,' Isabelle whispered. 'She wasn't well, she wasn't. No Eric anymore, and you were grey. She was sad and muddley in her head. Blueberry's always kind, wouldn't hurt anyone, so when she was low – *pop* – here I am. But I can't get back.' Isabelle began to sob so hard she could barely talk. 'Sometimes people don't want us anymore. It's the hardest thing, and it's often old people who need us the most.'

'Cortina said it was you. She said you betrayed Mum – she was sure of it.'

'Of course she did. She hates me, wanted to get her own back. She knows what can happen.'

'How did Mum let you go? We don't even know we have fairies.'

'Do you know how you blink? How your heart beats? Why your hair falls out?' She glanced up at the top of his head. 'It just happens. Sometimes we grow old with our people and fade away. Sometimes people don't want us anymore because they just want a quiet life. Sometimes they let us go because they've given up … Anyway, it doesn't matter what the reason is – it's horrible and it hurts. Everything happened in a flash that night, it did. When Blueberry let me go, I should have returned to the forest, but suddenly I was with you in your bedroom.' She shivered. 'I was frightened, I was. I didn't want to tell you Blueberry had rejected me so I made up the camera thing. It was good, wasn't it?'

She sat up a little and smiled.

'I started to like it. I should have gone to someone else straight away but the freedom was lovely … until I started to fade. It was then I got the idea about Cortina. I was sad and cross' – she frowned and folded her arms – 'so when I saw a chance to get rid of her I took it.'

Thomas shook his head. 'Well, your little plan didn't work. What'll happen to you now?'

'What do you mean?'

'You tried to get the queen dumped from her throne. Won't she arrest you, clip your wings or something?'

Isabelle laughed. 'No, of course not. We're always squabbling. That's what we do. We're sneaky. I think that's how she became queen in the first place.'

Thomas held his forehead. A headache was looming. 'I give up. I thought fairies—'

'Angels actually.'

'Don't you start. I thought angels were supposed to be good.'

Isabelle shrugged and held up her palms.

Thomas sighed. 'Okay. So where's my mum?'

'I don't know. All the lights went out so no one could see. I heard a man come into the house. He went in the bedroom … knocked things over and made lots of clattering. And then bang bang bang on the door and Blueberry went away with the lady from town.'

'But why? What's going on?'

Isabelle shook her head and sank to her knees.

'That doesn't work anymore. I know you're not ill. You can move between people.'

Isabelle lay down and pulled the cotton wool around her. Her wings fizzed a couple of times and a few golden droplets sputtered onto the bed.

'You stomped on me, you did,' she said, unable to disguise her temper.

'Yes, I know, sorry about that. But that was your wing.

You seem weaker all over.'

'You know nothing, you don't. You think you do now you've spoken to her. We can move between people if we want, but if we don't find someone, we fade away.'

'Can't you just choose anyone?' He laughed. 'How about me?'

'We got to be compatible – be together, think together, melt together, be in the same bubble every second of the day. I've heard you say *That person's in my space* and you don't like it. Well, we're there all the time. Think what that's like. Sometimes we don't fit.'

'How do you know?'

Isabelle shrugged. 'We just do. I can't explain. We feel stronger and happier.'

'And if you find someone, you'll be better?'

'Yes.'

'Well, that's easy then, isn't it?'

'It should be, but look.' Isabelle turned so her back was facing him. Her wing, broken and tied to the splint, looked delicate and painful. 'I can't fly,' she said. 'How can I find someone if I can't get out of this room?'

A few sparks fizzled onto the bed as she flapped her unbroken wing. They glowed for a few moments, then turned into a grey ash.

CHAPTER 33

Thomas went into town early so he could call in at Blue Tiger before his meeting with Marion. The news of yet another drama in his once-boring life had left him shaky. Being with Maria for a while would calm him.

The bookshop looked closed – front door shut, no lights on. He peered through the window at the counter. Was that Maria? Someone was over by the desk, their head cradled in their arms. They weren't moving.

He knocked on the door and went back to the window. Still no movement.

He banged hard on the glass. The figure stood. He could see her now. It was Maria. She seemed panicky, looking around the shop as if she were about to run. He caught her eye and she relaxed and took a deep breath. She came towards the door, opened it, dragged him in and locked it.

She wore a beautiful burgundy jacket and black boots, and despite the strangeness of the situation, Thomas couldn't help thinking how lovely she looked.

'Thank God, I thought it was them,' she said, and threw her arms around his neck.

Thomas froze, unsure what to do with his hands but as certain as he'd ever been that her breath on his neck was wonderful.

'Oh, Thomas,' she said, and began to cry.

'What's wrong? Who did you think I was?'

'Just hold me. Just for a minute.'

Willingly he wrapped his arms around her, held her against him and closed his eyes. She seemed to melt into him, as if they were sharing the same time and space. He heard a tiny gasp.

'Did you feel that?' She shook her head. 'I'm being silly. But it was the oddest thing … like I didn't have my own body, like I was just part of you.'

'Yes, yes, I felt it too – I thought it was just me. I haven't hugged anyone for ages.'

'Neither have I,' Maria whispered, and she gazed at Thomas.

'What happened? Are you alright?'

'I am now. But, man, I've been so scared.'

She took his hand and led him to the counter. Things had changed in the bookshop. Not just his orderly work; Maria had been busy too. It looked amazing – a cool sanctuary.

'The shop looks fantastic. You've been working hard,' he said.

'Yes, that's the problem. I went for a meal with Mr Lipscombe and told him I didn't want to sell the shop.'

'You don't want to sell?' Thomas couldn't hide his elation. 'That's brilliant news. But did he threaten you? I—'

'No. Far from it. I think he saved me.'

'What do you mean?'

'When I said I didn't want to sell, four gorillas surrounded us. They spread a load of papers on the table and told me to sign them. Threatened to burn my parents' house down – with them inside it!'

'*What?*' Thomas's belly began to churn.

'That's not the half of it. When I said I wouldn't, they dragged Mr Lipscombe onto his feet and wrenched his arm so far up his back I thought it was going to break. He was in agony.'

'Oh my God,' Thomas said, though a tiny part of him was struggling to sympathise.

'Then he dived forward. I don't know how he did it – the pain must have been unbearable. The table and the men went flying. I just legged it. I dread to think what's happened to him.'

Thomas felt a twinge of jealousy. He'd have liked to have saved Maria himself.

'I just ran here, and that's not easy in these boots.' She laughed half-heartedly. 'Locked up and tried to get some sleep.'

'I don't trust Lipscombe,' Thomas said, folding his arms. 'I think he's done something with my mum's house too. I got a call from his assistant. She's taken Mum to hers. Said it wasn't safe at home. I'm going to meet her at Secondsite. You should come. But first we need to ring the police.'

'No. Not the police. Not yet. Those men said they'll hurt my parents. Let's just see what this woman says. Perhaps she can throw some light on it.'

Thomas nodded, and Maria brushed her fingers down his arm.

'Come on, grab your coat,' he said.

'You've pulled,' Maria said laughing.

'Pardon?'

'Never mind.' Maria fastened the buttons on her red jacket. 'I don't need a coat.'

They dived into the bright sunlight, and to Thomas it felt like a beginning.

* * *

Maria tucked her arm through Thomas's and pulled him closer. 'Should have worn my coat.'

'Glad you didn't,' he replied, nudging her shoulder with his.

Many regarded the gold-coloured art gallery as a white elephant and an enormous waste of money, but Thomas loved Secondsite. The building was big and airy, and you could sit with a coffee and lose yourself in the unusual creations.

The door slid open and a ping heralded their arrival. While Maria found a seat at a table, Thomas ordered coffee and cake.

They sat by the window, letting the sunlight bathe their faces. Thomas didn't know whether to be worried about his mum, or happy to be with Maria, but it was clear Maria was still on edge.

'So what do you think of this place?' he said, trying to ease the tension.

'We're lucky to have it,' she replied. 'I saw some Warhol pictures here, and stuff by that chap Grayson Perry.'

'Yes, and the one who did all those little terracotta people. I loved that.'

'Gormley. He did The Angel of the North too.'

'Hello.'

Thomas and Maria turned as one towards the soft voice.

'I'm Marion. We met briefly,' she said.

Thomas nodded, introduced Maria and gestured towards the empty seat.

'Where's my mum?' Thomas said, looking around.

'She wouldn't come with me. I tried, but she can be very stubborn, can't she? She wanted to watch *Escape to the Country* so I left her snuggled on the sofa with my cat. I'll drive her home tonight. I just didn't want to miss our meeting and have you thinking I'd kidnapped her.'

'Haven't you?' Thomas snapped.

'No, I think I probably saved her, but you can make your own mind up.'

He listened with growing incredulity as Marion told them her story, about Tenerife and his mum's house, the suitcases full of money in the stationery cupboard and the purchase of the bookshop, the sinister telephone call of a man called Seth Ozil and the rescue of his mum.

Thomas was the first to speak.

'We have to go to the police,' He said, standing up. 'Your boss is a bloody crook. He swindled an old woman out of her house and tried to kill her. Come on,' he said looking at Maria.

She remained seated.

'If we tell the police, Mr Lipscombe will go to prison. He says he'll make it right.' Marion said.

'I don't care about Mr bloody Lipscombe. He's a total twat and deserves everything that's coming to him.'

'I know he sounds awful,' Marion replied, 'and I know he's done wrong. But he isn't a bad man. He was desperate. Got sucked into things way above his head.'

'And what about the threat to my parents?' Maria said to Thomas.

He could barely believe what he was hearing. 'Look, they tried to bump my mum off too remember. It's all the more reason for us to go, isn't it? That's what the police are there for.'

'You weren't at the restaurant, chuck,' Maria said. 'These people aren't your local petty criminals from the pub. They're mean and organised. They know what they're doing. They're more than capable of carrying out their threats, I know they are.' Maria swallowed hard. 'I'm terrified.'

'It was the same at your house, Thomas,' Marion said. 'They must've cut the electricity and sneaked in. There was a guy waiting outside. I could see the muscles through his jacket even in the lamplight.'

Thomas felt sick. 'So what're we supposed to do?'

'We'd better speak to Mr Lipscombe,' Marion said. 'Let's see what he has to say.'

Thomas shook his head. 'I don't see the point,' he said, regretting the querulous tone in his voice.

'Mr Lipscombe saved me at the restaurant,' Maria said.

'And he called me to get your mum out of the house,' Marion said. 'He's been a prat, but he deserves a chance, doesn't he? Maybe he's got a solution.'

'Oh God,' Thomas said. 'What's the matter with you two? He's a crook himself. And what about my mum's house? All they need to do is get her out of the picture. It's all signed over.'

'No,' Marion said, and smiled. 'It's not.'

CHAPTER 34

Peter switched on the coffee machine and watched the dark-brown liquid drip into his cup. He'd been pacing the office all morning and with every minute that passed, his hope that Ozil had changed his plans increased.

The phone rang, startling him, and his hands shook as he answered.

'Mrs Blueberry's safe,' Marion said.

The relief washed over him. He felt liberated.

One small victory.

He slumped to the floor, his back against the wall as Marion explained what had happened.

By the time she'd finished her story, he was close to tears.

'Thanks, Marion. I don't know what I'd do without you. I don't know what I'd ever do without you. You're my rock. I'm so sorry I've never said that before. I'm such an idiot.'

He could hear breathing so he knew she was still there.

When her voice at last danced into his ear, his pain disappeared momentarily.

'Thank you, Mr Lipscombe,' she mumbled.

'Call me Peter.'

She laughed, and the sound was more a chirrup, as if from a tiny bird. 'Okay. So, what do we do now … Peter?'

'I don't know, but I'll think of something. I promise.'

* * *

Peter checked himself over in the kitchen mirror. It would have been easier to sling on a pair of joggers and a sweatshirt given how much pain he'd been in when he woke up. But he'd been determined to keep up his grandfather's standards, and had chosen a grey pinstripe, white shirt and navy tie.

His suit was his armour. When he was little, he'd read how a knight would prepare for battle with his squire, each piece of armour precisely and purposefully placed. The past – not so much the dates but the social history – was another thing he had in common with his grandfather.

The knight's code of honour had impressed him, and he'd tried to live by something similar.

He shook his head. *Until recently.*

What a mess he'd made of everything; how easily he'd let go of his own honour.

He sat at his desk and a preternatural calm fell over him. It was strange, as though he no longer cared and had nothing to worry about. Mrs Blueberry was safe, and he had no intention of giving Ozil the transfer documents for her house. Marion had locked the cabinets and had the keys.

A long black car pulled up outside Lipscombe Property Associates. The driver got out and opened the passenger door. Seth Ozil emerged from within, donned in an immaculately-cut suit and designer sunglasses. Ozil nodded to the driver, who shut the door and followed behind as he strode towards the office.

Peter's chest tightened. He looked down – his hands had formed into fists, almost white at the knuckles. He unclenched them and tried to look nonchalant as Ozil opened the door.

'Ah, Mr Lipscombe, how lovely to see you.' Ozil slid his sunglasses to the top of his head and looked closely at Peter. 'I see my men failed to avoid your face. I will have to have a firm word with them. Detail is everything, don't you agree? The ability to follow simple instructions.'

Peter tried to return Ozil's stare, but lowered his gaze after just a moment.

'How is your eye?' Ozil asked.

'I'll live,' Peter said.

Ozil smiled. 'For now.'

Peter's heart thumped. 'Pardon?'

'Nothing, just thinking out loud.' Ozil pulled up a chair, and his driver moved to the front door, wrists crossed over his crotch. 'Now, to business. My evening didn't go to plan. I was hoping you would transfer both properties today and pay your debt, yet here I am, the owner of neither. You, it seems, have a conscience. But let me explain. You can't pick and choose. You can't have principles. That's not the way it works. You borrowed a substantial amount of money from me and the debt must be repaid. You don't get to choose how. I do.'

He banged his fist on the table and Peter flinched

'Did you help the old lady?' Ozil said.

The question was precise and clipped, and caught Peter off guard. He tried again to meet Ozil's eyes, but the man's stare – cold and resolute – punctured Peter's flimsy defences.

'No, of course not.'

'My men tell me a young woman went to the house. It was late. Why would she do that, Mr Lipscombe?'

'I don't know. A relative checking maybe? I think her son's away.'

Peter concentrated on his desk and traced the line of a pen mark with his finger.

'But why would they both leave in the dead of night?'

'I don't know. Why are you asking me? Perhaps she was frightened.' Peter looked across at the driver. 'Maybe she saw your oafs.'

'Perhaps. But it's quite a coincidence, and I'm not a believer in coincidences. There's usually a logical explanation.'

Peter shook his head but said nothing.

'Very well. We will leave it there. I am struggling to believe you. But you're not a foolish man, and you know the consequences of betrayal. Rest assured, I will find out. Now, the papers for the house please.'

'I don't have them at the moment,' Peter said, looking back down to the desktop.

'Mr Lipscombe, I don't know what's got into you. I told you I would collect them today. Why aren't they ready for me? I'm a busy man. I will ask you again, where are the papers?'

Peter glanced towards the cabinets.

Ozil smiled and nodded to his driver, who strode towards the files.

'You would be a poor poker player, my friend,' Ozil said.

The driver pulled the first drawer.

Locked.

He jerked it again and shook his head.

'The key, Mr Lipscombe.'

'I don't have it.'

'Who does?'

'My colleague.'

'And where are they today?'

'I've given her the week off. I don't know where she's gone.'

'So you would've spent the week working in an office with locked cabinets? Perhaps she had a late night too. Do you take me for a fool?'

Ozil stood. His cheeks reddened and the vein in his temple began to throb. It was the first time Peter had witnessed any emotion in the man.

'Try the rest. All of them,' Ozil barked, nodding towards the cabinets.

The driver pulled and shook each drawer but they remained in place.

Peter tried to maintain a look of concern, but inside he was smiling.

What are you going to do now?

The final cabinet flew open, and the driver toppled backwards into a table. Peter stifled a gasp.

Ozil walked over to the open drawer. 'What a stroke of luck, A to D and the only one unlocked. Don't look so surprised. You should be happy. Your poor security has done you an enormous favour.' He riffled through the files, handed one to the driver and snapped, 'Find me the deeds.'

Ozil returned to his seat. 'You thought all the drawers were locked. You had no intention of giving me the papers, did you?'

Peter shook his head.

'It is of little consequence. I have them now. It's only a matter of time before the house is in our possession.'

'Oprostite gospodine,' the driver said, his voice deep but reverent.

'English,' Ozil snapped.

'Excuse me, sir.'

'What is it?'

'These papers, sir?' He held them towards his boss.

'Yes, that's right. They're the ones. Give them to me.'

'But—'

'Give them here.'

The driver edged across the room and held the documents at arm's length. Ozil snatched them from him and flicked through the pages. Then he frowned, and turned the sheets back and forth.

'Is this a joke?'

'What do you mean?'

Peter had no idea what Ozil had found. He'd visited Mrs Blueberry himself, and she'd signed everything.

'These make no sense.'

'But—'

'Look,' Ozil shouted and threw the papers into the air.

Peter retrieved some of the pages and spread them over his desk. Mrs Blueberry's spidery blue signature appeared to be in order. 'I … I don't understand.'

'Are you blind? Look again.'

Peter focused on the words until the letters stopped moving. *Good God.*

> Beat the eggs and sugar together until light and fluffy. Add a quarter teaspoon of vanilla essence. Fold in the flour, being sure not to overmix. Divide the mixture between two seven-inch, greased and lined sponge tins and bake in the centre of the oven for about twenty minutes …

Ozil stood and hissed, 'I ask you again, do you take me for a fool?'

Peter couldn't help it – the image of a cartoon character with steam coming out of his ears came to mind.

'What are you smiling at?' Ozil yelled, saliva spraying onto his suit.

'Nothing. I don't know how that's happened.'

'I have invested heavily in your business. I was ready for some returns, and now it would seem that what we thought was in the bag was never there, and what we hoped to attract would never be enticed. And that's all down to you.'

Ozil spun around and nodded to the guard.

'No wait,' Peter said. 'I can sort it.'

'I know. You will sort it. You will fulfil your obligations.

And as with all business transactions, there will be penalties if you cannot deliver. I will return. But in the meantime, here is another reminder that you can always do better than your best.'

The driver walked towards him.

CHAPTER 35

Iris felt safe. She was home, on the sofa in front of Thomas, the two red bars of the electric fire warming her, and surrounded by ornaments and knick-knacks holding a lifetime of memories. She knew each one's history, where she'd bought it or who had gifted it to her. Capsules of love.

Marion had dropped her off earlier that evening and greeted Thomas so warmly that Iris had wondered if there was a friendship in the making. Thomas could do with it.

She felt her heart quicken as the memory of the previous evening came to her again. No matter how many cups of sweet tea she drank, it wouldn't soften. The car screeching through the quiet streets, Marion's frantic glances in the rear-view mirror …

Iris shivered. What had happened to her happy, comfortable life? When had she become so old? Eric's death had broken her for months, but this was different. Something was missing. She was grieving for herself – the Iris she used to be.

It dawned on her with horrible clarity that she'd likely depend on others for the rest of her life. She and Eric had taken wrong turns and dead ends, but it had been fun – a journey. Now she could see only a shackled existence – friends and family shepherding her down their own roads for her own good. She couldn't fault their concern; her absent-mindedness was getting worse, and now she was even misplacing the cards.

Was that what was in store for her? A slow glide down the final runway? She wanted a rollercoaster ending.

And only she could make that happen.

Thomas seemed agitated. 'Mum, what's been going on? Why didn't you come with Marion this afternoon?'

Iris smiled. Her refusal had been a small rebellion. Hardly Che Guevara, but it was a start.

She clenched her fists and looked at Eric's empty seat. It was now or never.

'Look.' She reached under her cushion, pulled out a handful of white cards and passed them to Thomas. 'I forget things. I made these to help me remember.'

Thomas looked up at her, puzzled. 'You never said. Why didn't you say?'

'I don't know. You've had a lot on your plate, darling. I thought it was just one of those things and might get better. And then it didn't, and I didn't want to go into a home. I thought I could manage.'

'What about the house?'

'I don't remember,' Iris said, and felt tearful as she spoke the words out loud.

'Don't worry. We can get it sorted,' he said softly, and unfolded a freshly-ironed handkerchief. He'd told her so many times not to bother pressing them. It was a waste of time, he'd said. But she always did.

He passed the hankie to her – a little act of love. This house was full of them. What had she been thinking?

'He said you'd have to pay thousands of pounds in inheritance tax. Said he was doing us a favour, that it would be a nice surprise. Eric told me not to sign it and to talk to you, but I thought I had it under control.'

'Eric?'

'Your *dad*,' she said, incredulous that Thomas should have to ask. Then she remembered, and mumbled, 'I've been seeing him too. He sits in his seat.' She patted the brown leather. 'We talk and he gives me advice – you know, like he used to.'

'Mum, that's cr— What did he look like? Is he okay?'

'He looks like he did when he was happiest. You remember, just after he retired. And he's fine. He really is.'

Thomas smiled. It was rare to see him do that. The last few years had been difficult. After the split with his girlfriend, he'd been so quiet and reserved. Maybe the bookshop and Marion were a new beginning.

Still, why he didn't phone the psychiatric hospital there and then was beyond her. He seemed so accepting. It made Iris feel hopeful.

'What are we going to do, Thomas?' she asked. 'Have I lost the house?'

'No, I don't think so. Marion says she's fixed it. I don't know how, but she said not to worry, and I believe her. But, Mum, why didn't you talk to me?'

'You'd have thought I was hopeless. I can't seem to do anything these days. I didn't want to end up in a home.'

'Don't be silly. You do great.'

'And you never want to talk. You've been distant since you came home. The redundancy and … and Kate.'

Thomas stared at the fire, the glowing bars turning his face pink.

'I know you don't want to talk about it,' she said.

'It's not that I don't want to, Mum. I just can't. When I think back it hurts too much. We had such a good life, and then we took it for granted and threw it all away. I don't think I'll ever find anyone like Kate again.' His eyes grew moist and he wiped them in one quick movement with the back of his hand.

'Of course you will. Marion's nice.'

'Mum! She's just a friend. And anyway, she seems to like that idiot Lipscombe.'

'But you've had a spring in your step lately,' she said, *and lead in your pencil*, she thought, remembering Eric's words.

Thomas was quiet for a moment, then said, 'I've enjoyed going to the bookshop, and the owner's nice. Her name's Maria and she's in the same boat as us. Lipscombe tried to stitch her up too.'

'There you are then. There's love everywhere, look around this room,' Iris said. She reached forward and took his hand. 'We all need it, we're all looking for it. Sometimes it goes and we don't know why. It's so strong one year and then it just disappears the next. But it must still be there, somewhere deep.' She squeezed his fingers. 'Sometimes we hurt people and we do stupid things and we can't say sorry and make it right. Sometimes we lose love. But it's never really lost. It's like the breeze swirling around us – you can't see it but you can feel it.'

Thomas shook his head.

'You can!' Iris said. 'And every bit of love that's created has to make the world better, I'm sure it does.' She paused for a moment. 'Thomas, love's infinite. It's never going to run out no matter how many people find it, or find it again. There's enough. You've been so sad since you've been home. Remember, you're allowed to enjoy yourself again. You don't have to be punished. It wasn't your fault, and your unhappiness doesn't make things right.'

'I know, Mum. It's just so hard.'

Iris passed the handkerchief back to him, and he blew his nose.

'Everything's been horrible,' he said. 'I tried with the book, but that's rubbish.'

'Don't say that. I like it.'

'Mum, you would say that.'

'I do,' she said. 'And you told me the bookshop's going to display it, so it has to be pretty good, doesn't it? And if you like the girl who works there then go for it. Be brave! Life's too short.'

Thomas smiled, and Iris held his gaze.

'So what are we going to do now?' she said.

'What am *I* going to do, I think you mean. You're going to the doctor's,' Thomas said.

'I'm okay. I made this mess, I can help sort it out. I'm not the frail old woman you think I am.'

'I've never thought that, Mum,' Thomas said, shaking his head. 'We'll get it fixed, I know we will. Perhaps everyone can meet round here and talk about what to do.'

Thomas stood, and Iris reached for his hand again.

'It'll be okay,' she said.

He walked past her towards the door. A buzz came from his jacket. Just his phone, no doubt.

* * *

Thomas lifted Isabelle out of his pocket and placed her on the bed. She was still grey and fragile.

'That's the very last time I'm going in there, that is,' she said, brushing the fluff from her dress. 'Don't you *ever* clean them? Have you ever smelt your pockets?'

'Nope, can't say I have,' Thomas said, grinning.

'Well you should. They're disgusting, they are. It was nice to hear Blueberry though.'

'Yes, she seems with it today, doesn't she?'

He knelt beside the bed and studied the fairy. The debris from his pocket made her look unkempt and dirty. Her tiny body seemed so thin, her arms were almost translucent, and her once gossamer-like wings looked smudged and frosty.

'What you staring at?' she said.

'You. You're looking worse. I think the house is going to be alright, but what are we going to do about you?'

Her wings buzzed. 'You know that lady who helped Blueberry? I think she's the one. When she's closer I feel stronger, and I think I have the same effect on her.'

'Marion? But …'

She seemed so mousy. But then Thomas remembered coming down the stairs earlier that afternoon. She's seemed almost to grow in stature as he'd approached. He thought she'd been pleased to see him, but now it made sense.

'Yes, Marion,' Isabelle said. 'She's going to be a star.'

CHAPTER 36

Thufir Hawat had made a welcome return to the shelves with his – her – opinions. Thomas was delighted. He handed Maria several copies of *Angel's Delight*. Maybe Thufir would decide to review it.

'Come with me.' Maria led him to the basement. 'I've applied to the council for an A3 licence.'

Thomas laughed. 'I've no idea what that means.'

'It's for a coffee shop. I know I can do it. We've got the loo over there and I'm sure we can get drinking water from upstairs. It won't be huge, just a cosy place for people to hang out and read. I'll get a couple of second-hand settees and armchairs. Big old leather things. Nice and worn.'

'You're amazing,' he said. 'A few days ago you were being threatened by Russian henchmen, and here you are planning a coffee shop.'

'You gotta keep going, pet. Can't let the bastards grind you down.'

She looked away.

'You okay?'

It was as though all the air had left her body. She slumped and reached for the wall.

'Thomas, I can't sleep. What if they come back? I feel frightened all the time.'

Thomas put his arms around her, hoping their bodies would merge again. He shut his eyes, willing the moment to last. Just him and Maria, all the worries and sadness gone.

She held him too.

'I won't let you fall,' she whispered and squeezed him tighter.

They spent the rest of the day tidying the shop. The last customer left and Maria locked the front door. Thomas looked down the aisle. So much had changed. It felt safe and welcoming, but relevant, too, in the harsh internet world.

'You've worked wonders,' he said. 'When did you find the time to do all this?'

'A lot of late nights. But without you I wouldn't have started.'

'Of course you would.'

'No, I wouldn't. You made me see it was worth giving it a go. You can't start a fire without a spark, and you were so much more than that. A flame that warmed my cold heart.' She laughed.

'Is that from a song?'

'No. Well, the Boss might have mentioned the fire bit.'

'I thought you liked Marillion.'

'I do, they're my favourite, and I owe you a dance, don't I?'

'Yes, you do. I've been catching up with the albums. They're good. I love that lyric about the blue sky above the rain,' he said. 'I've felt like that for a while. It's just been raining for so long though. I want some sun.'

'They're playing London in December. Shall I get us tickets?'

Thomas nodded. A date. Maybe. Sort of.

'Come on, it's nearly six. I'll buy you dinner,' Maria said. 'You can tell me all about it. Where do you want to go?'

'Anywhere but Luigi's,' he said, and she giggled.

They went to Noodly Noodles, shared a bottle of red, and Thomas told Maria about Kate. How happy they'd been, all their plans, and how their love had disappeared like sand through an egg timer.

Thomas waited for her to answer and finally she spoke. 'You're daft, man. Things change. I expect she's moved on and is happy again. I'm sure she'd want the same for you. Life's too short.'

'My mum's words,' he said. 'Now, I'm ready.'

Maria looked puzzled.

'For the blue skies.'

Maria leant forward and kissed him on the cheek. Thomas touched the spot where her lips had been.

'Don't rub it off,' she said

'I'm not. It just felt like angel wings.'

'How do you know what angel wings feel like?'

'I didn't until just now.'

'You daft bugger.'

They walked arm in arm across town. At the taxi rank,

he pulled her close, keeping out the late-evening chill. Slowly the queue grew shorter, and Maria looked into his eyes.

'I'll organise a meeting round my mum's in a couple of days,' he said, knowing that was not what she wanted to hear.

'That'll be great, chuck,' she said, gripping his hand tighter.

The last four people jumped into a taxi.

'I'll see you then,' she said, her head tilted.

A cab drew up beside them.

'Yeah, I guess ... um.'

'What?'

'Nothing.' He shook his head and opened the rear door.

She kissed him on the cheek again, and climbed in.

Thomas closed the door, and all the courage that had deserted him, shocked him into action. He pushed his face close to the window and motioned for her to wind it down or get out – anything.

As the glass descended, the taxi drove away. The last thing he saw was her smile lighting the night sky.

* * *

Now here he was, looking at that smile again.

His mum placed a tray of hot drinks and biscuits on the table, then pulled out a notepad and pencil from her pinny pocket.

'Right, what have you decided?'

Marion burst out laughing. 'Oh, Mrs Blueberry, we're hopeless. We've done nothing.'

There was a gentle knock on the front door.

'Who can that be?' his mum said, straightening her apron as she strode purposefully into the hallway.

Thomas looked at Maria and shrugged. There was a muffled conversation and the lounge door opened.

Lipscombe hobbled inside.

Thomas put his head in his hands. *What the …?*

'I invited him,' Marion said. 'We can't do anything without him, can we? The meeting's pointless if he's not here.'

'She's right,' Maria said.

'Cuppa?' his mum said.

'Mum!'

'That would be lovely, if it's not too much trouble,' Lipscombe said.

He looked down the table, and did a double take when their eyes met, probably remembering their previous meeting. He sat next to Marion, grimacing as he pulled out the chair.

'I don't know how you have the cheek to show your face around here,' Thomas said.

The man's appearance was shocking. His eyes were bruised, a jagged red cut slashed across one cheek, and his swollen lips made it difficult for him to speak.

'I'm sorry,' Lipscombe said. 'I know it's crazy but I've got no one else. I don't expect anything from you, but maybe you've got an idea.'

Iris returned and placed a cup and saucer in front of Lipscombe. She smiled. 'I remember you. Thomas, this is the kind gentleman I was telling you about, the man who's sorting out the house for us.'

'Mum, we spoke about this, don't you remember? This is the bastard who nearly stole the house from us.'

'Thomas! That's enough of that language. I don't remember anything like that.'

Lipscombe shifted in his chair and looked embarrassed. 'It's true, Mrs Blueberry. I'm so sorry. Your house is safe now though. You've got Marion to thank for that.' He turned to Marion. 'Tell them what you did. I've worked out it was you, but I've no idea how.'

Marion smiled shyly. 'It wasn't hard. Peter ...' She looked at Lipscombe and he nodded. 'Peter has dyslexia. It's been a struggle to run the business and —'

'I couldn't have done anything without Marion's help. And I'm sorry, Mrs Blueberry, but your son's right – I *have* been a bastard.' He covered Marion's hand with his.

Marion smiled and continued. 'I knew there was something going on, and I knew it wasn't right. I just couldn't let Mrs Blueberry sign her house away, so I changed the wording in the middle of the contract with the first thing that came into my head. I knew Peter wouldn't read it; I just hoped Mrs Blueberry wouldn't either.'

'So the contract's worthless?' Thomas said.

'Completely,' Lipscombe said. 'Unless you want a good recipe for a Victoria sponge.' He chuckled, then winced. 'That's why I'm a little worse for wear than I was after the restaurant.' He glanced at Maria. 'That's something else I need to say sorry for.'

'Aye, man, it was a terrible night. Not worth a free meal. Good food, mind. But you were like James Bond at the end. You saved me, didn't you?'

'After getting you into the mess in the first place,' Thomas blurted.

Immediately he felt embarrassed by his petulance.

'Why did you try and get Mum to tell me about the house if the contract was worthless?' he said to Marion.

Marion looked at Lipscombe and took a deep breath. 'I was in a state. I didn't know what to do. I didn't want Peter to know I'd gone behind his back. I wanted you to pull out of the agreement before the deadline so he wouldn't know what I'd done.'

Thomas shook his head.

'He's trying to put things right again now,' Marion said.

Thomas folded his arms. 'What are you doing here anyway?' He said to Lipscombe, trying to suppress the whine in his voice.

'I told you, I don't know what to do. Go to the police, make a run for it, or just accept my fate?' He sighed. 'And I've put you all in danger. I don't know if these men will go away or if they still want the house and the bookshop. I'm so sorry but I don't have anyone else to ask.'

Lipscombe's face turned ashen, and he looked close to tears. His head slipped forward and banged onto the table. Thomas lifted him back into his chair, Maria got water from the kitchen and his mum raised the glass to his lips, the back of Lipscombe's head cradled in one of her arms.

'I'm so sorry,' Lipscombe said again.

'Okay,' Thomas said, looking around. 'How do we get out of this?'

'Maybe the money,' Marion said. 'Peter's got six

suitcases stuffed with cash in the stationery cupboard. Maybe we could give it all back.'

They all stared at Marion.

'Why don't I think that's unusual anymore?' Thomas said.

'They'll want more,' Lipscombe said. 'I've already spent loads on my bills.'

'Surprise surprise,' Thomas said sarcastically.

He thought for a moment. Maybe there was a way.

The fairy queen.

'I know Jacobs Manchester,' he said. 'He owes me a favour.'

Every head turned towards him.

'*The* Jacobs Manchester? On the TV?' Marion said.

'Yes.'

'I love him,' Maria said. 'How come he owes you a favour?'

'It's a long story, but I'll speak to him. If he can't help, he might know people who can.'

'Maybe we can meet him,' Maria said, bouncing a little in her chair.

His mum cleared her throat loudly, and everyone turned to look at her.

She stood straight, hands pushed deep into her apron pockets. It was as if the years had washed away. His brilliant, vibrant, confident mum was back.

'I can help too,' she said.

CHAPTER 37

For most of the journey, Thomas and Maria sat close, hardly talking, their shoulders touching, moving in time to the gentle rhythm of the train.

The previous evening seemed an age away.

He'd told Isabelle about the afternoon's events and asked her to contact Cortina for help.

Isabelle had seemed stronger, perhaps due to Marion's presence. Golden dust had even fizzed onto the bed when she'd flapped her wings.

'Do you really think Marion's the one?' he'd asked.

She'd nodded, and he'd asked her whether he'd see her again when, if, she went to Marion.

No, she'd said. She'd have to stick to the rules.

He'd told her he'd miss her, and her reply had made him laugh.

'It's a shame you're not my person. You're not so grey now I've got to know you.'

It had been a compliment of sorts.

Not exactly enough to take his breath away.

Not like Jacobs Manchester's flat.

Thomas had contacted him that morning. To his surprise, Jacobs had seemed genuinely pleased to receive his call and invited them to visit. Had Cortina been at work?

Maria's mouth dropped open the minute they walked through the door, and a tiny gasp escaped. If the spectacle of the apartment wasn't enough, seconds later Jacobs Manchester strode across the room. Maria squeezed Thomas's hand so tightly it hurt.

'Thomas, how the fuck are you, hmm, hmm? And who is this *delicious* creature?' He took Maria's hand and brought it to his lips.

Maria swooned and Thomas shook his head. He wasn't sure, but he thought she'd actually curtsied. That or she'd gone weak at the knees. He willed Jacobs's wig to slip sideways.

'Come and sit over here,' Jacobs said, leading Maria to the massage chair. She sat and he switched it on.

Maria screamed and began to giggle. Jacobs increased the intensity and Maria shrieked and kicked her legs up and down. She jumped out of the seat and whispered in Thomas's ear, 'I think I just wet myself.'

'Are you all right?' Jacobs said.

'Absolutely,' Maria said. 'I love your show by the way.'

'Who doesn't? I'm fucking brilliant,' he said, and Thomas wasn't quite sure if he was joking or not.

'So,' Jacobs said, 'how can I help?'

'Well, I wondered if your brother, being in the business, might scare the hoodlums off.'

Jacobs looked puzzled. 'What business is that?'

'You know.'

'I don't.'

'Drugs.'

'What the hell are you talking about, hmm, hmm? He's a banker. I don't talk about him, he doesn't like the publicity.'

'But—'

'There's a lot of crap said about me, Mr Thomas hmm, hmm.'

'I know but what about the shooting? All the people you've upset.'

'What shooting?'

'When we met last time.'

Jacobs laughed. 'Oh, that. I was having you on. Just adding a bit more to the legend of me. Figured you'd tell your friends about it, mmm? I didn't think I'd see you again. It was on the news – some gang-related revenge thing.'

Maria took Thomas's hand.

'Don't worry, I still owe you one.' Jacobs said. 'You didn't know where the bullet was going, did you? Is this instead of reading your bloody book, though?' Jacobs sat on the sofa and patted the cushion next to him. 'Look, it seems you need money. I can get you on *If Fishes were Wishes* tonight if you'd like. The top prize is half a million, and the answers go like this: A, B, A, C, A, B.'

'ABACAB,' Maria said.

'You like Genesis?' Jacobs said.

'Yes.'

'I love them. They played for my fiftieth. I like your girlfriend, Thomas.'

'She's not—'

Maria squeezed his arm.

'It can't go wrong. I've done it before,' Jacobs said.

'You've done it before?' Thomas and Maria said in unison.

'Of course. We can't pay that sort of money regularly, can we?'

Thomas and Maria stared blankly at him.

Jacobs sighed. 'Our own people win it now and again, especially if we've had a glut of clever clogs. People like to see winners, gives the plebs something to talk about. No offence. Get down to the studio for two thirty. I've got to get made up ... not that I need it,' he said, and laughed.

'This isn't legal, surely,' Maria said hesitantly.

'Of course it's not, but where else can you make half a million? See you later.'

Thomas and Maria stood in disbelief, the whirr of the descending lift the only noise.

'I need to go to the toilet,' Thomas said. 'I don't suppose you need to go,' he said, and grinned.

Maria hit him on the arm. 'Cheeky bugger.'

* * *

Thomas shut the bathroom door and splashed water on his face. No way was he doing anything until he was sure the fairy wasn't going to appear.

Five minutes later he was still alone. He unzipped his fly.

'Hello again,' the tiny voice said.

'You do that on purpose, don't you? Is it something about the loo you like?'

'Oh, yes,' Cortina said. 'I love standing around in the men's urinals. The smell of piss is bliss. Or maybe I just want to see willies. I'm mad about them, you know.'

'Well, every time we meet—'

'Every time we meet,' she mimicked. 'Where else can I fucking see you alone?'

'True. Look, please stop swearing. It just doesn't seem right.' Thomas felt like a prude but Cortina's bad language unsettled him. She was so tiny and perfect; it didn't suit.

'Please stop swearing,' she said sarcastically. 'God, you're pathetic.'

'What's got into you today? You're being so nasty. And why did you tell me Jacobs's brother was London's number-one drug baron?'

'You still don't understand about angels, do you? We turbo-boost our people. If Jacobs tells you a story about upsetting people, I have to make it even better.' She crossed her arms and hovered in front of him. 'I'm in a bad mood too. I've had to leave Jacobs by himself. God knows what he'll get up to without me, and it's all because I owe you one for saving him and have to do what that slug Isabelle wants.'

'Well, at least you're still queen because of me,' Thomas said, trying to keep the indignation out of his voice but not succeeding.

'Yes, okay and fair's fair. What do you want?'

'Hasn't Isabelle told you?'

'Yes, but I don't fucking trust that bitch.'

'Will you stop it?'

The queen huffed.

'It's all true. We're in trouble,' Thomas said. 'An idiot got us involved in this mess, now I don't see a way out of it.'

'This is the bloke who got stitched up in Tenerife?'

'Yes. I think he's trying to make things right. He's been a dickhead but …'

'Thomas! Please don't use that sort of language.'

Thomas gave her a hard stare. 'Is there anything you or the fairies can do?'

'Angels. I don't know. I'll have a think. I've got an idea about Tenerife. If I can sort it, we're even?'

'Of course.'

'Fuckety fuck fuck fanfuckingtastic,' she said, and was gone.

CHAPTER 38

Eric was on the high stool by the fridge where he often sat while she cooked.

'So,' he said, 'what did you have in mind? I heard you saying you could help.'

'I'm not going to talk about it,' Iris replied.

'What? Hang on, we always talk about things.'

'I don't want to talk about this one though.'

'Why?'

'Because I don't.'

Eric was quiet for a while. When he spoke, Iris could hear the concern in his voice.

'Iris, you're not well – you know that, don't you?'

'Yes, I know. Don't fuss.'

'Well, you've got to be careful. You can't do the things you used to.'

'I want to. I want to feel alive again. I've been pootling

about the house, tidying up and cooking for Thomas. I want an adventure.'

Eric shook his head. 'You're too old.'

'We had adventures, didn't we?'

'That was a while ago. There were two of us, and you didn't forget things back then.'

'I know, but I can still do it. And if I can't, people will help. Look at whatshername.'

'Marion?'

'Yes, she helped.'

'You were lucky there.'

'I know, but I think people are mostly good, I really do.'

'Maybe, but as you get older you have to slow down.'

'Yes, slow down, but I'm stuck at a stop sign, watching my life pass me by. When the lights go green I don't want to drive straight into my grave.'

Eric laughed. 'I don't know where you think up these phrases. You should've gone into advertising. Okay, so you want an adventure – go on a cruise. I don't see how you can tackle the Latvian Mafia by yourself.'

'It won't be just me,' Iris said under her breath.

Eric thought for a moment, then his eyes widened. 'No, you're not going to see them?'

'You see, that's why I didn't want to talk about it.'

'Iris!'

'They were fine.'

'No, they weren't. You don't understand blokes like I do.'

'You were jealous, admit it.'

'I wasn't. What I said was true. Romeo's was run by gangsters, and they fancied you.'

'It wasn't, and they didn't,' Iris said crossly, busying herself with the drying up, but she knew Eric was right.

Romeo's was a nightclub. Iris had found a job there when Thomas had been young and money had been tight. She'd worked on the reception desk and worn a low-cut gold dress that was part of the uniform. This had caused the first of several disagreements with Eric.

'We don't need the money that much,' he'd said as she looked at herself in the bedroom mirror.

But Iris had enjoyed the attention and, if she said so herself, she'd been rather good at being the face of the nightclub. Soon her popularity had drawn the attention of the owners, two Italian brothers, Lucas and Federico.

Younger than Iris and rather suave, they'd worn smart suits and crisp white shirts that had shown off their dark complexions. For some reason, they'd liked her, and with that had come lunchtime meetings, parties at their houses and 3.00 a.m. lifts home after the club had closed. Eric had hated it, but Iris had enjoyed the independence, organising Romeo's by herself, allowing the brothers to concentrate on their other businesses. They'd relied on her and trusted her completely.

She hadn't understood what their other interests were, but had a feeling they weren't entirely above board. Frequently other young, well-dressed men would visit the office, and when she entered, the conversation would stop.

One night after the club had closed, Lucas sat down beside her.

'Federico is in love with you.'

He'd sighed and clasped his hands together, told her

how they were one of the oldest families in Italy, that they lived with integrity even though she might consider some of the things they did dubious. He'd talked about old values – respecting your elders, honour amongst thieves, and the sanctity of marriage.

He couldn't let her work there anymore, needed Federico focused on the business. 'You've been more than an employee though; you've become a part of our family. If we can ever be of help to you, then we are here,' he'd said.

That had been over forty years ago. Iris had left that night and not seen the brothers since.

'They said they would always help, Eric. You know that.'

Eric folded his arms across his chest. 'I know, I just wonder why.'

'Look at you getting all hot under the collar,' Iris said, and laughed.

'It just drove me mad. They were better looking, had more money. I'm sure they were more fun. You couldn't know how much I loved you and how inadequate I felt.'

'You twit, it was always you. There could never, ever, ever have been anyone else. It never crossed my mind. When he told me, well … it was a surprise.'

'Told you what?'

Iris hesitated, annoyed with herself.

'It doesn't matter. It was a long time ago. You've been the love of my life all of my life. I miss you so much. Every day it's like a piece of me is missing, and every day I get through it and then it begins again. Perhaps me becoming forgetful is nature's way of easing the pain. The past becomes more vivid and the present pales. When I lost you, the world didn't seem worth being in anymore, that's how much I loved you. I've got a mountain of memories made of you and me, and I climb it most days. The view from the top is wonderful.'

Iris began to cry. Eric stood and moved towards her.

'Don't come closer,' Iris said. 'It's too hard. I want you to hold me. I want to snuggle against you. I can't smell you anymore. The cupboard with your suits in used to be full of your scent. It's gone. You're going too, aren't you?'

'I'll never go as long as you love me. And, yes, I was jealous. You were a single golden flickering star and people were drawn towards you. They couldn't help it.'

'But you were the only one I wanted,' she said as tears of longing and frustration welled in her eyes.

'I can't keep doing this,' Eric whispered. 'Coming back to see you, I mean. I'm not sure how many more times I'll be able to. I just wanted you to know that I heard you tell Thomas that love was infinite, that it wouldn't run out. No matter how many people find it, there's enough. So find some more … for me.'

'I don't want to.'

'Try. The world is still a beautiful place, and you have time.'

'It's not as easy as that,' she said, wiping her eyes.

'Of course it is. You're so lucky.'

'Why?' She was smiling now.

'Because you're alive.'

* * *

As the bus meandered away from the town, the roads became wider and the houses bigger. It seemed as though she had taken this same trip only yesterday.

Iris alighted opposite a tree-lined cul-de-sac. The large, imposing house at the end of the road hadn't changed except for the front garden, which had matured.

Feigning a confidence she didn't feel, she strode up the long drive, knocked on the door and waited.

She heard shuffling from inside, then the door slowly opened.

A small elderly man, slightly hunched, leant heavily on a walking stick, and seemed to struggle to catch his breath. He wore jeans and a white cotton shirt.

Iris squinted and tried to see the young man she'd once known through the thick white wavy hair and wrinkles.

She could not.

An elderly woman hurried along the hallway.

'I've told you not to answer the door,' she said in a concerned voice, taking the old man's arm. 'You never listen. You just have to do it, don't you? Have to prove you still can.' Her voice broke as she spoke.

Iris noticed a cylinder of oxygen by the hall table.

The man shrugged the woman away.

'Sorry about this. Can I help you?' the woman said.

For a horrible moment, Iris couldn't remember why she was there. She panicked and a wave of heat flushed through her body. She looked around, searching for a clue, and then she met the old man's eyes.

In an instant, the years peeled away. He was smiling.

'La mia bella principessa,' he whispered. 'It is Iris, yes?'

'Yes,' she said.

The other woman laughed. 'My beautiful princess. He doesn't say that very often these days.'

'It has been so long, and you have hardly changed.'

It was Iris's turn to laugh. 'Now I know it's you, Lucas. You and your flattery.'

'Come in, come in,' Lucas said. 'Wine? Coffee?'

He leant against the woman, his breathing strained. They moved through the house to a large oak conservatory overlooking a manicured garden complete with statutes and a small fountain.

'Forgive me. Where are my manners? This is my wife, Gabriella. I think you had left the club before I met her.'

They exchanged pleasantries and Lucas told Gabriella about Iris's role at Romeo's. He painted a far more perfect picture than she could remember.

'It was as though this woman had a special aura about her,' he said, taking Iris's hand. 'Wherever she went, she turned heads and left her mark. Poor Federico, he never had a chance. He fell in love but Iris was a married woman.'

There was an awkward silence.

'Where is he?' Iris said, looking down at her hands. 'Is he okay?'

'In Italy. Bellano. A beautiful town on the shore of Lake Como. He still does a bit of work, but most of the time he just relaxes. He's happy. He didn't marry' – Lucas shook his head – 'but he is healthy. He was always lucky in that respect. He's fitter than me. Must be the Mediterranean diet.'

Gabriella went to make coffee and Lucas stared at Iris.

'My good friend,' he said, 'how time passes us by. The three amigos. We were full of life and bursting with possibilities.'

Iris laughed. 'We were, but my husband hated it. I miss him. He died.'

'I'm sorry. I am sure he didn't like the business or us. I know I wouldn't have done. He must have been a strong and wonderful man to have first attracted you and then to have kept you. Forgive me, but he never sparkled like you did at our parties.'

'I know, but he was solid. He was my foundation. Without him I wouldn't have had the confidence to try anything. Now he's gone, I ...' Iris looked about the room.

'But you came here.'

'Yes. You said if I ever needed help ...'

'I did. So you need help? I wish you hadn't waited until I can't breathe to reclaim the debt.' He struggled to laugh and then coughed.

Gabriella hurried back to the room with a tray laden with coffee, biscuits and cakes.

'What are you doing? You must calm down. No excitement. How many times must I tell you?' She fussed around Lucas, brushing his hair with her hand.

'Agh.' Lucas waved her away. 'Forgive my wife. She would wrap me in cotton wool and have me sit on this sofa all day. That's no life. Tell us about you.'

Iris told them about Thomas and Eric and how she was struggling to remember things.

'Getting old, it's not for wimps, is it?' Lucas grimaced. 'I have emphysema. My own fault. Too many cigarettes and cigars. You remember?'

'I do – sometimes you couldn't see for the smoke. I had to cut my way through it.'

'Those were the days. I wouldn't change them. Even though I don't have much time left.'

'Stop it,' Gabriella said. 'You know I don't like you talking about that.'

'It's true. I'm going to die. Shout it to the heavens. All these medicines I take just let me die more slowly, it's cruel. I have no spark, nothing to get me out of bed. This is no life at all. Iris, you understand?'

'Please don't,' Gabriella said quietly.

There was a glint in Lucas's eye, and he wore the tiniest of smiles.

'You have something for me, don't you?' he said, leaning towards her.

'I need your help, but I didn't know you were so ill.'

'Pfft, don't you start. Tell me about it.' He glanced at Gabriella.

Iris took out her notepad and told them about her house and Mr Lipscombe and his change of heart. She described Seth Ozil and her midnight escape with Marion. Finally, she spoke of the bookshop and Maria and how helpless, desperate and frightened they all were. When she'd finished, she looked from Lucas to Gabriella.

Their expressions could not have been more different.

Gabriella was ashen, her lips tight, her head shaking. She turned to her husband, and her expression said, *Oh no you don't.*

Lucas, in contrast, was beaming, his cheeks flushed. It was as if he sat straighter in his chair.

'I feel so much better,' he said, reaching for the notepad.

CHAPTER 39

The tiny red boat was better suited to a cartoon than the ocean. The warm-up man had already whipped the audience into a frenzy, and they stood, applauded and whooped as Jacobs Manchester made his way down the jetty in time to the jaunty theme tune. Cannon-like lights swung manically around the studio until Jacobs reached his spot. They whirled in unison and highlighted the star as he emerged through the smoke.

Thomas had to concede it did look effective.

He felt excited and nervous. He glanced at Maria beside him, like a child at Christmas, enthralled. She wore new red trousers and a white shirt. Make-up artists had styled her hair and made up her face, and she looked even more beautiful. She smiled at him, and it was as though they were alone on the sea, the boat rocking gently, all the glitz and razzmatazz gone.

What? she mouthed, her smile widening.

Thomas could only shake his head in wonder.

Their names were announced and, as instructed, they waved into the camera.

In the first round, Thomas answered the questions and Maria fished for prizes. Jacobs had told them to take the red boat; the yellow one was modified with hidden holes that the producers could open remotely. They'd been gobsmacked.

'It's where we put the duffers we don't like, or ugly plebs who are no good for ratings' he'd said.

Then he'd reminded them about the order of the answers: A, B, A, C, A, B. 'Then take the rod with the red mark. That'll be half a bloody million. Got it?'

They'd both nodded.

The couple in the yellow boat used the buckets as soon as Thomas answered a question wrong, and Maria was soaked, her top sticking to her skin.

Thomas felt protective and nodded at her shirt. Maria looked down and laughed, pulled a prize from the water and raised it high above her head.

When their opponents had answered five questions incorrectly, Maria ran across the jetty and began emptying the buckets into the yellow boat. After three, it listed.

The audience jumped up and cheered. *Jaws* music blasted through the speakers and the spectators sung along. Maria raised the final bucket and poured it into the yellow boat. It sank, leaving its occupants splashing in the water surrounded by red-suited divers.

A producer escorted Thomas and Maria to the green room while Jacobs introduced Kylie Minogue. A muffled medley of her hits washed through the walls.

'You can't beat a bit of Kylie,' Maria said, and began to dance around the room.

'You're crazy.'

'Come on, chuck. Let's see your moves. We're about to win half a million.'

The door opened and a neat young man escorted them back to the studio. The crowd welcomed them into the arena like gladiators. The noise was deafening as the lights whirled around.

This time they sat in a boat with at least twenty fishing lines dangling in the water. At the stern were two golden fishing rods, set as if to catch a marlin. At either side, huge cartoon-style black whales bobbed on the water. Jacobs stood on the jetty in front of a colourful board with a pyramid of fish.

The lights lowered and three white beams highlighted the star. A pulse thrummed through the speakers like a beating heart. Jacobs spun around, his arms half-raised.

'So, Maria and Thomas, you've made it to the final. All that stands between you and half a million pounds are …'

The audience joined in.

'Six questions, two whales and one perfect storm.'

The cheering increased.

'Are you ready to play?'

They nodded.

'Ok, for every question you get right you can pull up a fishing line and catch a prize. You can bail out of your boat at any time, in which case you can keep whatever prizes you have won. If the boat sinks before you bail out, you lose all the prizes. If you answer the last question correctly, you can choose a golden fishing rod. One of the golden rods will have hooked a fish worth half a million pounds.' The watchers whooped. 'Choose the wrong rod and the boat sinks. Is that clear?'

They both nodded again. Thomas could feel his heart racing.

Jacobs stood back, mimicked an angler casting off, and bellowed, 'Then let's fish for a wish.'

The water around the boat became choppy and Thomas grabbed the sides of the boat. Maria slipped and hauled herself up using Thomas's knees, her smile beaming through the spray. The lights darkened and fake lightning flashed across the studio. A wind machine took their breath away and the whales spouted water into his face.

'It's brilliant, isn't it?' Maria shouted.

'Yes, great,' Thomas yelled clinging to the boat for dear life.

Jacobs's voice boomed over the PA. 'Question one. In what year was Mount Everest first climbed? A, 1953, B, 1954 or C, 1951?'

In unison, Thomas and Maria shouted, 'A.'

'Can't hear you,' Jacobs said.

'A,' they repeated, this time with the help of some excited audience members.

'Correct – pull up a fish.'

There was wild applause.

Maria reached for the closest line and reeled in the prize. It was heavier than it looked, so he helped her heave the fish into the boat.

A voice came through the speaker. 'You've landed an all-expenses-paid family holiday to the Bahamas!' The sponsor's details flashed onto a vast screen behind them along with images of the prize. Thomas thought it strange seeing people relaxing in the sun while all around them a storm raged.

He tried to bail out some of the water from the boat, but it was a losing battle.

'Question two …' Jacobs yelled.

They answered correctly and the screen displayed a small car. Then came a digital radio.

'Are you going to be brave or bail?' Jacobs yelled.

'Brave, Brave, BRAVE,' the audience chanted.

There were only one or two dissenting voices.

'Brave,' Thomas and Maria shouted.

'Okay. Next question …'

Thomas moved close to Maria and cupped his hand around her ear.

'What question is this?' he said.

'I can't remember.' Maria said. 'I think it's the fourth one.'

Thomas panicked. Wasn't it the fifth?

'I need an answer,' Jacobs said. 'You're getting close to sinking.'

Maria grabbed his arm and pointed to the screen.

'Look! Three prizes.'

They looked at each other, grinned and held hands, shouting, 'C!'

Maria pulled another prize from the water – a speedboat trip down the Thames.

'Brave or bail?' Jacobs shouted.

'Brave.' They said, timing their reply with the audience's frenzied chants.

Their answer earned them £20,000, and Thomas gawped at the fish, not quite able to believe it.

'Brave or bail,' Jacobs shouted excitedly.

The water was now up to the rim of the boat. They tried to clear some of it using the fish they'd reeled in, but the spouting whales just spewed more into the boat, and the choppy water now sent waves over the side.

The audience was less decided now, and a cacophony of conflicting advice ensued.

Thomas and Maria looked at each other. 'Brave,' they shouted into the wind.

Jacobs took the last fish from the top of the pyramid and read the question. The storm abated and the audience quieted, leaving just the thrumming heartbeat.

'What is the longest known journey for a message in a bottle? A, 20,000 miles, B, 25,000 miles or C, 30,000 miles?'

Thomas and Maria looked at each other and pretended to confer. Then Thomas nodded and Maria said, 'B.'

'Correct,' Jacobs said.

The storm began again, and the audience erupted with applause and advice.

'Left, left.'

'Right, left.'

Thomas and Maria moved towards the golden fishing rods at the stern. Breathless, Thomas spotted the red mark and pointed at the rod closest to Maria. He tilted his head back, closed his eyes, and laughed as Maria turned the handle of the reel.

The audience gasped and he opened his eyes, ready for Maria's arms.

On the end of the fishing line was a dark shape.

A white spotlight picked it out.

Even then, it took him a moment to understand.

His brow furrowed against the wind.

There, on the end of the line, was an old boot.

* * *

Thomas passed Maria a towel for her hair. 'What just happened?'

'We lost the lot, man, that's what.'

Thomas shook his head.

'I know,' Maria mumbled, and took his wet hand in hers.

The door opened and Jacobs Manchester walked in, beaming.

'Oh my God, that was TV gold, hmm? *Hmm?* Your faces. Su-fucking-perb.'

'What do you mean?'

'We zoomed in. You were like so sure of the half a million! The disappointment, you could almost see it oozing out of you and dripping onto the floor. Amazing.'

Thomas stood up, his hands clenched by his side. 'We *were* sure. You told us. We needed that money.'

'I know. One of those things,' Jacobs said. 'Shit happens, hmm? Producer said we didn't have enough cash for a big win this month. I thought we'd better make the best of a bad job.'

'You used us.'

'Well, it would hardly have been brilliant TV if you'd known, would it?'

Thomas felt as if he were about to explode.

'Look, you can keep the prizes. How's that? Well, not the money one, but all the others.'

'We don't want the bloody prizes. We needed the money. Don't you understand? You knew we were desperate.'

'I know – it made it even better, didn't it? Life or death. Your faces!' Jacobs laughed, looked at Thomas, and took a step backwards. 'I'm sorry. Get dry. I'll buy you dinner.'

'What're we going to do now?' Thomas said.

'Come on, chuck, let's go.' Maria said quietly.

She took his arm and pulled him towards the door. He felt dazed, as if he were dreaming and looking down on the room from above.

'I'll do the book launch,' Jacobs called after them.

* * *

Maria's arm was warm, entwined with his, and they swayed gently to the movement of the Tube train. Despite everything, Thomas felt happy. He smiled and stared at himself in the concave window, adjusted his position and watched his reflection stretch.

'You silly egg,' Maria said and squeezed his arm. 'And I've a bone to pick with you. *We don't want your bloody prizes*?' I could've done with that car.'

On the way up the escalator, Thomas stood behind Maria, his head on her back, hands holding her hips. She reached down and covered them with hers.

There was just the odd black cab prowling for passengers as they walked arm in arm through the quiet streets. It was a warm night and Thomas wished the hotel was further away but after only a few minutes they were standing in the foyer.

The receptionist seemed tired, bored and affronted that he should have any customers at all. With a huff, he checked the reservations and activated their passes.

'Who wants the biggest room?' he said.

Thomas nodded toward Maria.

Hers was on the first floor. The hallway had seen better days – worn carpet, the skirting scuffed – but to Thomas it was the best place he'd ever been.

'It was an adventure, wasn't it?' he said.

'Aye, it was,' Maria replied.

'We'll sort something out, won't we? We have to.'

'Of course we will. It'll be okay. Maybe Lipscombe's got something up his sleeve.'

They reached Maria's door. He wanted to kiss her but just said, 'Night, night then. Sleep tight.'

'Thomas, it sounds like this room's enormous. I think I might suffer from claustrophobia.'

'You mean agoraphobia.'

'That too,' she said, trying not to laugh.

'Do you need me to come in and make sure you're okay?'

'I think I do.'

She kissed his cheek softly, the barest of touches. He thought of angel wings again.

'Please come in,' she whispered.

CHAPTER 40

Thomas spent the next few days in Blue Tiger Books. Maria had obtained permission for the basement coffee shop, and despite the smothering shadow of Seth Ozil, those hours spent researching providers and sourcing materials had been some of his happiest.

At the end of each day he kissed Maria goodbye. He could sense her wondering why he didn't stay and go home with her. She would never say so, but Isabelle and his mum were pulling him in different directions. His mum had seemed a little better since the visit to her friends, but Isabelle was deteriorating fast. On his return from the city, she'd barely been able to lift her head. She'd tried to sit up and buzz her wings, but there'd been no noise, no shower of gold dust.

'I don't know why Blueberry doesn't want me,' she'd whispered into her pillow.

'Mum's not well herself, but she wouldn't want you to be ill. She'd want you to be happy.'

'But I'm not. I want to go back to her.' Isabelle had turned towards him, her eyes blazing.

'Can you?'

'No, I don't think so.'

'Well, don't even think about it then. We need to get you with Marion, don't we?'

'Yes, but what if I don't like her?' She'd wrapped her tiny arms around herself.

'She seems nice, not fiery or anything. But you can do that, can't you?'

'Yes, I know, but I won't see you anymore either.'

'We'll both have new lives,' Thomas had said, pushing the lump in his throat away. 'Isabelle, everything's changed since I met you. The world's exciting again. It's not all good but I feel alive.'

She'd laughed but held her stomach. 'It's nothing to do with me, it's not. It's all in your head, silly.'

'Well, it just feels that way.'

He'd wanted to kiss her tiny cheek but instead had blown a kiss towards her back. Her wings fluttered at its touch.

Now, here he was in the living room, and it was surely the strangest council of war imaginable.

His mum hadn't sat still for more than five minutes, fetching tea for every visitor as they arrived. Marion was quiet and composed, slipping tiny glances at Lipscombe, who'd arrived suited and booted. If he'd been hoping his pinstriped armour would give him confidence, it didn't appear to be working. His leg bounced up and down, shaking the table until Marion put her hand on his knee and stilled it. Marion seemed pleased. After the meeting, he'd have to get her close to Isabelle.

Maria floated into the room in a flowery blue dress, bracelets jangling, and Thomas found it impossible not to feel happy.

'Afternoon, chuck,' she said, and kissed him on the cheek.

He glanced awkwardly at Marion and Lipscombe. They were both staring at the table but he was sure they were grinning.

'So what's been happening?' Lipscombe said.

'We haven't had much luck, have we, Thomas?' Maria said. 'Turns out the fishes held empty wishes. Didn't even win a telly.'

Thomas nodded, feeling cross all over again. 'No, it didn't go as planned.'

'I met my friends,' his mum said, and sat down next to him.

'Mum, we spoke about this when you got home. It's great you want to help, but all your friends must be ancient. Unless they've got a load of money to give us, I don't see what they can do.'

'But they said they'd help. They're looking forward to it.'

Thomas sighed. 'Okay, Mum.' He really needed to be more patient. 'How about you, Peter?'

Lipscombe jumped. 'Well, you won't believe it, but I've had this letter from a professor.'

Marion shook her head and tried to stop Lipscombe's hand reaching into his pocket.

'I don't know, Peter,' she said. 'He sounds like a crackpot. Maybe just don't read it. See what happens.'

He shrugged her off. 'You never know. We're clutching at straws anyway. This could be it. Listen. It's from Professor Buttons McQueen at the National Autonomous University of Mexico.' He waved a small white oblong card in front of them. 'It says he's an adventurer in antiquities. It sounds like *Raiders of the Lost Ark*.'

Lipscombe passed a letter to Marion and she read it aloud.

Dear Mr Lipscombe,

Greetings from Mexico. I trust you are well.

I am conducting research into Francisco Pizarro, the Spanish conquistador. You may know his history, but in case the name is unfamiliar, here's some background.

In 1530, Pizarro captured the Aztec emperor, Atahualpa, and murdered many thousands of his followers in a brutal ambush. Atahualpa agreed to pay a ransom for his release and selected a large hut. He offered to half-fill it with gold objects and fill it twice over with silver objects. Despite completing the task, Pizarro executed Atahualpa three years later.

It has always been a mystery as to what happened to the treasure, but I believe I'm on the verge of discovering its whereabouts. I've tracked a ship that sailed from South America to Spain. It left laden with gold, but

```
arrived in Cadiz empty, its manifest
altered accordingly.
    However, on examining the captain's
log, I've concluded that the ship
docked at Tenerife for two days. The
question is why? Further research
revealed letters from a sailor who
declared they'd buried 'riches beyond
belief' on the island. The coordinates
and description match the hillside on
land belonging to you.
    I'm writing to ask for your
permission to begin excavation.
    I need not tell you that should I
discover the treasure, you'll become
a very wealthy man, and I'll have
contributed something truly remarkable
to the world.
    I look forward to hearing from you.
Yours,
    Buttons McQueen
```

Marion folded the letter and handed it back, her lips a thin line.

'What do you think?' Lipscombe said.

Maria shuffled in her seat.

Bookshops, fairies, gangsters and now El Dorado.

Cortina had said she'd had an idea. Could it be her doing?

'I thought we could show Ozil the letter and offer the land plus the money that's left in the cupboard,' Lipscombe said.

Thomas shook his head and folded his arms. 'It sounds far-fetched, but what else do we have?'

'It's ridiculous,' Marion said sharply. 'He's obviously a crackpot. Ozil will want something more than that.'

'But what can we do? Have you got any other ideas?' Lipscombe said.

Marion sighed, staring at the table. 'No.'

Lipscombe put his hand over hers and squeezed it.

'I'm just so worried about you,' she said, sniffing.

'Okay. It's agreed then. Let's try that,' Maria said, though Thomas could see she was unconvinced. 'If it doesn't work, we go to the police. Have you heard anything more from Ozil?'

'Nothing,' Lipscombe replied.

'Can you make contact?' Thomas said. 'Say you'll meet him at the office at 7.00 p.m. this Friday, and that you have a proposal.'

'Okay.' Lipscombe said. He seemed to be barely breathing.

'We'll all be there with you, won't we?' Thomas said.

Everyone nodded.

'I'll ask my friends to come too,' Iris said.

'See how it goes, Mum. But it might be best if you stay at home for this one.'

'No! I want to help. I'm not a doddery old woman. I want to be there too.'

Thomas conceded; she wouldn't remember this conversation in two days' time anyway.

'Marion, before you go can I show you something?' Thomas said.

'I can't right now,' she said, glancing at Lipscombe. 'We're in a bit of a hurry.'

'It won't take a minute. Just upstairs.'

Maria laughed. 'You can't take a young lady upstairs to *show her something*, chuck.'

Marion looked at Lipscombe. He nodded towards the hallway.

'Next time for sure,' she said, and made for the door.

'Wait,' Thomas said, louder than he'd intended.

'What's the matter, chuck?' Maria said. 'Are you alright?'

'Nothing,' Thomas said. 'It's okay.' But a chill slithered down his spine as he watched them leave and thought of Isabelle upstairs.

Fading.

CHAPTER 41

It felt odd. Peter had never been to the cinema with a girl.

The idea had come to him spontaneously, as he'd wracked his brains for something that would dilute Marion's evident disappointment. She hadn't wanted him to mention the letter from Buttons McQueen at the meeting. She thought the man was a fraudster. But Peter was desperate. If someone had told him Maxwell the Third could predict the lottery numbers with a twirl of his tail, Peter would have given it a go.

Now here he was, warm and cosy, the past hours forgotten. Well, almost. *I'm just so worried about you*, she'd said. He'd not forgotten that.

Their arms touched, and Peter sat statue-still, not daring to move lest he broke the spell, even though his neck ached. Marion's fingers found the tips of his and a warm tingle rippled through his body. He explored her hand, feeling the lines of her palm and the space between her fingers. He was still rigid, but dared not move in case he lost her. Then, as if she'd read his mind, her head lowered gently onto his shoulder. He released the breath he hadn't realised he'd been holding and moulded into her.

His phone buzzed in his pocket. He glanced at the screen.

Seth Ozil's name pulsed, lighting up the seat in front of him.

He pressed Decline.

Mr Ozil could wait.

CHAPTER 42

They waited in silence at Lipscombe Property Associates, Lipscombe at his desk, Marion at hers. Thomas and Maria perched on a table, their legs swinging.

'We should've just gone to the police,' Marion said.

'I'm beginning to think you're right, chuck,' Maria said. 'I was just so worried about my parents, but I don't see we've got a choice now.'

'I'll ring them,' Thomas said.

'We're here now. Let's just see what Ozil says,' Lipscombe said. 'It might be okay.'

'Peter, they're not going to accept that crazy letter. They're really not.'

'Let's just see, can we?'

No one spoke for the next twenty-five minutes.

Then two vehicles pulled into the car park, their headlights elongating the shadows in the office. The doors slammed and footsteps crunched on the gravel.

There was a loud rap at the door.

'I'll go,' Lipscombe said, and stood unsteadily.

'Mr Lipscombe, how lovely to see you again. Ah, I see we have company. The gang's all here.' Ozil laughed, but there was no joy in his voice; it was cruel and mocking. He nodded to each of them. 'It's like my favourite film, *The Magnificent Seven*. You've all come to the aid of a poor defenceless nobody. You realise he's dug his own grave by being greedy? An unfortunate choice of words perhaps, but they could be apt. We'll see.' He smiled as three burly men in dark suits stepped through the doorway. 'You have a proposal for me?'

'We do,' Lipscombe said.

'And it's not a complete waste of my time? It's Friday night. I could have been enjoying a meal at Luigi's. That's your favourite restaurant, isn't it?'

He smiled at Maria. She looked away.

'I think it's an excellent offer,' Lipscombe said.

He tried to keep his voice steady, but Thomas heard the fear in it. Marion shook her head and mouthed, *Don't.*

'I have this letter from an eminent professor. He thinks my land in Tenerife may have Aztec treasure buried on it.' Lipscombe unfolded the letter and handed it to Ozil. 'I thought I could give you the land and return the money still left in the suitcases and we'd call it quits.'

Ozil's smiled as he read, then looked at Lipscombe in silence, the seconds stretching until he spoke.

'What in God's name do you take me for?' He screwed the letter into a ball and slapped Lipscombe hard across his face, sending him staggering across the floor towards Marion.

'Stop,' she shouted, and helped Lipscombe to his seat. 'Leave him alone. It's a perfectly good offer.'

'The land is worthless,' Ozil said. 'I should know. It was me who set the fool up with it. You've printed the letter yourselves. There's a term – fool's gold – isn't there? But I'm no fool. I'll take the land as compensation for all the delays. No doubt I can sell it on. But I can't launder money through a worthless chunk of rock. I want the house or the bookshop. It's up to you which one. Look at me being generous.' He laughed again and looked at his henchmen, who murmured their appreciation.

'You can't have either.' It was Maria now who stood and took a step towards Ozil, her voice high and shaking.

One of the goons grabbed her arm and held her still.

'Leave her alone,' Thomas said more bravely than he felt.

'My, my. You three really are magnificent. It's a shame your friend here' – he looked at Lipscombe – 'has never shown such backbone.'

He nodded at the man holding Maria, and he let her go. She rubbed her arm where his fingers had been.

'He was pretty damn brave at the restaurant,' she said. 'Your thugs didn't expect that, did they?'

Ozil just smiled.

'You can't do this to us. We'll go to the police. Enough is enough.' Marion said.

'But that's just it, enough is never enough. It never will be, I'm afraid. You're in the spider's web now. Live with it. Embrace it. Now, I have something to show you.' He reached into his pocket and handed Maria a photograph. 'Recognise it?'

Maria's legs buckled, and Thomas grabbed her.

'It's my parents' house,' she said.

'So, we will hear no more talk of the police,' Ozil said, looking at each of them.

'Some of your money's already in the system,' Lipscombe said.

'It's a trifle compared to your promises. And you haven't kept them because you found a conscience. And that will never do.'

'At least he's got a conscience. That's more than you'll ever have,' Marion said, her voice small and hopeless.

'Enough,' Ozil snapped. 'I reject your proposal. I want the house or the bookshop, otherwise there will be penalties. This is what we agreed.'

Lipscombe stood and used one of his arms to control the tremble in the other. He straightened his back and took a deep breath.

'Neither property is mine to give away, and these kind people don't wish to lose their homes or their businesses. Why would they? They're prepared to go to the police and face anything you throw at them or their families. It was me who asked them to delay so we could have this meeting. I suggest you look for some other outlet and leave them alone.' Lipscombe licked his lips. 'I have nothing more to give you, I'm afraid, and I accept whatever it is you're going to do to me.'

He glanced at Thomas and looked at the floor.

Ozil clapped slowly and deliberately, the sound echoing around the quiet office. 'A noble and fitting final speech, Mr Lipscombe.'

He nodded to his men.

CHAPTER 43

Iris hadn't seen Eric since he'd told her she was lucky to be alive. He was right, of course, but most days it didn't feel like it. Every day was the same. Thomas was often out so what was the point of cooking something nice just for herself when scrambled egg or beans on toast would do? She cleaned, watched the telly, enjoyed all the soaps. Then she cleaned, watched the telly and enjoyed the soaps again. When Eric had been alive, there'd been holidays to look forward to, friends for dinner, the cinema, theatre. The days had flown by. Now it was as though she watched the second hand move in slow motion. Often she had no idea what day it was.

Today, though, was an exception.

Today, she had a purpose.

Today, she, Iris, was going to make a difference. She was going to prove that despite her age and frailty, she could still turn heads … that she was still important, still alive, and the world was lucky to have her.

* * *

Lucas wheezed as he opened the door, Gabriella fussing close behind.

'Why are you so stubborn?' she said.

'Because it's all I have now. Can you imagine what that's like? The one thing I have to look forward to is beating you to the front door.' He turned to Iris. 'Forgive us. We're two cranky old people with too much time on our hands.'

'Speak for yourself,' Gabriella said, and swiped at his bottom.

Lucas turned and wrapped his arms around her.

'Forgive me again, Iris, but my predicament has taught me that every hug may be my last. To feel my wife warm, close to me, her body pressed against mine as I have always remembered it, that would be a perfect ending. So I hug her every chance I get – just in case.'

'Lucas, stop it.' Gabriella wriggled free. 'Don't talk like that, I've told you before.'

Lucas laughed. 'My wife doesn't accept reality. She's like an ostrich with its head in the sand. She thinks if she doesn't talk of dark things, they will not come and visit us. They will. We must accept them. If we can do that, our fear will be gone.' He reached for Iris's hand. 'Where are our manners? Please, come inside.'

Iris perched on a dark leather armchair, notebook in her lap and told them about the plan. Lucas's smile beamed wider; Gabriella's lips remained thin.

'I doubt he'll accept the treasure letter,' Lucas said. 'I think he's going to need further persuasion.'

'You can't go, darling. I won't let you,' Gabriella said.

'It won't just be me. I'm going to make some calls.'

'I'm going too then.'

'You are not.' Lucas said.

Gabriella crossed her arms. 'If Iris is going, then I'm going.'

'Iris isn't going either, are you, Iris?'

'I most certainly am,' she said. 'I want this as much as you do.'

Lucas laughed and shook his head. 'It seems I've been outgunned. I may govern this house and my business, but it is Gabriella who commands me. Kipling was right – the female of the species and all that. I am disappointed and beaten, but I may yet have an ally to save me from humiliation.'

The patio door juddered open – whoever was behind it was having a job.

'Talk of the devil,' Lucas said, and called out, 'The sun has turned you feeble.'

'Look who's talking – the walking wheezer,' a man with a pronounced Italian accent said.

The curtains parted and a slim elderly man wearing a blue polo shirt and cream chinos pushed through. His hair was thick and dark, though Iris suspected he'd dyed it.

Federico.

He stopped when he saw her. His eyes were full of tears.

'Bella donna amore mio,' he whispered.

'English, Federico. Where are your manners,' Lucas said.

Federico moved easily across the room and knelt in front of Iris. She felt both embarrassed and flattered.

'My beautiful lady,' he said. 'My love.' He took her hand, raised it to his lips and kissed it. 'You have not changed.'

'Your brother said something similar. You're both terrible flirts.'

'It is true. Your eyes still sparkle as they always did.'

Iris laughed. 'What about the rest of me?'

'As you get older, it is the inner beauty that becomes important.'

'Now I know it's you, Federico. You were always full of nonsense. I'm sure a sexy young woman would turn your head.'

'Iris, I met you forty years ago. I am still single. No one has ever come close to your star.'

'Don't be silly.'

Iris retrieved her hand, but Federico remained kneeling.

'It's true, Iris. When Lucas told me of your predicament, I caught the first flight. I've been waiting here for you ever since. He also tells me your husband died. I am sorry. I know I was a fool all those years ago, but I was young. Anything was possible. My heart ruled my head. I was wrong, I lacked morals, but my mistake could never change the way I feel, and now we are both single.'

'Federico! Enough,' Lucas barked. 'The woman has barely sat down. And for God's sake, stand up or you'll be in that position all afternoon.'

Federico shook his head and used the arm of the chair to lever himself up.

'Lucas, you more than anyone should know we must live every moment.'

Lucas dismissed him with a wave, but he reached for his wife's hand.

'Things change too quickly. Happiness has always been a butterfly flitting in and out of my life,' Federico said. 'That is my ridiculous, stupid fault, but this room is full of butterflies, full of happiness. Their wings are bursting with life and they have the most vibrant of colours.' He turned to Iris. 'As soon as I walked in here, I felt free. It's you, Iris Blueberry, here in this space.' He smiled as he spoke her name. 'Because of you, I can do anything. Because of you, I can't close my mouth or open my eyes. I am smiling too much. Everyone has a right to a room like this, full of butterflies, full of future happiness.'

'Have you finished?' Lucas said, and Iris thought he was trying to keep a straight face. 'Always the poet. Sit.'

Federico went to sit on the arm of Iris's chair.

'Not there. Over here.' Lucas pointed to a seat by his side.

'But—'

Lucas gave him a hard stare, and Federico did as he was told.

'I'm sorry about my brother. As you know, he is a hopeless romantic.'

'But he's right, isn't he, about happiness?' Gabriella said, and winked at Iris, who could feel herself blushing.

'Don't you start.' Lucas tapped his wife's leg. 'Now look. We are embarrassing our guest.'

'I'm okay,' Iris said. 'I'm just not used to this attention. I've been an unnoticed old lady for too long. Federico, what you said was lovely, but I'm not the person I used to be. I don't think you'll want me now.'

'All I want is your hand in mine. Time is precious.'

'Federico! Will you shut up? We have work to do. Iris, tell Federico what you told us.'

Iris ran over the plans, Lucas made some telephone calls, and then Gabriella led them out to the garden.

As they feasted on salad and French bread, it seemed to Iris that Federico's butterflies surrounded the table, each taking the form of laughter and memories.

She caught her reflection in the patio window. An old woman stared back, but for once it didn't bother her. The person inside was the real one, still there, not ready to surrender. Behind her stood Eric, his hands on her shoulders. He was smiling. She blinked away a happy tear and reached up to touch him.

But he was gone. Only the reflection of the sun remained, low in the sky but bright as ever.

* * *

'Time to go,' the man said.

Iris stood. 'It's been lovely. Thanks for arranging the taxi. I won't be too late home now, will I?'

The same man looked at another and frowned. 'We're all going. You need to show us the way.'

'You can't come home with me,' Iris said indignantly.

A woman took Iris's hand. 'Iris, sit down. Are you alright?'

'Of course I'm all right. I want to get home to my husband now. It's been lovely.'

Iris looked around the room and began to sob. 'I don't know who you are. I don't know where I am. I can't remember anything.'

CHAPTER 44

Marion placed herself between Lipscombe and the men. 'Leave him alone. This isn't a gangster movie. You can't just go around beating people up.'

The men stopped and looked at Ozil.

'She's right,' Thomas said. 'We're going to the police. You'll just make it worse for yourselves. Leave him alone.' His voice was shaking and he struggled to breathe, let alone speak.

'Just go, man, and we won't say another word. It's over,' Maria said, but she sounded unsure.

Ozil smiled. 'You've all jumped to the wrong conclusion. I have no intention of hurting Mr Lipscombe.'

There was an audible sigh of relief.

'But I'm a businessman. There's a code of honour amongst people in my profession. If something's not done, there are penalties. It's the same in any business. If the

Olympic stadium's not finished there are repercussions, are there not?'

Thomas nodded.

'My men will think I've gone soft if there are no sanctions and will attempt to usurp me. It's the way of things.' Ozil relaxed against a desk. 'I told you a story once, Mr Lipscombe, about how encouragement can always improve your best. Do you remember?'

'Yes,' Lipscombe said breathlessly.

'I have another story, this one is about failure and how you can encourage people to avoid it.' Ozil sat on the desk and put his feet onto a chair so his knees were almost level with his chest. 'When I was twelve, my father set me targets for my exams. He told me that if I failed he would punish me. I was at an age where the possibilities were endless and the summers were long; failing a few exams would have no effect on the rest of my life. He'd disciplined me before, but a few slaps of the belt were worth an evening or two with my friends. So I didn't study as hard as I should have done, and when I received the results, they were poor. I took the letter to my father and – rather like you, Mr Lipscombe – I prepared to take my beating. Instead, my father looked disappointed. He opened a drawer, pulled out a gun and shot my dog.' Ozil licked his lips. 'I launched myself at my father, but he was a grown man. He beat me to the floor again and again. But it taught me something – that unless you're a psychopath, you would rather endure pain than let someone you love endure it for you. I never failed another exam.'

Thomas mulled over the words. Lipscombe was doing the

same. Their eyes met and Ozil's meaning dawned on them.

'No,' Lipscombe shouted, and hurled himself towards the guards.

One of them grabbed him around the waist, sweeping his legs from under him. Ozil nodded, and the other man seized Marion's wrist.

She screamed. Maria started yelling at them. Thomas had never felt so powerless. He needed to get help, but the third guard had positioned himself in front of them. There was no escape.

'I have an hour. In that time we will use Marion as our teaching tool. Our lesson today is: failure is not an option. Do you know where that phrase comes from? No? *Apollo Thirteen*. Lay her on the desk.'

'I'm going to kill you. I'm gonna bloody kill you, you bastard,' Lipscombe writhed underneath the guard on top of him.

Spittle ran down his cheek. The guard pressed his knee into the small of Lipscombe's back, and his cry became guttural. The guard then grabbed Lipscombe's hair and twisted his head towards Ozil.

'Where shall we start? The face or the feet? You choose, Mr Lipscombe.'

'Fuck off.' Lipscombe screamed.

Thomas felt terrified, and utterly impotent. Maria had curled into a ball beside him and Thomas tried to speak, but even his mouth wouldn't work.

'That's not very polite. In that case, I will choose. The face it is,' Ozil said, and nodded to the far desk. 'Pass me that letter opener.'

The guard gave it to Ozil, and he held the blade against Marion's cheek.

'Keep her head still.'

'The feet, the feet, you bastard,' Lipscombe shouted.

'As you wish,' Ozil said calmly. 'Though it was Hobson's Choice, if I'm honest. The arch beneath your foot is one of the most sensitive parts of the body. But at least you don't see the marks though. Let's see then.'

He pulled off Marion's shoe. 'Hold her legs.'

Marion squirmed as Ozil slowly pushed the point against Marion's skin, turning it white.

Marion begged him to stop, her voice desperate.

'You can have the bookshop.'

Maria wiped tears from her eyes.

'Thank you, but we need to finish the lesson or we'll be none the wiser.'

'We don't need a lesson,' Thomas said, trying to keep his voice calm. 'We understand now – we do.'

Ozil pressed the point of the blade and Marion's scream was like nothing Thomas had ever heard from a human being. Animal-like.

All Thomas wanted to do was run.

Anywhere.

Away from that feral sound.

Ozil removed the knife, leaving a red line that began to bleed. Then, like a surgeon, precise and unhurried, he peeled a sliver of skin from the wound. Marion's screech was unworldly.

Ozil stopped and looked over at the door. 'Well, well, what have we here?'

Thomas followed his gaze.

There, accompanied by two elderly men and another woman, stood his mother.

The other woman was supporting one of the men and holding an oxygen cylinder.

Ozil pointed to each person in the room. 'One, two, three, four, five, six, seven. Would you believe it, Mr Lipscombe? You really do have the Magnificent Seven coming to your rescue.'

His mum looked frail and tiny, her companions even more so, like they'd escaped from an old people's home.

The man with the oxygen mask removed it and said, 'Release the woman.'

Ozil guffawed, but it seemed overly loud to Thomas. False and hesitant.

'It is good to laugh,' the old man said, 'especially if that laughter is the last thing you'll ever hear.'

Ozil nodded to his men, who moved towards the four elderly people.

Lipscombe scrambled up over to Marion and cradled her as if she were a child.

The old man lifted his hand towards Ozil's men, an unspoken stop.

The men stopped.

'My name is Lucas, and this is my brother Federico.' He took a gulp of oxygen, and removed the mask again. 'This is Mrs Blueberry, whose house you tried to steal.'

He nodded towards the woman supporting him, and Thomas could have sworn he winked. 'This is my beautiful wife, Gabriella. And you are Seth Ozil, a tiny piece of excrement who has delusions of grandeur.'

Ozil laughed again, but the glare in his eyes and the flare in his nostrils told another story. He took a step forward.

'Stop,' Lucas said. 'Never interrupt me. I am Lucas Genovese. That may mean nothing to a lowlife like you, but it will mean something to your superior. Call him now.'

Ozil nodded to one of his men. 'Finish them.'

'You may wish to reconsider,' Federico said. 'I have six men outside, Make the call first and see what transpires.'

The guard paused and glanced at Ozil, who was looking out of the window at two large dark cars parked next to his own. He rubbed his lips.

'Very well, I will humour you.'

He pulled a mobile from his jacket pocket, pushed a button and spoke in a language Thomas couldn't understand. Still, there was no doubt – Ozil was being reprimanded, and his expression, illuminated by the screen, had lost its assuredness.

'Jebi ga,' he said under his breath. He straightened his back and stretched. 'It seems I have been mistaken. You're free to go.' He turned to Marion. 'My apologies to you. It was nothing personal. We will take the suitcases and the matter is closed.'

Marion stared at him, not moving.

'You're total scum,' Lipscombe said.

'Come now, let's depart as friends,' Ozil said, glancing warily at Lucas and Federico.

Thomas heard a buzzing, and looked around the room. The guard who'd wrestled Lipscombe to the floor pulled out his phone and put it to his ear. He didn't speak, just stared coldly at Ozil, then nodded, pocketed the handset and strode towards him.

'What are you doing?' Ozil said. 'Get the suitcases for me. Now.'

The guard flipped Ozil around, wrenched his arm high behind his back, and bent him face down over the desk. Ozil shrieked.

The guard spoke to his counterpart who retrieved all but one of the suitcases and took them to the car.

'Listen, we can make a deal,' Ozil said, panting. 'We don't need the bosses. We can go it alone. There'll be more money.'

The guard jerked Ozil up into a standing position.

'Failure has penalties,' Lucas said quietly.

'We can sort things out. We can. It's just a misunderstanding. Let me talk to the boss.'

The guard frog-marched Ozil to the exit. Ozil tried to wedge his foot against the doorframe, but a third guard stepped forward, raised his boot and brought it down, crushing Ozil's ankle.

Ozil screamed and collapsed. The two guards carried him outside.

An engine revved, then backfired. Thomas ducked and looked at Maria, who stared back wide-eyed. *Was that …?*

'It is done,' Lucas said. He turned to Gabriella. 'Hug me just in case.'

His wife hurried over to him and the two embraced for several minutes. No one spoke lest they spoil the moment.

Lucas pulled away from her. 'God damn it, I'm still

alive. That would have been the perfect time to perish – in the arms of my wife after such a success and such excitement.'

Thomas grabbed Maria's hand and pulled her over to Lipscombe and Marion. The four formed a joyous circle and held each other.

They were free.

'Thank you,' Lipscombe said to Lucas. 'And please thank your men, too.'

'Think nothing of it. My brother and I would not have missed it for the world. And there are no men, just us pensioners.' He laughed. 'Our reputation preceded us. It was a good bluff.'

A bluff? Thomas gawped. 'Mum? That's—'

Was he seeing correctly? She was in Federico's arms. They gazed into each other's eyes, faces only inches apart. Then his mum planted a soft kiss on Federico's lips.

Thomas felt a strange warmth in his chest. Happiness. Pride.

Maybe a little nausea.

CHAPTER 45

They drove back to his mum's. Thomas sat shoulder to shoulder with her in the back seat and stared out at the empty roads. In the darkness, his mother's frail body and his own grown-up one were invisible. It was as if he were a child again, warm and safe.

'We nearly didn't make it,' she whispered. 'I couldn't remember the address.'

Thomas squeezed her arm. 'But you did in the end. That's all that matters.'

She wiped her eyes. 'You won't believe it, but it was your dad. He told me where to go.'

'Mum, I believe it. I believe it with all my heart.'

* * *

His mum busied herself in the kitchen, making tea despite Federico's insistence that only champagne would do for his *bellissima principessa*. She giggled in a way that

Thomas thought a son should never hear, and decided to check on Isabelle.

She was not on his bed. He straightened the quilt, thinking she might be buried within the creases of the cotton, but there was no sign of her.

'Isabelle?'

He looked on the floor, under the bed, above the cupboard. Nothing.

The earlier elation evaporated, replaced now by acid emptiness in his stomach. He'd been so engrossed in the house and his mother that he'd neglected Isabelle. Was he too late?

The towel on the radiator next to the bed twitched. Thomas peered down into the gap between the bed and the wall.

There she was. He lifted her gently onto his pillow. Her wings were crumpled and still, dark lines drawn into nothingness. No golden dust, no shimmer.

'Isabelle, what happened? What can I do?'

She opened her eyes and winced. 'I rolled and went down the side, I did.'

'Thank goodness. I'll get Marion. You'll be all right now. I—'

'I think it's too late,' she said. 'I feel so weak. I think I'm going to fly.'

'No. Wait. Just a little longer. She'll be here soon, I know she will.'

'I can't. It's like I'm being pulled away towards a bright star.'

Thomas's chest tightened. 'Just hang in there a few more moments. Please.'

'Don't worry. I'm not frightened anymore. I'm not. Nothing could be as bad as losing Blueberry.' She closed her eyes.

The front door opened and Thomas heard more cheerful voices. He dashed to the top of the stairs.

'Marion. Come up here. I'll get you some stuff to bandage your foot.'

She waved a hand and said, 'In a minute. I'm fine. Your mum's just made tea.'

Maria poked her head around the lounge door. 'You alright, chuck?'

'That letter opener was filthy. We should clean the wound. Sepsis. I had it once. It nearly killed me,' Thomas said.

'He's right, chuck. I'll help if you like.'

'No,' Thomas said too loudly. 'You chat to Mum. I can do this.'

Maria shrugged, and Marion frowned but made her way up the stairs.

'Wait in my room. I'll get the Savlon,' Thomas said when she reached the landing. 'There's something on the bed you might be interested in.'

He grabbed disinfectant and plasters from the bathroom, then went back to his bedroom. Marion was sitting on the bed reading *Angel's Delight*.

Isabelle was watching, but Marion seemed oblivious to her.

'You wrote this?' she said.

Thomas nodded.

'It's amazing. I like the cover.'

'Is that what made you pick it up?'

'No, you told me to, something interesting on the bed?' Thomas laughed and pointed to the pillow. 'I meant Isabelle.'

She looked stronger, and gold fizzed from her wings. She raised her arms and shrugged.

Marion just looked confused.

'Isabelle the fairy … well, angel. There.' He pointed again. 'On the pillow.'

Marion's frown only deepened. She leant forward, now inches from Isabelle.

Angel's Delight fell from her lap and thumped onto the floor. The book landed spine up, supported by its bent pages.

Thomas looked back at the pillow.

It was empty.

CHAPTER 46

Thomas added the final touches to the display and stood back. It looked good, he had to admit. Copies of *Angel's Delight* were stacked in the window, some face out so that Jacobs Manchester's endorsement on the cover was visible to all.

It was only 8 a.m., but already a crowd had formed at the front of the store and several police officers were trying to clear a path on the pavement for passing shoppers.

Jacobs had been true to his word and was coming to the bookshop for the launch. The publicity and excitement had taken the small town by storm. Thomas had interviewed in the paper and on the radio. Look East was going to cover the story on TV too.

The front door jangled open.

'Morning,' Becky said. 'It's manic out there. You can barely cross the street. The police say they might shut the road.'

She hurried down to the basement. Thanks to her the coffee shop had been up and running far quicker than they'd expected.

It was going to be a busy day. Thomas hoped he could cope with the excitement. He was tired. The previous evening, Maria had taken him to the Marillion concert. They'd stood near to the stage and held each other close, swaying in time to the music.

'This one's lovely.' Maria had said and she turned to face him, the words of the song swirling around them.

> *You landed in my life*
> *Like a new and brighter light*
> *That made all my past seem in the shadow*
> *I always used to believe*
> *That beauty was skin deep*
> *But I need a new word to describe you*
> *No one can take you away from me now*

He had felt as if he would burst with happiness. His mum had told him that there was enough love in the world to last for all time. It didn't need to be rationed, it wouldn't run out.

Love was his again.

He'd breathed into her hair, and looked into her eyes. And in that moment the sensation that they were one body had returned, leaving him light-headed.

She'd kissed him then, and without warning the auditorium had been full of snow, floating through beams of colourful lights and onto their hair. She'd worn a mustard-coloured jumper and Thomas had taken a picture of the snowflakes falling from her dark hair onto the gold.

It was the most beautiful thing he had ever seen ...

* * *

'You alright, chuck?'

'Just thinking about last night.'

She took his hand and squeezed it. 'You ready?'

'Yes, nearly there.'

'Who'd have thought? I'm going to get the till ready.'

Where had the time gone? So much had changed.

Peter had sold Lipscombe Property Associates and moved to Tenerife with Marion. They'd written several times and seemed very happy particularly once their cats, Deirdre Reynolds and Maxwell the Third, had joined them on the island.

His mother was on an extended holiday with Federico and Gabriella. Thomas wished she'd been able to come to the book launch but the winter sun had done wonders for her health. As had love, Federico had told Thomas, though that had been a little too much information.

Lucas had died not long after the showdown with Seth Ozil. He'd passed away in his wife's arms after asking for a hug ... just in case.

A lump formed in Thomas's throat.

A commotion erupted outside and Jacobs Manchester's voice rose above the hubbub.

'It's lovely to meet me, hmm, hmm? I know it is. That's it, that's it. No touching now. If fishes were wishes. Yes, yes, lovely to meet me, I know. No, I don't want to kiss the baby.'

Jacobs turned towards the bookshop as people piled forwards for his autograph. Their eyes met and Jacobs mouthed *Help*. Thomas smiled and shrugged.

'How you doing, fuckface?'

Thomas spun around. Cortina hovered in front of him.

'Makes a change not seeing you in the loo with your willy sticking out.'

'Please, you're a fairy. You—'

'Angel.'

'Angel. And a queen at that. You should set an example.'

'You're no fun. Look who I've found – goody two shoes herself.'

'Isabelle!' Thomas said.

The fairy shimmered in the sunlight. Her wings had healed and golden dust showered the carpet as she flew.

She beamed at him. 'I made it, I did. It's a long way to flies, it is.'

'It's a long way to flies, it is,' Cortina mimicked. 'When will you learn to talk like a grown-up?'

'Leave her alone,' Thomas said. 'It *is* a long way to fly.'

'I wanted to be here for the big day. Where's Blueberry?'

'She couldn't make it. She's in Italy on holiday.'

Isabelle looked sad.

'But she's really happy. She's with Federico.'

'Ah,' Isabelle said. 'He likes her from way back, he does. I remember.'

'Are you with Marion?'

'Yes. It's nice. We're doing lots of new things. She's good, you know.'

'I do know. I thought you'd flown though. You could have told me.'

'I couldn't take the risk. It might have broken the bond, what with it being so new. We hadn't set, we hadn't.'

Cortina shook her head. 'God, you get on my nerves, you do. Fuckety fuck, now I'm doing it. Tell him why you're here.'

Isabelle flew in front of Thomas.

'Well, we're fairies, right?'

'Angels,' Thomas said.

'It doesn't matter. Listen. Every fairy has one wish they can give, they can. Blueberry didn't need it and I think Marion's got hers already. So, you deserve it. You looked after me. You've got one wish.'

'You're joking. That's like a fairy story,' Thomas said.

'Well, it is a fucking fairy story, but it's true,' Cortina said. 'Hurry, Jacobs is about to lose the crowd. Make your wish.'

Thomas glanced at the door. The handle turned. He looked at his pile of books. *Angel's Delight* ... after all this time ...

'I know,' he said.

NOTE FROM THE AUTHOR

Dear reader,

If you don't believe in fairies – or angels – this next paragraph is for you:

In all probability, Thomas and his mum are suffering from methane and carbon dioxide poisoning because of a crack in the geo-membrane under Iris's house, which, as Peter Lipscombe mentions in Chapter 6, is built on a landfill site.

As well as other serious side effects, these gases can cause confusion and hallucinations.

If you do believe in fairies, or have an open mind, please carry on. It's only a few more pages …

EPILOGUE

Isabelle flitted around Blue Tiger Books. She was impressed. The store looked fabulous – nothing she could do to improve it – though she had to admit, the number of books piled onto tables and shelves had come as a surprise. Still, Baby Blueberry would be very happy here. He loved books.

She flew to the front of the store.

There he was – Thomas – his back to her, diligently arranging his single novel, written in hope at a time of sadness.

Angel's Delight.

An odd sensation fluttered in her stomach. She couldn't quite put a name to it but maybe this was how Blueberry felt when she looked at Thomas – proud of her boy, all the greyness now gone.

A golden shower fell over the books – a little fairy dust never hurt after all.

The flight from Tenerife had been long, and her wings, though healed and strong, were stiff. The island's climate was different to the changing seasons of England. Warm nearly all the time. She wasn't sure she liked it, but would learn to. It was where her person wanted to live so she would adapt.

Marion had been a perfect choice. With Isabelle's help she'd soon become part of the ex-pat community – arranging dances, quiz nights and trips all over the island. Hers and Peter's house parties were the talk of the community. No guest left feeling anything but warm and loved and needed.

Peter had settled well into island life too. Every morning he'd get up just as the sun was rising over the sea and set off to work. He and that professor – Buttons McQueen – were excavating the hillside of his abandoned property. Every day was an adventure, full of promise and possibility. In the evening, dusty and exhausted, he'd fall into Marion's arms, and they'd curl up next to each other, their cats purring in their laps. They had never been happier and Peter would talk to Marion about how he and Buttons would find Eldorado gold tomorrow.

And in a way, they already had. A few weeks after they'd arrived in Tenerife, Peter had received a letter from the Spanish government. An extension to the express motorway from the airport was destined to pass through part of his property. The land would be compulsorily purchased at a premium. Peter and Marion had held out for an even higher price and insisted the hillside remain untouched by the road. It had all been agreed with surprising ease.

Isabelle looked across at Cortina who had come to the bookshop with Jacobs Manchester. The Queen winked as if reading her thoughts.

Blueberry's absence made her ache a little. If only she could tell her that she'd once been her fairy, that all the things that had happened in Iris's life had happened in hers too ... that Isabelle had given them a power-up, but that Blueberry alone had been the reason for all the love and happiness.

If Isabelle had the chance to start over and could choose her person, it wouldn't be a pop star, or an athlete, not even a great leader. It would be Iris Blueberry.

She heard Cortina swearing at Thomas and shook her head.

The queen was a disgrace, she was. Isabelle flew in front of Thomas's face and dusted it in gold. He looked up and laughed, his face full of joy. It was good to see him so happy. She'd witnessed all his wonder disappear as the humdrum of the world weighed him down. Now it was back. If he'd been grey before he was a rainbow now. He deserved her gift; he'd come a long way.

'You're joking,' Thomas said. 'That's like a fairy story.'

'Well, it is a fucking fairy story, but it's true,' Cortina said.

I really hate her, Isabelle thought. One day, she'd be a proper queen.

Thomas looked at his pile of books and smiled.

'I know,' he said. 'I reckon Jacobs Manchester will turn these into a bestseller so ...'

He held out his palms. Isabelle landed, and he lifted her

up close to his face and whispered. 'Can you make Mum better and let her have lots of adventures?'

'That's two wishes,' Isabelle said.

She buzzed her wings, sending golden flecks into the air, hiding the tears that were prickling her eyes.

'Oh fuck it,' she said. 'What the hell.'

And Isabelle suddenly felt very regal indeed.

* * *

So you read it to the end, even you non-believers. I'm glad.

It could be because you wanted to get your money's worth. I don't blame you – these books aren't cheap. But I'm hoping it's because there's a spark in all of us. Just a tiny ember of curiosity that keeps us forever looking.

The world is full of magic, and just like love, it will never run out.

ACKNOWLEDGEMENTS

Ordinary Angels was written during lockdown, I had been working on three different ideas but this one came to the fore because I wanted something to take me away from the monotony of it all. It's different to *Cold Sunflowers*, more escapism and I hope you can forgive my self-indulgence.

My thanks come in two parts.

First, those who helped with the writing and book production: Averill and Louise for the formatting and editing. Penny for early editing, proofreading and cover ideas. Eleanor, Eleanor and Barbara for the final proofreading. And Andrew at Design for Writers for another beautiful cover.

Second, those who've made the past couple of years a bit more bearable: Andy, Brian, Brian, Cameron, Dave, Don, Eleanor, Clive, George, Jo, John, John, Julie, Keith, Lee, Marcus, Mark, Ollie, Pat, Pete, Paula, Paulette, Penny,

Ralph, Richard, Rob, Terry, William – for the weekly Zooms, football, games nights, tennis and pub.

Fred and Pauline at the Ale House and Pete and Geraldine at the Live and Let Live – what would we do without you?

My daughters – Eleanor, for keeping us all going, with lifts, trips, takeaways and for the best company, and Poppy for second chances – I love you both.

Sean, for being a thoroughly nice bloke and for providing some of the best days when we were VIPs at Portsmouth FC.

Mum – well, you know, for everything.

Georgina – still in my corner – thanks.

The rest of the gang – Mike, Debbie, Chris, Lucca and Katie.

Mary K for your wonderful words of encouragement.

Lucy Jordache and Steve Hogarth, for kind permission to use the lyric from 'No One Can' in Chapter 46. I always wanted to sway to that song. The story mentioned by Thomas in Chapter 27 is *"Repent Harlequin!" Said the Ticktockman* by Harlan Ellison.

Finally, thank you to everyone who read *Cold Sunflowers*, especially those who contacted me or left a review. It's amazing what a lift that gives. Keep spreading the word. One day, Mr Spielberg …

ALSO BY MARK SIPPINGS

Cold Sunflowers

'Everything happens for a reason.'

It's 1972. Raymond Mann is seventeen. He is fearful of life and can't get off buses. He says his prayers every night and spends too much time in his room.

He meets Ernest Gardiner, a gentleman in his seventies who's become tired of living and misses the days of chivalry and honour. Together they discover a love of sunflowers and stars, and help each other learn to love the world.

Ernest recounts his experiences of 1917 war-torn France where he served as a photographer in the trenches … of his first love, Mira, and how his life was saved by his friend Bill, a hardened soldier.

But all is not as it seems, and there is one more secret that will change Raymond's life for ever.

Cold Sunflowers is a story of love.

All love.

But most of all it's about the love of life and the need to cherish every moment.

'a beautiful, awe-inspiring book that made me laugh, cry and feel all the emotions in between … Thank you again for creating such magic in words and a story I will never forget'
– Angela.

'It is the most wonderfully uplifting book and I absolutely loved it.' – Brigitte

'I'm finding it hard to say goodbye to Ernest and Ray.' – Lareese

'Such a heart warming tale of love on so many levels I just gobbled it up over a few days and have recommended it to my friends.' – Denise

'… truthful and real, full of kindness, love and hope. It has touched my heart and soul on so many levels and has taught me to appreciate life and keep going on even when things are tough. And of course staying kind and having a dream or two up my sleeve.' – Mary

NOTE ON THE AUTHOR

Mark Sippings lives in Colchester, England.
His first novel, *Cold Sunflowers,* became a best-seller
in the United States;
Ordinary Angels is his second novel.

www.marksippings.com

Made in the USA
Las Vegas, NV
09 October 2023